OTHER BOOKS BY MARGE PIERCY

FICTION

*Going Down Fast**

*Small Changes**

*Woman on the Edge of Time**

*The High Cost of Living**

*Vida**

*Braided Lives**

*Fly Away Home**

*Gone to Soldiers**

POETRY

Breaking Camp

Hard Loving

*4-Telling (with Emmett Jarrett,
Dick Lourie and Bob Hershon)*

To Be of Use

Living In The Open

The Twelve-Spoked Wheel Flashing

The Moon Is Always Female

Circles on the Water: Selected Poems

Stone, Paper, Knife

My Mother's Body

Available Light

PLAY

The Last White Class
(Coauthored with Ira Wood)

ESSAYS

Parti-Colored Blocks for a Quilt
(Poets on Poetry Series)

*Published by Fawcett Books

DANCE
THE
EAGLE
TO SLEEP

Marge Piercy

FAWCETT CREST • NEW YORK

A Fawcett Crest Book
Published by Ballantine Books
Copyright © 1970 by Marge Piercy

ISBN 0-449-20114-7

Manufactured in the United States of America

First Fawcett Crest Edition: October 1971
First Ballantine Books Edition: July 1982
Fourth Printing: November 1988

Contents

AT age eighteen, Shawn was officially loved by sixty thousand four hundred and eleven girls registered in his fan clubs. His parents found this bizarre and in questionable taste, along with the change in spelling of his name from Sean. If they had been less permissive, they would have stopped the whole episode. Shawn was the second generation born out of the Church, and his name was a sop to the quarter Irish in him. His father was a partner in a prestigious Philadelphia law firm. His mother owned buildings, had studied psychology and been analyzed by Jung, and was still beautiful in a gaunt silvery way. For a rock singer, Shawn was enormously protected and counseled and underexploited.

All three members of The Coming Thing—Frodo and Shep and Shawn—went to the same prep school, where they roomed together and kept up their grades to acceptable levels. When they had to miss exams, they made them up as a group. Their concerts were scheduled inside the rhythms of the school year, and they recorded intensively over vacations. Of course they had their share of bad scenes—oversold concerts in dingy halls with mushy acoustics and twitchy lightshows, and now and then a producer would try to chisel them out of their take. But on the whole, they were exploited as a careful investment, not as a quick-turnover commodity.

Falmouth was ossified in comparison to the primary school they'd all gone to as kids. That was a school almost without walls, a beautiful place with human teachers, and they had played mathematics and music and rattled on in French and German together since they were fat sloppy toddlers.

> I am not an ice cube or a stone,
> I am not an ice cube or a stone.
> Honey, even teddy bears don't like to sleep alone.

7

At Falmouth they were popular but aloof. Frodo called it the Pimple Farm. The lead guitar, Frodo was small and squat and mean-looking and by far the most talented musically. He saw the world as a series of references to earlier rock and rhythm and blues. He was rough with the groupies sometimes, and perhaps Shep and Shawn could only remain in contact with him because they had had that common childhood. Shep was slender and fair with long fine brown hair, as much dandy in his dress as he could get away with at any given time, the only one who ever took an interest in their finances.

At Falmouth the other boys had hang-ups. Shawn was at ease with his creativity, at ease with his brain, at ease with his body. His first sex had happened with Melanie Clinton, whose father made airplanes. She was a year older but in the same language group: they had no formal grades. They got undressed under the sprinkler in the garden of the Clintons' summer home on the Jersey shore. Melanie was as blond as he was, and they had both just begun to have pubic hair, golden under the sun as tiny wires from jewelry making. She had no breasts, and they were both coffee-tan and fishbelly-white.

"It's so cunning," Melanie said. "I wish I had one like it." They both laughed, because they understood she was saying something the school psychologist would seize on. They tried to perform what they understood of the sex act. The water made her slippery, and there really seemed to be no extra room. Still it was pleasant and exciting as he lay on her cool slippery body with the droplets from the sprinkler and the sun on his back, warm and cool, warm and cool.

He finally accomplished it with her later that summer on the shore. In the twilight, their bodies were pale and warmer than the air, though the sand was still warm under them. He tried kissing her but he was awkward. It seemed silly, faking it, as if they were pretending to be adults. It was better to play with each other. He stretched her with his fingers, and finally he got his prick slid in. They moved around and worked out the ways that felt good. He kept at it till she got sore.

He was too young to go out with her, and anyhow they were both very busy. A liberal school didn't mean an easy one. But they were both in band, and sometimes after rehearsals they would hang around and screw on their nested coats. Melanie did not like the word fuck. She said it had negative connotations. He thought fuck but said screw to please her. He was playing drums then, and she played clarinet. Sometimes when they were rehearsing, he would get a hard-on looking at her and hoping. In the middle of the spring her periods started, and then she was afraid to, so that ended that.

> Nights spent alone you're better dead,
> Nights spent alone you're better dead,
> I need you, gal, to hold down the dark half of my bed.

> My back gets cold, I might come down with flu,
> My front gets cold, I might come down with flu,
> Don't want no electric blanket, all I want in bed is you!

He didn't like going to a boys' school, but his father had gone to Falmouth, etc., and Shawn had a girl in town. He heard the boys talking all the time in the house about how to make girls, and the talk choked him. A girl will let you know, she knows what she wants, he would have said, but they didn't ask him. They were shy of him about sex.

The school said he was undermotivated, meaning mostly Bs. They blamed it on his success. He always had money, but it flowed in mysteriously and invisibly and went away to make more of its own. Specialists bred his money, like trainers taking care of a racing stable. When he was seventeen, he insisted on buying a blue Porsche he sometimes drove fast. Otherwise the money was a process negotiated among his lawyer and agent and the record company and impresarios of tours and the corporate package that was the group and the trust funds that silently siphoned it off.

The truth was that in classes just enough juice flowed to light a few circuits; but when he was working with the group every switch turned on. All the adults he knew outside the music business might imply and coerce and assume that English history and physics were real and rock was frivolous, but he knew what engaged him all the way through and what just tiddled along in the front of his brain and caused his tongue to repeat empty phrases. Besides, his future yawned like an immediate pit, like the future of everyone else his age. The Nineteenth Year of Service was coming. Since Congress had legislated it into being two years before, it had sat there like a tollbooth across his way. He knew that for him those eighteen regimented months would not be dangerous, of course, but they would be a drag.

Two things were real. Two things gave off energy: One was making the music, working it on out together; finally recording, though that was something else and already into another specialist's scene, who could mix you into his kind of salesroom baroque. The other real thing was connecting with an audience—promise and delivery into that hot maw. Yet all draggled off into bad smells. For instance, at first they'd read their publicity: what they came to call Yetch Comix, or Three Clean Boys to Cream Over. They couldn't take it. They were weak, and it was strong—the godawful commerce of manipulating acne-fears and wet dreams. They pretended it didn't exist. They pretended that their concerts were conspiracies between them and kids almost like them. But the serious promo fizz was poisonous too, twaddle about the sonic revolution and the great significance con. They tried to keep each other sane. They tried to remember for each other who they were. The groupies were sometimes human, and at times it all seemed nothing but a clever way to get laid a lot. Then they went back to school and crept under the damp covers of Falmouth.

> Well, girl, you put me down
> cause you don't know who I am.
> Behind these glasses and this nose
> Look out! Stand back! Hold on! It's CAPTAIN WHAM!
> I'm the shocking electric man.
> Just let me at your socket.
> Baby, I got the juice to turn you on.

Then it came, the Nineteenth Year of Servitude, shit on wheels. Right at the beginning of the White Knight's first term, his task force on youth problems had come up with The Plan, presented as a great victory for the peace groups and the public-spirited and the draft protesters. Most guys still ended up in the Army, and a great many went into the street patrols and the city militia. But a number were channeled into overseas aid and pacification corps, the rebuilding programs in the bombed-out ghettoes, and the pollution clean-up corps. Girls who weren't pushed into the nursing corps worked in the preschool socialization programs in the ghettoes or as teachers' aides or low-level programmers for the array of teaching machines. Of course, students in medicine, engineering and the sciences just kept trotting through school.

School records, grades, and counselors determined some of the channeling, but the prime tools were the mass exams everyone took, separating out levels of skill and verbal intelligence, and locating potential troublemakers. Anthropologists praised the Nineteenth Year of Service for providing a rite of passage, and sure enough, everybody could tell the nineteen-year-olds from their younger brothers and sisters, because they all had their hair cut and wore uniforms. There was an absolute gap between kids and adults, a *before* and an *after* that could never meet. The sexes were segregated and sharply differentiated in function. The elders had no more trouble telling the boys from the girls and keeping them from joining their small differences. Sex officially ended at eighteen. For two years now, the Nineteenth Year had bottled up the so-called Youth Revolution. Now it was bottling up him.

Of course they weren't going to ship him off to Guatemala to stand guard over the embassy and United Fruit. The Coming Thing were assigned to the Youth Services Bureau in Philadelphia, which meant they played for teenage functions at schools, settlement houses, or in the park, and got sent to other cities for similar use. They played at the big assemblies where spokesmen (called pigeons by the kids) from the different forces made pitches. He had to put in an appearance at the bureau five days a week. He was supposed to punch in and punch out for a nine-to-five day plus performances extra—they were big on discipline—but the office manager was a good scene, and after a while she took care of that.

Mrs. Kapp was twenty-six. She'd been married and divorced, and running an office full of privileged kids made her nervous. Mostly, they treated her like a warden or a piece of nasty equipment. She wasn't pretty—she had a small, pug-nosed face, and she wore glasses too big for it—but she had good solid bouncy breasts and her hips curved out like a cello. He saw right away that she was shy of him and expecting to be ignored or put down. He sprawled in the visitor's chair, while she gave him those quick looks and went on stabbing at the blotter with a letter opener. "A woman my age trying to manage this circus," she said about five times until he gave her his slow grin.

He picked her out to spend time with because she gave off unhappy vibrations but not hard ones. Most of the kids were on jackhammer ego trips of their own. The only other human in the place was a black girl from a trio, the Shar-monts. She was their lead singer, a little girl with a big sexy voice. She cried a lot, and she was bitter and mean as a fist. Her whole family had been wiped out when the Army shelled Bedford-Stuyvesant during the bloody summer of the last year of the King of Clubs, when the president had announced his policy of "limited disciplinary retaliation" for uprisings. She hated whites and she let him know it.

Mrs. Kapp, he found by looking in the file, was Denise. He began calling her that when they were alone. He stopped by her office when he was bored and asked her questions and made her talk till she opened up like a daisy. He wasn't out for anything, except maybe to keep himself as comfortable as he could, to ease the bite of discipline on him. And he had to stay human. So he made her talk. First about the office and then about herself and her bad marriage and her crappy family and her loneliness. He liked to watch her come slowly to life.

She showed him pictures of her kid, Stevie. Did it shyly. She had to be asked everything twice, because she didn't believe anybody could be interested. They had really got to her and begun to grind.

Shawn was bored for the first time in his life for most of every day. He felt cut off from the kids they played for. It had been their thing, and they did it because it felt good. Turning people on. Now their group was part of the pacification program—caught themselves. They even had to have their programs approved beforehand. So they stayed cool and detached.

Frodo said that it was no different, that they had always been selling something, or what did they think was the name of the game anyhow? Frodo affected a sudden severe cynicism. The only thing that bugged him, he said, was that they were being taken. They could be making piles, and instead they were being used to sell somebody else's product. Yes, they were used. Rock meant liberation. It meant opening up your head to those sounds. It meant blowing their minds. It meant rebellion, freedom, sex. Now they were selling Today's Swinging Army. The coming thing for these kids was being channeled into servicing the empire and then back to school for training and then into a niche. It meant co-optation, manipulation: it meant the rest of your life doing Their Thing. It meant, if you don't fit we'll snip off the pieces that stick out, baby, and then you'll fit just fine.

So there they were, they played the music, and the kids screamed in sort of the same old way and shouted for their old songs. But it felt meaner. It felt like the kids knew they were being conned and were even more determined to rip off a piece of flesh. The Coming Thing were organ-grinder's monkeys, but the organ-grinder was the state, and they were showing the other little monkeys how groovy it could be to work for the organ-grinder too. They all felt the pressure, the deadness, and they shrank from each other.

Her eyes were hazel, sometimes brownish, sometimes greenish. He would sit on the desk while they talked. Shyly she would touch his arm, retreat. Nothing more. It was taking forever, he thought, then listened to himself and realized he had decided to go to bed with her. Why? Why not? Because she wanted to and never would. Because he wanted to take off her clothes. She would look better that way. It seemed like something nice.

So one afternoon he slid off the desk, picked her up out of her swivel chair and kissed her, taking off the owl's glasses. She went soft and woozy in his arms and then grabbed him hard. Let go all at once. Stared at him with her mouth slightly open. He reached for her again. "Not here," she said.

She gave him her address and instructions. She had to draw a map for him. She was flustered and clumsy. She would not look at him and then she would stare hard, her glasses back on, trying to read his face. Are you fooling? Are you teasing me? What do you want? Aw, come on, Denise. He felt gentle and sure with her. His big soft goose.

He was a ridiculously long time driving around and around before he could park his Porsche. Dingy narrow noisy streets. A little three-room walk-up flat over a drugstore. He could hear kitchen noises from the next apartment. There was a kid, a real live kid—Stevie, aged five.

They sat at a metal table in a corner of the kitchen and ate hamburgers and instant potatoes and overcooked frozen beans and store-bought layer cake. Denise was embarrassed and tried to make Stevie mind his manners at the table.

Afterward she gave Stevie a bath in a tub full of sailboats and submarines and a red and blue Noah's ark that floated. Stevie slept in the box-sized bedroom. When she had put Stevie to bed, she came back and turned on the television. They sat on the couch staring at it. Funny how he could hear people stirring all over the building. He put his arm around her, and she began to tremble and look suffocated. He pulled her onto his lap. At once she began to kiss him back passionately and all her soft full flesh to move against him and quiver.

"Let's get undressed," he said.

"This opens up."

They pulled the couch out into a double bed, and she unrolled the bedcovers from the closet. Then they both very rapidly undressed and got in. Her skin was soft, plushy. He felt as if his fingers left prints. Her hands on him were avid and yet gentle. She was easy to please. She started coming almost as soon as he entered, yet she kept her head and moved with him. It was nice—very, very nice. They watched a movie on television and then got back into bed. He fell asleep in a relaxed coil and spent the night.

She rose early and put on her clothes and tried to get him up. He did not feel like budging.

"Stevie will be getting up."

"But not me. Not yet. We can't go into the office together anyhow, right? So sign me in, and I'll mosey along by the middle of the morning."

She was nervous and hurried the kid through his cereal and milk. But she had already lost the ability to fight Shawn. Too insecure, too nice, too genuinely soft. He went back to sleep in spite of the building noises.

When he got up, there was a ticket on his car and a brand-new scratch on the street side. Two kids were climbing on it. Damned nine o'clock side-changing. She didn't have a car. "That's a hell of a neighborhood for parking," he told her in the office.

"But it's convenient on the bus to work ... Maybe you

could come on the bus? Your car looks a little conspicu-
ous."

It was a blue Porsche, the color—as many girls had told
him—of his eyes. She was still watching, holding her
breath to see if he was in fact going to come again. He
laughed and patted her fanny. Not that night. He had a
concert. But the next. When the next night came, he took
a cab.

He spent two or three nights a week with her, then
three or four. His parents did not like it. Tough. Very
tough. She was a lousy cook—partly because she was tired
when she got home and partly because she didn't buy
good ingredients. She was always adding up bills. He was
getting her in the habit of punching him in and out and
covering for him, so he took to making dinner the nights
he stayed. She would sign him into a practice room at the
bureau and lock the door. Jesus, if he spent one third the
time practicing he was signed up for, he would have made
a one-man technical revolution by now. He'd buy a steak
or chops and put together a salad. And fruit, lots of fruit.
Not like suppers at home, but not bad. He learned to
make spaghetti.

He had never shopped for food. He had never cooked.
He had never washed dishes. Food had been something
that came on a plate. But this was how people lived. They
kept house. It was part game and part nuisance and part
voyage of discovery. Tripping into the ordinary.

Stevie was in kindergarten in the morning and playschool in the afternoon. The woman who ran the playschool drove a VW Microbus and delivered the kids
home. Stevie had his own key. He could just about reach
the lock. Shawn had his own key too now. Stevie was glad
to see him when he got home. Sometimes Shawn would
wait to do the shopping until Stevie could come with him,
because they both enjoyed that. Stevie really dug being
asked what they should have for supper. Denise had a
whole set of muddled guilts about being a bad mother
because she worked. She would read some idiot in the
Sunday papers about how to raise kids and go into a
dither that she was doing something wrong. He could not
understand how she could let the Sunday paper make her
feel guilty.

She bought his records. He couldn't stand to hear music
on her diddly little phonograph. It was a pain in the ears.

He bought some components and put together a decent hi-fi, working all day. Turned it on to surprise her when she got home, and in ten minutes the neighbors were pounding on the walls.

"It's a shitty apartment, you know? Not even a bedroom." Roaches in the sink. She had a can of bug spray she was always using, but all it did was give him a sore throat and roughen his voice. Roaches ate it up like candy. Probably got high on it.

"It's only a hundred and ten a month and it's right on the bus line to the office."

It all came down to money. Everything in her life had price tags hung on it. Cash register whirring away all the time. She got forty bucks a month child support. Jesus, she couldn't keep a dog on that. Stevie wanted a dog too, by the way. Then the playschool and bus fare and utilities and the dentist and she was taking the pill now and everything went jingle, jingle on that cash register in the closet. They did not pay her enough. Yet she was frightened of losing her job. She saw it as great security and she clung to it with her nails and teeth, even though she hated every minute. She had a terrible drone of fear going on all the time that she would lose her job and Someone (the State, her exhusband) would take Stevie away. It was the best-paying job she had ever held. Shawn used to spend as much as her weekly paycheck in an evening and not think twice.

Stevie was a funny kid with a shock of brown hair, already wearing glasses that looked big on him too. He met the world with a nervous but enthusiastic giggle. He liked school pretty well. He liked most things that a kid could be halfway expected to like. He didn't get much. A hotbox to sleep in. A plastic Noah's ark that floated. Magazine pictures of dogs taped on his wall.

It seemed strange for such a soft silly woman to be part of the apparatus of the state for controlling its restless members. In some ways she saw the apparatus clearly enough. "Well, you see, this way there's a pool of labor available for all manner of social service, and it tends to stabilize the kids."

"Social service: Like policing. Like municipal strikebreaking."

She shrugged. "It's supposed to stabilize the rest of society too. I mean, it seems to be working. Since they rounded up the militants and the agitators and started this, everything's been quiet. So they must be right."

She did not want to talk about the Nineteenth Year of Service. More than anything else, she was afraid they would find out about Shawn and she would lose her job. She could not manage to save anything, and whenever she thought of the future, she shut her eyes and turned her face and shivered. Money had been an ambience to him. But to her it came in little miserly clumps—never enough, never enough. It was finite and each dollar could be spent only once and for one thing, and always there were other needs and bills. It gave money a totally different character. It made money skinny and shrill and always butting in.

The first time Shawn took a bus to her apartment he couldn't believe the trip. People crammed against each other, poking into each other, sweating and heaving and blowing and pushing like they'd all have heart attacks on the spot. All taking it.

"That's just rush hour. That's the way it is."

"Every day? But it's insane. Why don't they run more buses?"

She shrugged. "It's rush hour. I don't know. I guess it would cost too much."

The daily cattle drive. He learned to avoid those hours, but he could call up the physical sensations at will. He puzzled about that endurance. Somehow she was trained to endure. Maybe it started very early, with school. In the schools most kids went to, they learned to shut down, shut up, sit still.

Lots of old people lived in the neighborhood. When the sun shone at all, they would bring out folding chairs or kitchen chairs and sit by their stoops staring at nothing, hoping to talk. Yet when he came by, they sniffed and gave him the cold eye of fear. People were afraid here. Denise was scared silly when she had to come home late and alone. She had been followed on the street several times. Once her purse had been snatched. When she had to walk on the streets at night, she scuttled along thinking about being raped or beaten or hit on the head or cut up with a knife.

The city smelled bad. Kids screamed all evening in the street, because they had no yards. Stevie played awkward catch with him in the living room until they broke a lamp.

He got an air conditioner, and that helped sleeping. But the fuses blew once a week. Fucking archaic wiring. Whole place could go up like a kerosene-soaked rag. When he took Stevie to F. A. O. Schwarz and picked up a train that hooted, there was hardly room for it to make a good circuit on the livingroom floor.

It all came down to the damned apartment. The city pressed in on it and sweated on the walls. The street was shabby, the paint peeled in the hall under the wee myopic bulbs, the doors did not shut right, nothing was lightproof or impermeable to sound. Everything leaked and creaked and sagged and shifted uneasily. Even the newer pieces of furniture were already seedy. The water made him gag. It was the ordinary city water, but he had never had to drink it before. It tasted like a rat had died in the pipes. Half the time the water wasn't hot enough to shave with. He liked to shave. He shaved slowly, grinning with clenched teeth into the mirror, using a straight-edge razor. It was his major affectation. He liked to strop the razor. One of the few things Denise ever insisted upon was that he keep the razor on top of the bathroom cabinet, out of Stevie's reach. The bathroom opened on an airshaft, and as he sat on the toilet he could hear a dozen other people flushing and running showers and yelling at each other.

"Well, this is just how people live!" Denise said waspishly, and then got apologetic. They climbed into bed. Soft against him, bouncy under plush. "You're so big," she would say and suck on his prick till he moaned. "You're so beautiful." She would run her hands over his long body again and again. She would fondle him with that soft avidity and stare and stare into his face. Then she would get on top and start almost at once, Ooooh ooooh oooh, and squeeze it out of him. It was nice, it was nice and easy and it went on.

But the bed was something else. Not a proper bed at all. A couch lumpy and bumpy with a canyon in the middle between the two halves. He liked to sleep all wound around her, but there was that canyon gaping. The bed had metal sides he barked his shins on. He hated bruises. Like mushy spots on fruit.

He decided to move her out of that open sore, into a place with a yard and thick walls and a bedroom with a door and water that was hot and wiring you could plug things into without everything going black. It's true that what fascinated him was the ordinariness, the sense that he had penetrated into The Way People Live, but there was no point overdoing it. It had been very interesting, rush hour and fuses that blew and roaches, but enough was enough. She argued with him, scared. He took off her clothes and shut her up. Then she argued more. He sulked for a week. Laid other girls and waited. When he came back, she wept and clutched him. Through the filmy layers of argument, he read her fear. He would buy something outright. See? She'd own it for a change. No sweat, right? For the kid. It was easy to be crafty with his plump goose.

An agent found them a duplex, the left half of a house with an upstairs and a downstairs and a slot of yard, real rooms and doors that shut. It was a fine toy. Everything was somehow miniatured, but after those stinking three rooms, why, they'd have a room just to stand and yell in. $22,500. Cash, he said. Then the gears stopped meshing and the machine ground to a halt on his hand. Because he had only just turned twenty, and the money had come in and gone out to make more and always it had been managed, and now he found how little he controlled—all that invisible money he had raised strutting and shouting for hot squealing audiences. Somebody had it. Lawyers, his parents, trusts. But not Shawn.

His parents thought he was in the clutches of an aging adventuress. They said the affair was squalid and that he had lost his mind. "I want to help her and the kid," he said. He talked about the street where old people sat looking at blank walls like television, and the buses where people were into each other without joyful groping—just meat on the hoof. He talked, and they shut off. Bang. Slam. They refused to empathize.

Jesus, it was simple enough. He wasn't even in love with her. He just liked her. He liked the kid. He liked her climbing on his prick and burbling her funny noises and milking the come out of him. He liked her praising of him. Why not? He turned her and the kid on, and they would go along with Stevie's always damp hand gripping his, and his skinny legs pumping away and his face under the shock of slicked-back brown hair turned up like a sunflower in a silly grin. It was another world. It was through the looking glass into Everybody. But just from the old personal-comfort point of view, he wanted to

drive over to see her and park on a street where kids
wouldn't cut designs on his car, and listen to music so he
could feel it in his head and body, and climb into a real
bed in a room with a door that shut. If he was an average
shmuck taking care of his woman, nobody would make a
fuss.

But they blew up a giant shitstorm, and then Denise
was not in the office. They got her fired, man, like that.
And she disappeared. Gone, his weeping plush goose and
the kid, gone. Well, if they could pull a disappearing act
and disappear his woman, he could put on a little magic
show, too. He felt stripped and sore, sore in his body and
mind, sore through. He went with what was on his back
and in his pocket. Took the bus to New York—he was
practically acclimated to buses—and headed for the Lower East Side. AWOL. Eat shit. There were always kids
down there hiding out. Runaways and AWOLs and kids
dodging the eighteen months of slavery. He was on the
street for a day and a night, and then he landed in a crash
pad. Four rooms, railroad flat, with ten kids bedded down
wherever they could.

There was a redheaded kid with a sleepingbag—sixteen?
seventeen? She said eighteen. He didn't believe it. Didn't
care. "Shawn?" she said. "I'm Joanna." She had a funny
voice, metal that caught in her throat. Lots of kinky red
hair, mounds of it falling on her back and shoulders. A
skinny kid wearing a striped tank top with no bra and
dirty denim bellbottoms and sandals on dirty scarred feet.
"You want to ball? Take off your clothes and let's get in
the bag."

Little feather points stuck through the cloth. It was hot
and stuffy, and they sweated like pigs. She was bony after
Denise, sharp hipbones that poked him, low breasts that
flattened against his chest. She bit her lip and held him
firmly by the buttocks with her nails digging in. She
frowned with concentration and worked, worked, worked
him into her tight cunt. Came with a muffled sigh and a
grimace. Let him finish while staring at the ceiling and
thinking about something else.

"I boosted some meat this afternoon, but I'm hungry
again. The stew's all gone. You got any cash at all?"

They struggled out of the sleepingbag, and she dressed
without wiping herself. Rank salty smell. A fat boy was
rolling joints, and they smoked for a while, and then she

fell asleep on top of the sleepingbag, kitten curled with her mouth slightly open. He nudged her over, spread out the unzipped bag, and lay beside her back to back, bone to bone. Spines in hard tangent. She mumbled in sleep. He fell under and drowned into nightmares of flight and confrontation.

The third night the pigs arrived. Lined the kids up against the wall and came down the line. They used their night sticks in the small of the back, slammed heads against the bared bricks, taking identification and dragging the kids out one by one knocking on the steps. When they got to the redhead, she had no ID on her.

"How old are you, kid?"

"Eighteen."

"In another five years. You might as well finger the guys who've been into you right now. Be sorry if you wait till the matron turns you inside out."

"Get your motherfucking hands off! I'm eighteen and it's my business."

"Some business," the pig said genially, and pulling her back by the hair they worked her over, both of them punching her breasts and belly and back till she went down vomiting. The bigger one kicked her, and she sat forward bleeding from the mouth. Then yanking her by the hair to her feet, they carried her out cursing and wriggling and bleeding and still drooling vomit.

When they came to him in the line, one rabbit-punched him in the kidneys while the other turned him around by his hair. Then one of them said, "Hey, don't this look like our sweet baby?"

They did not work him over. One seized him by the legs and the other by the shoulders, and they carried him out, only striking his spine against the steps from time to time. They were throwing the other kids in the wagon, making a bang as the bodies struck metal or a thud when they landed on each other. But they took him off in a car.

He had his court-martial and got what was considered a light sentence to brig. There they beat the shit out of him, but did not break him. They did what the Army was supposed to. They made him a man—one man: Shawn the Prophet, who saw light rising out of hell as he lay with the guard's foot on his neck in his first shit-splattered latrine.

THE attack was a thing Corey associated with early childhood, partly because he could not remember when he had been without the fear of it, and partly because that fear was so total it made him a baby again. It came out of exhausted sleep or near-sleep. He would wake up feeling he could not breathe. He was suffocating. His chest was in a vise, his heart beat hugely and shook his bones. He knew he was dying. But he could not lie still, no. He had to keep moving, to thrash and roll on the floor and run from room to room. He would pinch himself and bang his head on the wall. Inside his skull was a sense of mounting pressure. Everything rubbed on his nerves. His hearing grew so sharp he could detect sounds in the next house, he could hear all the fluids of his body sloshing like an old-fashioned washing machine.

Gradually the thing would recede. For hours, his chest would feel tight and sore. He could be sucked back under. He could not stand to be alone. Then that blind dependency made him despise himself. It was an eagle that stooped on him as he slept and tore into him, that carried him bleeding high up so he could not breathe, and dashed him to the ground.

As well to think of the attack as a bird as to think of it as a disease. The few times he had tried to describe it to some doctor—in school, once in a clinic—they tested his heart perfunctorily and told him to stop worrying about nightmares. They asked for a history of epilepsy in his family. They checked his reflexes. In high school the doctor asked what drugs Corey used. Ho, ho. "Aspirin." Corey made his face blank and innocent. "Once I had penicillin." To relax with any stiff in the whole bureaucracy was to lay traps for himself. They were there to stand on his head.

Once he had had an experience on acid that was similar but not bad because spaced out, without the pain. Since his vision, he had not dropped acid, just as he had not smoked cigarettes. Gone from two packs a day to nothing, watching his nerves writhe like a tortured cat.

"The white man's gifts to the Indian were smallpox and cholera and rum." He said that in a report in American History class. He stood hand on hip, looking evil: the face that scared uptight people. His darkness against them. "The Indian's gift to the white man was lung cancer." The kids giggled knowingly: he was putting down tobacco because he dealt grass. He did it for the money and the style and to buck the system. He dealt the best he could get, which was saying little. Sometimes he could have sprinkled it on pizza and nobody could have told the difference, and sometimes the cat would go crazy and try to claw into the bag, and then he'd know what they had cut it with that time. Like everybody else he turned on, but he was not a head. Not any more. Islands sealed in by fog.

He was tired of dealing. Tired of the tension. Knowing that any time they chose, they could burst into his locker and paw through whatever he had there, notes from Ginny, secret things he wrote to himself. They had done that once but missed his stash. Ah, he was tired. Dealer: hero and parasite. Something in the scene rubbed on old sores. "Kid, how come you're so dark? You don't look like a nigger in the face. Did you know your pa, kid?" One of their neighbors in Franklin's Ditch. They didn't talk to him that way any more. He hadn't had to cut anybody in a while. Proving himself over and over on a score that never balanced, never would. Fighting on all fronts, he courted complete collapse and surrender. He seldom risked open bravado in class any more. The frustrated, embittered lumps who taught at Franklin High were good at one thing: hating.

In the tenth grade they had taught him a valuable lesson: there was no right or wrong there, only the powerful and the powerless. He had got into a fight with Old Man Prit-Shit when Corey said in American History I₂ (they had him tracked into the boob class) that the whites had practiced bacteriological warfare against the Indians way before the Revolutionary War, intentionally spreading smallpox among the Delawares with infected blankets and handkerchiefs. Old Man Pritchett had contradicted him, finally thrown him out of class. He had come back with a library book to prove it, and been suspended from school for a week.

Yeah, he owed a big debt of gratitude to Old Man Shit
with his paunch and his prejudices and his mean, safe digs
to goad the boys he hated most to that spasm of anger
when he could dump them out of school for good. He
owed him a big debt. Old Man Shit assigned the class a
book report. They were supposed to go to the public
library and get a book and read it. Of course it was a safe
bet that most of the kids would never do it. The library
was in Valley Acres, and most of the kids in z track came
from Franklin's Ditch, among the old canals and marsh
against the steel mills. But he could get a lot of mileage
out of role-playing in places where he didn't belong. Then
the thing happened that wasn't supposed to: he found out
there were books in the library about how things had
been, and he got mad enough to read them. He could read
well enough when there was a reason for it. And he read
himself right out of the bag they'd shut him up in. It all
started with the first lie: Columbus discovered America.
The white man had stolen the land and attempted to wipe
out his people and lied to him to make him ashamed.

The school was a prison scene anyhow. Indians loved
their kids, but the white man feared and hated his children. You couldn't even take a crap without a teacher
standing there hurrying you. There weren't even doors on
the john cubicles for fear the kids would smoke or shoot
up: all sins were equal. You had to get a pass and carry it
to go anywhere. He had a collection of forged passes and
passes he had conned teachers into signing, on which the
date was written in pencil or the old time could be torn
off and a new one added. But beating the system was only
grooving on his own slavery.

When he got out of school, Ginny was hanging around
his rusty old Ford in the parking lot and she begged a ride
home. She lived in the Ditch too, upstairs in a two-family
frame house the color of smoke from the mills. Finally
when he was dropping her off, she couldn't stand it and
she had to ask him if she was going to see him that
evening.

He sat there at the wheel pretending to think it over.
She was easy to tease and torture. Ginny was okay. She
had big boobs and she put out. She wasn't really dumb,
but she'd do anything he told her to, because she wanted
so much to please. She had an old man who was always
knocking her around and five brothers and a couple of

babies to take care of. Her mother didn't do anything but
lay babies around the house. Her mother was after her
to quit school and get a job, but she hadn't done it yet,
because she wanted to hang around him. She was a pretty
girl who acted like she didn't know she was pretty, with
her round wistful face with the pointy chin and her sandy
eyes lighter than her hair. He had picked her out in home-
room the first day in September, but he'd never let her
know that. Publicly and privately she was his property.

He drawled at last, "Yeah, I guess so. Why not?"

When he came home, Linda was twitching up and down
in front of the house in a pair of their mother's high
heels and an old lace tablecloth. "Well, here comes the
bride."

"Shut your mouth. They almost fit, see?"

Almost, by two inches. Linda was ten and lighter than
both his mother and he were, with light brown hair like
Ginny's. Her father was a white man, while he had some
of his Indian from both sides, Oglala Sioux from his father and Choctaw from his mother. He respected the
combination. Sure he had learned his heritage from shitty
cowboy movies, in which the Indians died grunting in the
dust, and then out of the library. He had not thought of
himself as an Indian until high school. He had learned
his identity out of books, but he had made it real the old
way, by fasting and vision. He had made himself real.

His mother was in the kitchen. He looked in the pot.
"Fish and dog stew." His literary joke.

"Cut that out, sugar. That's short ribs and onions.
Supper'll be on the table in twenty minutes."

She always cut times in two. He took his semiautomatic
.22 out back by the stinking canal to shoot cans. "Honey,
the neighbors are going to report you," she called softly
after.

"They're chickenshit, honey. Get on with my supper."

She shook her head over the stove, and Linda came out
behind him. His mother didn't bug him to watch out for
Linda, because he took care of the kid as much as she
did. Mother spoiled him as well as she could, with leaning
on him the rest of the time, but she hadn't needed Linda,
hadn't wanted her. Damn Polack took off as soon as her
belly started to show. Not that Corey had minded seeing
him off. Cheap at half the price. Used to get drunk and
tear up his ass like Ginny's old man. Linda was an okay

kid, although sometimes he wished she had a little more
sense. Took after his mother. Too easy for people to push
around, including him.

"Sure, go on, make a couple more babies," he would
tease his mother. "We got room."

She would get angry and carry on, but she knew he
halfway meant it. It was a drab, thin life for her. He
wasn't around much, Linda was no company in the evenings, and all day she stood on her feet behind the counter
in the doughnut shop in the plaza. Mostly fat kids and
housewives eating themselves sticky and not bothering to
leave a tip. Though he was only five seven, he'd always
felt tall, because she was just five one. He hated to see her
running back and forth behind the counter.

His father didn't sound like he'd scored high on brains
either. Next year Corey would catch up with his father
and pass him, forever. His teen-age old man off to the
Indo-China War and splattered all over the jungle by a
shell his first week in combat. Here comes daddy home in
a box. A couple of photographs of his parents crammed
into a booth giggling at Riverside Amusement Park. A
bundle of illiterate letters full of complaints about the
weather and the food. A green check suit he had once put
on for a joke, and his mother wept, wept. Then he realized with a shock his father had been real, a man, a lover.

He drilled the tin cans that sat in a row on the broken
dock. No reason to fix it. He had had a good childhood
along the canal with the other kids, with a leaky rowboat
to explore their junkpile wilderness among the slag-heap
outposts of the steel mills. In his games the Indians were
heroes and the Indians won. They played Tarzan too. He
could swing pretty well by the arms and beat on his chest.
Cottonwoods grubby by the canal, scrawny sumac trees.
Grassy hummocks and islands and weedy hidden places.

"Die, Yankee dog!" He shot the last can and emptied
the spent clip.

"Now can I look through it?"

He gave it to Linda clean and steadied it against her
small shoulder. "Die, Yankee dog!" She made pow noises.

Just stride into school cool and easy some morning with
the rifle on his back like a guerrilla fighter. Better a
machine gun. Line up the faculty. Torture the principal to
learn where they kept the anxiety gases and the chemicals
they put in the soup to make the kids stupid and passive.

He used to try in school. He used to be all ready to prance and dance and memorize the lies in the textbooks so teach would pat him on the head and say Good Doggie. Though down in z track, they didn't want you sounding off much. He remembered forcing himself to sit through a test without writing anything. Because then he knew he had outlasted them. They could no longer play on his wants and fears. They could no longer cut him off from his brothers and make him try to outdo them.

The teachers mocked him in class and threatened him with expulsion and the cops and reform school and jail. But he had learned to cool it. The worst they had been able to do was suspend him now and then. He had learned not to be tempted into defiance they could crush. The only thing they had on him was that he did want to stay in school for the time being, because his people were all gathered there for him.

The pressure was constant. Never could you think you were a man, never could you forget you were under their laws. Sit here. Shut up. Platoon B, line up waiting for Platoon A to gobble their slops in the lunchroom. No talking. Keep your hands to yourself. Don't look like you're enjoying yourself, ever. Don't laugh out loud over your peanut butter sandwich; don't get into excited conversation about anything you care for.

So you're trying to find out who you are, huh, kid? and you like the way you look. Well, get a haircut. Take off those obscene pants. Go home, girl, and wash that stuff out of your hair. Because we know you're dressing for each other, and we won't let you. We're going to make you look ugly, if we choose. You got no rights, kid, and don't forget it. You're our property to shape or break. We can humiliate you as much as we want to, and we want to a lot. What else do we get out of life?

He had been enormously excited when he learned that even the long hair bit was anticipated by his people. Earlier in the century, Washington had tried to shear them too, sending orders that all male Indians must cut their hair. Indians who refused were handcuffed, chained and shorn. It was always symbolic castration.

Nowadays he dressed like a slob. He had been into that hip dressing scene; that's where the take from the grass had spent itself. But he had gone through a repulsion. He was done supporting teen industries. He saw that style was

another way to hook him. All the energy that went into
dressing cool and pursuing fads kept him in his place. His
people had been tricked into selling land for beads and
gewgaws. Now the teen industries were fattening off the
fact that the Nineteenth Year of Service made parents all
the more ready to fork over money to buy their kids
records, clothes, a car and a phone of their own because,
after all, it would end. Bad as it was, high school was
obviously paradise, soon to be lost. The coming regimen-
tation hung over them all. Afterward, nothing would carry over, nothing could remain the same. The teen culture
was sealed and cute as baby clothes. By the time the
twenty-year-olds got back, they were ready for job training and the speed-up. They were hot to buy houses and
settle down. They married in droves and began laying
babies around. He felt he had nothing in common with the
guys who came back to the neighborhood. Some growth
mechanism had been shut off in them, permanently.

Not that he wouldn't some day want children. Everything useful that he knew (the history that led to him,
how to shoot, how to stay out of jail, how to handle
somebody on a bad trip, how to talk to people to move
them) he had learned on his own, and like a tribesman he
would pass on what was truly worthy. To find the woman.
He imagined her Oriental. Delicate flower body with the
downcast mysterious eyes and the mystic sexual lore of
the Orient and a rifle on her back. He would not have to
decide. It would happen to him like a grenade exploding.
Maybe love was all bullshit. Tough and silent as a shadow, she would follow him.

Linda was making faces. "Corey! Listen to me. You
didn't hear a thing I told you. Corey?"

He took the rifle back. "Time to clean up for chow."
Sitting Bull swaggered from under the house and stood
meowing by the door. Gray tabby-striped male with big
balls and bigger scars. Chewed ear and a bald spot, fleas
and a randy smell. "We are two of a kind, compañero,"
he said, and stooped to scratch the cat's chin.

> Let it be reported that I was the last man of my
> people to lay down my gun.

But he laid it down. And they shot Sitting Bull down, the
dirty Indian cops sent out to murder him. He was a chief

and a medicine man. A great leader in a people rich in
great leaders. They knew they could not bring him in
alive, and so they determined to kill him where he stood
among his people, disarmed and starving in the lousy
reservation at Standing Rock.

He washed, glowering in the bathroom mirror. Black
hair straight and coarse, long sideburns, high cheekbones
that jutted out of swarthy skin. Sullen eyes. The half-breed
villain about to pull a knife. So he gave the mirror his
dazzling smile—big oversized white teeth gleaming, yeah,
charm turned on at the flip of a switch. Now turn it off.
His morose evil look. Tough now. He pulled his mouth
tight, turning slightly sideways to sneer from narrowed
eyes down that hooked Indian nose.

"Corey's making faces at himself! Corey's loving himself
in the mirror!" Linda sang.

> "Oh baby, I'm so good,
> Oh baby, I'm so pretty.
> If you get down on your knees
> I will squeeze your little titty!"

He pinched her arm hard enough to hurt, feeling his
meanness as she cried out in pain and surprise. Sometimes
he felt crushed by them, his silly sister, his silly mother.
He would leave, he had to to breathe, and then where
would they be? Then he hated them for their clinging
weakness. He made ugly noises in his throat and pushed
past Linda to the table. Sitting down, he reached over the
table for the pan of short ribs, took a huge helping and
began to shovel it in without waiting for them. Pig Corey.
Yes, look. See what I am. Choke and let go.

After he picked up Ginny, they went to the drive-in and
saw two bombs, a science fiction freak-out about giant
computers that took over men, and the other a spy movie
with a duel between astronauts outside spaceships. They
cuddled during the pictures, and he felt Ginny up. She
was warm and ready and kept sticking her tongue in his
ear. It was four hours of eating caramels. His brain felt
rotten. He parked with her and started to make out, but
suddenly he felt blank and bored, and he stopped and
took her home. She looked miserable, but she was too
conned by the system and by him to challenge anything.

She'd go inside and change her deodorant or her toothpaste.

He intended to do his homework. He spread out the plastic books on the kitchen table and tried to eat them like cardboard breakfast crunchies. He sat there grinding his brain against the books and getting angrier and angrier and more disgusted with himself. The radio was on and the real rock kept nudging at him to remember he was alive.

> Oh baby, take my hand
> 'cause the night is hard and long.
> Your living hand to take my hand
> 'cause it will be a long time
> a long time till the dawn
> and the dark, the dark
> the dark is coming on.

Harsh electronic wail like the pattern of a nervous system flashed on a screen. Shawn's human voice cutting through, sailing through golden and living.

> Oh baby, take my body,
> it's too dark to see your face,
> my living body baby in your own
> 'cause we are sinking in the night.
> This is our only time and place
> 'cause the long night,
> the long, long night is coming on!

Voice like a naked male swimmer cresting the wave of sound. Shawn's voice always moved him, like a friend speaking, like a friend urging. To touch people directly fucking them all at once in their minds, instead of having to talk to them one at a time, one at a time, trying to make them see what was happening. To move people naturally that way. Everybody knew what that song was about except adults, except the enemy. They'd ban it. Soon the recruitment assemblies would start, pigeons from the different branches of servitude making their pitches. Because they wanted you to knock yourself out at those exams. They wanted you to try real hard to make street militia and be crushed if you ended up in a shovel detail. Imitation choices. Brand A or Brand B death.

Even Shawn the golden was caught, pinned fast. But he had tried to escape and now he was in stockade. You couldn't just quit the whole thing; you couldn't even get a job. What Shawn did and what Corey was doing were about the only ways adolescents could make it on their own: rock singer, dealer. But somehow They used you anyhow. He snapped off the radio, depriving himself of its useless pretense of solidarity. At least Shawn had tried to escape. Here he was grinding his brain against the programed learning texts, making a last-ditch effort to make it in their system, to keep from being shipped off to be killed overseas. A lemming like all the rest. All his rejection had caused him to do was give up smoking: by that standard, the Surgeon General's office was radical. He reached no one, he moved no one. All his relationships were lies. He had settled for a sullen inner alienation and the ethics of a small businessman, peddling grass for a fair price. He would take the exams, he would bow his head, he would march under. Follow his father into the great incinerator.

He went into his room and slammed the door. On the walls, quotes he had scrawled with marking pen. *"Kill and scalp all, big and little; nits make lice."*—Chivington's instructions for genocide against the Cheyenne. *"I am determined not to live until I have no country."*—King Philip of the Wampanoags, who saw his people lose their land to the Puritans his father had been naïve enough to help. *"My idea is that, unless removed by the government, the Utes must necessarily be exterminated.... The State would be willing to settle the Indian problem at its own expense. The advantages that would accrue from the throwing open of twelve million acres of land to miners and settlers would more than compensate all the expenses incurred."*—Governor Frederick Pitkin of Colorado.

The ancestors he loved best among the Sioux—no, the Dakota, don't use white names—were those like Crazy Horse and Sitting Bull, who had excelled both as warriors and as holy men—men in touch with what is. That he had some sense of what that meant, he owed to acid, but now he must do without chemical aid. On his wall too was a photograph he had ripped out of a library book—because it belonged to him. It showed frozen half-naked bodies stuck in grotesque attitudes of flight and terror and defiance, mostly women and children, the women with their thin shawls pulled up to try to protect babies, some of the bayoneted children scarcely old enough to run before the soldiers of the Army of the United States. It was a photograph taken after the last "battle" of the Sioux Wars, the Battle of Wounded Knee.

All the Dakota who had been forced onto reservations and promised so many things were starving that winter when they began the ghost dancing, the dancing they believed would bring back the world they could still remember, the world in which things had been happy and good and right, when there had been buffalo for all to eat. In the dance they would remember small things, even the games they had played to pass the time, and the intensity of joy and pain would cause them to faint. They danced to bring back their dead, to bring back the buffalo, to bring back the world that was good and made sense. It all ended in the snow at Wounded Knee. They were his people. So he had stolen the photograph to study and learn.

When he went to bed, Linda and his mother had been asleep for hours. Small noises nagged him, but finally he slept. Then it came down on him in deep sleep. The eagle stooped on him, dug its beak into his chest and gouged for his heart. Every nerve jumped.

He rolled from the bed, hit the floor. Rose, stumbled into the wall scrabbling for the light switch, pushed into the kitchen, turning on every light. How the air leaned, solid. Everything was edged with black, the blackness pressing on the film of light that pressed hard on his eyes. He swept a glass from the table and heard it break. He fell groaning and clawed at himself. He would die now, now.

Ran the cold water at the sink over his hands, splashed his face, drank. Then the cold water slid down into his stomach. His heart thumped. His blood seethed in each and every vein. Fear had him by the nape, shaking him so he would break open.

He came storming into her room. "Mama, mama, wake up! Wake up, goddamn you, wake up!"

The next day he was burnt out. After an attack, he could not sleep. The fear kept him from letting go of consciousness, slipping down. He stayed in bed until first Linda and then his mother left. Then he squatted among the rumpled sheets in his underwear searching for pimples to squeeze until the blood came. He warmed up the breakfast coffee and drank it, but he ate nothing.

When he heard their noises, he locked his door and would not answer to their knocking and pleading. Finally in midevening, he let his mother come in with a plate of food. When she had gone, he locked the door again. Then he crossed to the window, raised the screen and emptied the plate on the hard earth outside.

He considered it possible that he was crazy. They would judge him crazy, sick. But he had learned from his Indianness that he need not necessarily remain closed in his shame. To be different was to have a different path. Each man excelled his earlier stages, proceeding on his own way. Out of the raw agony of the attack he might penetrate to something he must know.

He disgusted himself like something gone rotten. He smelled like stinking meat. He could do nothing but wait and let the bad thoughts work in him. As long as they swarmed, nothing else could come. Fantasies. Women crawled through his bed like pink maggots. Tableaux of torture and humiliation. Slowly he slit open the cavities of his enemies. He lay in mounds of severed breasts. He stole Ginny's cunt and had it installed: he was self sufficient. He lay on a pile of breasts fucking himself while his enemies were burnt in segments at his feet.

He felt heavy as stone. Thick oozes poured from him. All the people fooled by his grin and easy charm, they should come and behold him on his dung heap. He would put their heads up on posts on his palisade. Ginny hung on the wall weeping for her stolen cunt, Ginny whom he could not love. He did not know why he could not love her. Somehow he did not doubt that she loved him, any more than he doubted the love of his mother. He thought his inability (or unwillingness) to love her had to do with the fact that he did not love himself and she did not love herself.

His mother brought him food like a jailer—food that he dumped out the window so that at night dogs fought for it out there and rats scuffled—but he was the jailer. His mother and sister lurked and scuttled and talked in whispers, trapped by him.

Fraud, he accused himself, pimpled fraud. You're no more an Indian than your little sister. What do you know about it all? It's something you read in a book. You might

as well decide to be an Eskimo or a Zulu. He remembered
the time he had driven into Chicago to the address he had
secretly copied of a sort of social hangout of lots of
Indians. He had parked nearby and walked by, walked by,
and finally he had run away. He had felt ashamed. They
would look at him and they would see he was as much
white as Indian, and that he had never known anything of
where he came from. His father had been born on a reservation in South Dakota, but his mother had never been on
a reservation in her life, and neither had he. The Choctaws
had been terminated by the government. He had never
even met his old man's family. He had made it all up. He
was nobody. He was a lie.

Diarrhea left him empty, light as a dried leaf. Finally
his head cleared and settled. Now he was only waiting.
Now he sat crosslegged, and all was dry and clear and
chilly within and without him in the late-April twilight.
The frogs sang under him, under the house set up on
cement blocks, like the high floor of a ritual hut where he
squatted waiting.

In the dark, he smelled the buffalo. There it was—gamy,
harsh, warm, rank. Then it spoke to him with its huge
head hung over the bed, bearded, mammoth, and streaked
with gray. The grandfather buffalo took him up on its
broad humpy back, and he clung to the greasy wool and
was carried jogging through the long grassy night of the
prairies, westward from the mills, westward from the ex-
pressways and the clutter of little houses, westward from
the vast blurred skyshine of Chicago.

"I was the bread of your people. I was the house and
the shirt and the blanket and the bow and the belly. I was
the tool and the stuff that is worked, I was the hand of the
maker. Your people lived on me as on a mountain. The
grass waved and I ate it as far as the clean fresh wind
blew.

"Then I was burnt and left to rot." And the grandfather
buffalo set him down on a high hill. And as far as he
could see was the long grass of the prairie, dense with
millions and millions of buffalo and pronghorn antelope
and elk and herds of wild horses running before the wind,
and the winds were heavy with the fluttering of prairie
chickens and wild turkey. Then as he watched, the white
men came and began killing, quickly, so that money might
be made and the Indians starved to submission and death.

They brought better and better guns till they could kill as fast as they could shoot. "And the wind turned bad and blew the soil away. I was killed and left to rot. I became garbage. It had been beautiful, the world made out of my flesh and my bone, my hide and my sinews. The people danced each season on my back. If there was plenty, all shared it. If there was nothing, they moved on or they starved. But what each man and each woman did was real and good and belonged to each like his arm. Every man had his song and his name, which made him strong and gave him dignity. The word was real, and every man had his own poem to connect him to himself.

"Now what is there? My people starve. They have no good work to do. They die of the white man's diseases in bits of desert allowed them. And what have they done with the good land? Are those who seized the land happy?

"Now there are people in boxes, their heads full of noise, their lungs full of smoke and poison, their bellies full, but their flesh sour. They do what they are told. They call the waste of their hours work, yet they are not making things others need—healthy food, strong clothing, pleasant shelter. At the top are a handful of men who buy and sell the mountains and the rivers, who pollute and explode and set aside as preserves all the lands of the earth. The people are barnyard animals who give milk and butter to their owners and decide nothing, not even the hours of their slaughter. They are chained together and crippled by shame. They cannot dance. Only the young are alive a little while to dance and feel and touch each other."

He was standing on a hill to watch. Young boys and girls were throwing their clothes into piles and running away to dance together around bonfires. The music was drums only. Naked people dancing together who had left all things behind and wanted only each other. So they became more real to each other than gadgets and fantasies. They left everything and came out of the rotting cities to dance together.

Then he was lying on his back in bed and the buffalo stood over him with hooves on his chest, a mountain crushing him.

"You see and do nothing. In seeing we begin, but you have not begun. Lead the tribes to water. Soon there will be no more people. Your generation is the last. You must lead the tribes to water. You must save your generation."

Corey sat on his bed, alone in the first false gray before dawn. Tears crept down his face. To begin. To commit himself to his sense of the good that could flower out of his muck. Somehow he must manage to trust himself if only as crude instrument. The world that wanted to be born was pressing on him.

It seemed clear enough in a general way what was to be done. It did not matter that he was not an Indian among Indians. The children of the people who had plundered the land were being themselves consumed by the greed of the plunderers. They could turn away from the ways of metal to the ways of the flesh. They could learn the good ways of being in harmony, of cooperating, of sane bravery in defense of each other, to be one with their bodies and their tribe and each other and the land.

The children would turn away from being white. For the whites were crazy. The whites were colonizers and dominators and enslavers. The whites always defined themselves out of nature, on top of the landscape. They came to rob and steal and develop and conquer. Already the children wore beads and headbands and smoked ritually. They were awaiting the coming of the real tribes.

Did he believe in the grandfather buffalo? What did that mean? There was a force powerful enough to kill and give birth, to create fire out of flesh, and that force seized him. The pillar of light: from top to bottom all things lined up in clarity and fire.

His totem was the mothering, fathering buffalo, body of the tribes, and his enemy was the eagle, bird of prey and power that had sold out to the conquerors, that savage, war-mad, torturing cannibal streak in the people, which had joined with the old horde terror and greed in their conquerors and become the major mode of the land. With the strength of the buffalo, he was to destroy the eagle of empire and lead the tribes to water.

Billy Batson and the Teentsy Revolution

HIS mother came into Billy's room and turned on the air conditioner so that it blew on his back. When she left, he shut if off. When she came back in again, he pretended to be totally absorbed in the problem he was working on, but she was determined to extract some conversation from him as her price for leaving again.

"Is that homework?"

He thought of lying, but it was not worth the effort. "Not directly. It's just an interesting problem."

She peered over his shoulder. She hated not being able to understand what he studied. She was intelligent, wasn't she? It was perversity. It was more cheating of her. She had been deprived of an education. What did not bore her was the closet drama of her martyrdom. Out of the corner of his eye, past his glasses, he scanned her face. She was a plain, rather squarish woman who boasted she didn't carry an extra ounce of fat. She looked like the ex-teacher she was, but inside she was Hamlet and Juliet and Lady Macbeth. He was Horatio and the good gray nurse and the audience too, the actor trained to feed her lines. Would she really let him go away to Cal Tech? She had to. To let him make good and come home laden with trophies. Never enough.

"What is this gaudy-looking object?" She pounced on the issue of *Grassfire* with its squiggly letters proclaiming NO MORE PIGEONS, NO MORE SITTING DUCKS. ALL POWER TO THE STUDENTS.

"Something the kids put out." Corey and his boys had run it off, a typical pornographic rag screaming for student power.

"You mean the school lets them get away with this nonsense?"

"It's not official, if that's what you mean."

"What are you doing with it, Billy?"

"Nothing. They were handing them out."

She tore it across and dropped it in the wastebasket.

"Don't get involved in any monkeyshines in school. After all the trouble I went to to keep the mention of therapy off your record, don't foul things up. It's not too late to ruin your chances at Cal Tech."

"I'm accepted. What more do you want?" He was not being recruited. He was excluded from the channeling exams. Of course he was staying out of the anti-pigeon agitation. What did it matter? All assemblies were displays of formalized bullshit: superb training in sitting being doused with propaganda and empty ritual while elaborating your chosen ability to produce sadistic or success-oriented daydreams. "I'm in, Mother. If you have to worry, pick out something real."

"You're not in yet, Billy-boy. And you didn't make MIT."

"Cal Tech's just as good."

"It's not as famous."

She had wanted to be a doctor. Her family had thought that unseemly for a woman. Instead, she had married his father, helped him through school, taught, and then there were children. His father was a pale gray drag. Started out as a high school math teacher and ended up as a middle-echelon man in a company specializing in auto insurance. He had been bigger than his father since he was fifteen, and his father had always regarded that as a breach of manners. His father read the paper and detective stories and watched television as if it were speaking to him. His mother had taught Billy a quiet scorn for his father without giving him anything else to love. Billy was to make up the world to his mother, to act out her dreams and bring home the grades and prizes and scholarships that proved her sacrifice was golden. Whatever he did would never be enough.

He waited; he held his big shoulders rigid, hoping she would leave. His refusal to arouse only irritated her. She patted at his hair, marched to and fro, peered again at the page he kept before him as if eager to get back to it.

"Sit up straight. You'll grow up round-shouldered."

"How much growing do you think I have left to do?"

"Well, your head's big enough. Being such a great clumsy boy doesn't mean your bones have set. The first thing people notice is your posture, Billy."

"Nobody looks at me, Mother. I have a label on me—genius, freak, science major. I wear an invisible white coat." It might as well be a monk's habit or a priest's vestments, it reduced him so purely to function.

"That's only high school. They're just ordinary children, the sons of men who work in the mills. What do you expect? College will be different." She imagined she was comforting him.

"I imagine it will be. That's where they start getting ready to use me."

"With an attitude like yours, I'm not sure they'll bother, Billy."

Everything in the system had a double edge, a second and contrary interpretation. The little privileges of the school turned out to be unpaid labor in disguise, such as the Science Club, which scrubbed glassware and washed beakers, or the Biology Club, which cleaned animal cages. Even his name, for instance. Billy: not William, as he was named formally, or Bill, the manly shortening. Billy belonged to early identification with Billy Batson, the crippled newsboy who could turn into Captain Marvel. He had not yet found his SHAZAM, only that he could master any consistent construct: chess, quantum theory, calculus, topology. He collected his science-fair prizes and headed the mathematics team for the glory of Franklin High, and remained Billy, the crippled newsboy—genius and freak. No one expressed resentment any longer because he knew the answers; they just looked through him.

"In ten years you're going to have backaches from slouching and wonder why. Then remember what your mother told you. There's pain enough in store for all of us without looking for it." Her hand glided suggestively over her heart.

He wanted to scream that she was healthy as a horse. Once she had been able to play him like a little violin, extracting from him all the squeals of sympathy and pain and guilt and tremulous desire to please that she wanted. "If you think I'm not getting enough exercise, I can always take up football again. I bet they'd be glad to have me back."

"And break your neck? That's a sport for ruffians, for boys who have no other means of making their way."

He was big and strong enough and he liked the rough action. He had liked his anger on the field. But she was right: the science would take him through. He wasn't giving them one extra bit of him. Two years before, even then, she had been able to make him feel guilty at will—guilty for making her worry. He had felt that he must somehow be in the wrong, be an insensitive lout, to enjoy football so much and worry his martyred mother.

She picked up the old glass paperweight from his desk. "I don't know why you want to hang on to this shabby object. It's not like you to be sentimental. You're not the least bit sentimental about your father or me, for instance. Why cling to a piece of childish rubbish? You're old enough to show some taste."

"It amuses me." He held out his hand until, reluctantly, she put the glass paperweight into his palm. At last she left him. He slumped forward. He had not let himself be roused. But he felt exhausted. He laid his head on his arm and looked at the paperweight in which the fake snow swirled soggily. Faintly he let himself smile. She would never know why he cherished it.

He had heard a fairy tale once, read by a substitute teacher. He had not been given such books as a child. Secretly he had read comic books. What shame when they were discovered by her, as later she found condoms on him. He carried them like the other boys, carefully tucked into his wallet. Aging there. Little tickets to normality. See, boys, I am just like you. Ignored. Once he had run water into one and watched it swell like a balloon until it burst.

The fairy tale was about a princess who lived on top of a glass mountain that she made the knights who constantly came to court her attempt to ride up. They slid off, naturally. They fell down in a heap and died below. The glass mountain got rid of all the pesky unsuitable suitors. Finally one guy made it over all the bones and rotting bodies and horseflesh and rusting equipment, all the way to the top. The goal post. My hero, she said, and prepared to make the grand sacrifice and accept a mere mortal mate, because he had won fair and square. But all the corpses had turned his stomach, and he said No thanks. He didn't want a princess who had to be conquered like a glass mountain. He went home. She leaped off and killed herself. That last was the fairy tale part.

America was a glass mountain. School was a practice glass mountain. Growing up and marrying and playing football and taking exams and everything else. Sometimes working on a problem, he thought he had got off, but afterward he found that that pleasure, that excitement, was just their means of getting him to climb a little faster, a little higher. They had pretty aesthetic systems to turn him on, but it developed that what they wanted were glass mountain missiles and glass mountain nuclear plants and glass mountain satellites. The systems were daydreams of the knights climbing before they slid down and were smashed. Or before they made it to the top and married the glass princess and began to wonder just what they had done wrong.

They had conned him plenty of times. Like the brotherhood bit. He got his own black boy to tutor, slow reader to bring up to age level. He was pretty excited about it all, a regular bleeding heart liberal prepared to share his enlightenment. He had worked hard and Joe had made steady progress. Then he took a good look one day at the books they were using. *Bobby's Career in the Coast Guard. Jim Gets His Wings. Dick Flies His First Bombing Mission. Jack Goes Down to the Sea in a Submarine.* They were instructive, all right. After that, he couldn't ignore that he was coaching Joe to get him up to the level where the Army could use him.

After that they talked some. He found out that Joe was quicker than he had been in figuring it all out. But what could Joe do? In the Army he would have money in his pockets anyhow, and it was better than rotting in Gary and doing the welfare shuffle. With luck, they might even teach him something he could make a living at afterward. But Joe cast a cold eye on that too, for he had seen too many black guys come back to the neighborhood trained at things they couldn't get hired to do. Then they had to find a hustle, or re-enlist. Likely they were pretty soon in jail or back in the barracks.

It had never before occurred to him that Joe was not stupid. Joe was a certified slow learner. He was in the dropout track. But stupid he wasn't. He had seen himself as Joe's liberal teacher, but Joe was giving him more real and more useful instruction than he was giving Joe. He felt as if a box had been taken off his head. He was naïve enough to try to explain to his parents his excitement, and they immediately lost their enthusiasm for his tutoring. He could see they were scared of something.

"I know you're lonely, but you'll only cause yourself and him damage by trying to pretend you can make a friend out of a boy so different from yourself. Why, he doesn't even know what you're talking about half the time." She crossed her arms, clucking.

She had a way of putting a finger on sore spots. Part of the trouble was, after he invited Joe over, Joe kept saying that coming from a nice home like that, he had nothing to complain about. Nice? He hated its banality. Even his mother was always saying it was nothing but a disguised tract house. When he visited Joe, he envied him his easy rapport with his family and his brothers and sisters. He knew that in a fancier way he was just as trapped and manipulated as Joe, but he could not explain to him how it was so. What really drew him was pure mathematics, but everybody had always shunted him ever so firmly into physics. In school, he could not study anything he really wanted. There was the assumption that what was really pretty and interesting belonged to a "club," and physics was the bread and butter reality.

Anyhow, it looked good on the record, the tutoring deal, and the Science Club and the Mathematics Team, though they remained to him mainly occasions of shame: how he had been conned for a while. How satisfying it would be to let them know he saw through. But where and who were They?

He sat up and fished *Grassfire* out of the wastebasket— woven bark with a brass eagle on the side: it would be called Colonial Something. His mother was big on Colonial Somethings. He pieced the halves of *Grassfire* together. It was as gaudy as she had implied. He felt as if the dayglo colors would bleed on his fingers. WAKE UP, CATTLE: YOU ARE THEIR MEAT. NO HAMBURGER TOMORROW: JAM TODAY. FIGHT FOR THE MAN OR FIGHT THE MAN.

Corey's boys were amateurs of hating. They hadn't studied who was using them and how and why. He was careful to remember that the teachers were fools who were never going to make it the way they were programed to feel that they should, that the teachers were merely the assembly-line workers and occasional shop stewards in a corporate factory. Corey's boys hated the teachers as if they were the enemy. He tried to remember he only had to suffer their bumbling malice a few months before he achieved the high-pressure, more interesting oppression of the university, to prepare him for the job where he would be paid extravagantly and might even be allowed to play sometimes. Always he would be a fish in somebody's aquarium. But he did not confuse the stupidity of the teachers with power. They were like the corner cop: they could make you very uncomfortable on their turf, but their turf was small and they could be easily removed from above. Only as long as you were clearly under them would they think of threatening you.

After all, the school had ways of using the kids to control each other. The "good kids" would man the corridors, demanding to see passes, would act as monitors, would do the unpaid labor that kept the school functioning. They would join the clubs and write the school paper, dull and full of photos of other goodies, and make civic speeches and sit on the sportsmanship council and be cheerleaders and run for the school elections on the platform of a straight, bland smile: perfect training in elections as popularity TV contests that never threatened the economic status quo.

He watched Corey's boys marching around and yelling and writing mindless slogans with magic marker. THE SCHOOLS ARE YOURS: TAKE THEM. UP THE BODY! Noisy, silly, easily stampeded, they waved their pricks like bombs. Then they took the school and that arrested him where he stood. They took the school!

Corey found him in the physics lab and told him he could still leave. "We aren't keeping anybody who doesn't want to fight." Corey leaned in the doorway squinting at him and speaking gently. "They aren't even after you, so we'd understand. Like if you stay, you might lose your science deferment."

"Think they're doing me a favor, don't you, boy? If I'm not a good slavey, they won't let me do my thing. But it's not my thing, it's theirs. I could do mine sitting at the bottom of a crater."

Corey sat down on a lab stool, swinging slowly to and fro and turning a bunsen burner on and off. Whoosh, whoosh went the blue flame. "If it's their thing, why do it at all?"

"It's more amusing than getting stuck in the Army."

Corey's face spread with a slow beatific smile. "So you're caught too. Balls in the vise, like the rest of us."

"Does that give you a thrill?"

"I don't believe people come over except because it's bad where they are. So don't work for them. Technology for the revolution. Do it for us." The burner spat fire and went out. Tongue of fire, hiss, hiss, dark pure blue.

"Why should I care if it's their thing or yours I'm doing?"

"*Our* thing—yours too. Maybe you have to do our thing before you can do your own private thing and have it come out good, good for you, for everybody. Science has turned into a cancer." Corey tapped his knee. "I want the good technician working in the good society in a human way . . ."

"I'm a mathematician who will be forced to study physics. I am not some sort of super plumber."

"What can they give you for being their toy physicist?" Corey held out a bony dark finger. "Exemption from the Army and other grinds. A house out past the expressway, a split-level you can spend your life paying for and filling with kiddies and electric can openers and electric blankets and outboard motors and electric fry pans and floor polishers and coffee grinders and power drills and three-speed lawn mowers and large shiny books about the history of locomotives to lie on the Danish coffee table. A hi-fi they can hear in Toledo. Two shiny cars that don't work. A sex manual next to the bed about how to fuck your wife so she'll be magically satisfied with being locked up in a box full of kids and gadgets . . ."

"I call it the glass mountain. I don't think it's worth rapping about. Could you spare me the rest of the spiel?" He glared around the empty lab.

"But a lot of kids haven't seen it yet. How do we know you see, if you keep it to yourself?"

"Who's us? The shepherd and his flock."

"They're turning on to themselves. We're building a real community here. That's what we can offer you, Billy. First, exemption from the Army—"

"Through your pull with Congress?"

"We don't go, Billy. We say no, and mean it. We build our own nation in the belly of this one. We make a good community for each other, based on cooperation and starting right now."

"Until tomorrow, when the police come and throw us out."

"We're practicing here. But I think we can hold it a few days." Corey looked up at the ceiling. "They built this school without windows to hold out a neighborhood, to hold out living, to hold out distraction—a fortress of a school. I think we can keep it long enough to change the people inside."

"Playing games, that's all." Billy got up and stomped around the long lab table. "You should be ashamed to talk about revolution. Just playing games. Have you read Marx? Have you read Lenin? Che? Mao? Do you have any idea what you think you're doing playing hide and seek in a school building?"

"Moncada was just a building too. And they didn't even hold it briefly. You start where you're at and where you can't stand any longer to be. You start saying no to the system and yes to each other."

"Rhetoric. Bullshit. You have no analysis and no strategy. You have no program." Billy sat down sneering.

"But we have a thousand kids in motion. Don't we?"

To that he had no answer. That was what had kept him there. Maybe it was simple curiosity to see forces in confrontation.

"What would be the use of having an analysis right now, when the kids wouldn't be ready for it?" Corey bent forward, touching Billy's knee. "This is what they're ready for, and this is going to make a lot of difference in them."

"A few holes in a few heads."

"Are you going or staying, Billy? Are you staying with us?"

"What does it look like I'm doing?"

"Come around with me and review the defenses."

Billy shook his head no. But the picture amused him, him and Corey the raging delinquent strolling arm and arm through the rabble looking at "defenses." He shook his head no, but waited.

Corey smiled. "Come on. Want to see what you think of them. Get your thoughts on how we can improve our positions. We're buying time, remember, time to organize each other."

He saw that he could not simply sit out the siege in the physics lab. He wanted to touch that sense of motion. He would be busted with the rest of them, so he might as well plunge in and satisfy his curiosity.

"They'll be surprised to see me."

"Maybe."

"You were surprised to find me here."

"Maybe." Corey grinned. He got up, stretched himself

like someone much taller, and motioned him toward the door.

Billy got up heavily, emphasizing his bulk and sticking his belly out. "But now I'm part of the master plan, uh?"

"You'll be part of making it, won't you?" Corey led out. In the hall kids were sitting in loose circles, kids were scrawling slogans on the walls, and a boy was working on jimmying the lock on a storeroom door. Everything was much more diffuse than he had imagined. People had broken into small details and everything seemed to be happening at once in all directions without coordination or direction. Corey did take Billy's arm, but his fingers were unconscious. He was alert only to the scene. Nobody paid much attention to them.

Corey explained in brief snatches. "We're taking turns sleeping up on three, so that there's always somebody on duty." They stood watching the kids working on the barricades inside the doors. Chairs, shop benches, tables, desks were heaped up bristling.

There were meetings going on all of the time in one or another room, big meetings in the gym every few hours, constant announcements over the PA system and rock music blasting away. Their talk had excited Billy. He knew he was a fool to take any of the gab seriously. Corey was just trying out his charisma on a new sucker. But on the other hand, something was happening here. Action combined the niceties of game theory with the shock of collision. Close to five hundred kids had taken the school. They occupied the lunchroom and fed each other. They served on the sanitary and food and building squads. They had meetings at which they argued about what they wanted in their lives and what kind of world they would be willing to live in. They danced and smoked grass and played basketball in the gym. They took down the pictures of George Washington and the Superintendent of Schools and put up posters of Che and the Rolling Stones. With all the art department supplies for the rest of the term liberated from the storeroom, they were making a huge collage and painting a mural in the cafeteria depicting themselves and their culture heroes seizing the school and the Franklin shopping plaza.

Corey assigned him a crew, and he set them to making smoke and stink bombs for the defense of the doors. This was the longest time in his life he had been away from home except for camp. He had hated camp. Here he was not under anyone. He could go away from them into a room and shut the door and work on a problem. Mostly the problems did not engage him long. He would hear noises outside and want to know what was up. His curiosity surprised him. He did not want to miss anything.

Corey asked him, "Is everybody treating you well?"

"Aren't specialists always treated well? *They* do that too." He liked and hated it at once. Respect. He wandered around the edges of the groups. He hated the dancing. Obscene movements. Some of it was naked and that was worse. Taunting him for being fat, for being awkward, for being him. Not overtly, of course. They were respectful. Indeed, they treated him like Captain Marvel wandering through in his red plastic suit. Gee, look who's here, how are you, old man? You want to dance? He turned on with them and went high up into the pinnacle of his head and looked down on the motes in Brownian movement and no longer cared.

He found his interest in the cookbook fiddlings of chemistry revived. Pick out the active ingredients in grass and synthesize them cheaply. Or play other changes on the chemistry of human absurdity. Corey would provide him with the volunteers he needed. Yes. When they lost the school, he would return to chemistry.

Corey had assigned him a girl; he was sure of that. Her name was Ginny, she said in a soft voice and slept beside him on a table in the physics lab. The second night he had sex with her. He was grimly determined, though scared she would figure out he was new to it, but she acted pleased and friendly. She seemed relieved that he wanted to.

With her soft hands she rubbed his back and belly and then his penis. She told him she was sure he was very strong and he told her gruffly that he was. He did not like her body much. It was soft and spongy and she had big jiggly breasts and a round belly somehow in the way. But he managed to stay in her, and he closed his eyes and pumped away with her making cooing noises. Odd thoughts distracted him, such as that someone might come into the lab and see them. The picture rose of the whole physics class sitting around them calmly taking notes while he humped away on her. She was wet inside, and somehow that distracted him too. That it was wet and runny like a mouth or a dog's nose.

When he finished she sighed and rubbed against him and said that was the way she liked it, going on for a long time. Most men didn't. He patted her on the shoulder and turned over to try to sleep on the hard table. On the whole, he was glad he had done it. He still did not know how to talk to girls. The idea of having to go up to a girl and start talking and make a pass at her or however people got into those things, was enough to give him a headache or make him itch in his clothes, for instance when he had to go to parties.

All things considered, therefore, he was more or less glad Corey had assigned the girl to him. He did not know if he was glad or sorry to think that she would probably be there the next night too, but he had the hang of it now. With her, anyhow, it would not frighten him. Only he was not sure how he was supposed to act with her the rest of the time, so during the day he kept busy with his crew and pretended he didn't see her when she came in. His crew were learning fast and he was pleased with them. He was getting a lot better results out of them than the school ever had. One of his best men was Chuck, who'd never been allowed to take anything more demanding than Life Science.

Ginny hung around and finally out of embarrassment he put her to work with the crew. It turned out she wasn't stupid. He could not say why he had assumed that she was. She even asked good questions. He forgot to be worried about how he should act. He treated her like the rest of the crew and that seemed to work.

Why had he assumed that Ginny was stupid? It was Joe all over again. It was because she came from the Ditch, not from Valley Acres, because she was tracked into "general studies," which was the dropout track. She wasn't even good enough for "commercial," which would train her for a typing job—a job she would always think of as temporary if she spent forty years at it. No, she was down in "general," where she would, if she was persistent enough to hang around to graduation, be able to get a job in a department store or filing or running messages.

He kept thinking about tracking. He spent time going through records in the principal's office. Sometime in grade school, already your fate was settled, your social class was established for the rest of your life. Unemployment or welfare or with luck into the mills, for the guys in "general." Typing and clerking and maybe secretaries or bookkeepers for the girls in "commercial." College and afterward semitechnical or social work or teaching for the "academics." If you weren't in the academic track and the fast classes, nobody would try to teach you much, just keep you busy.

Ginny's parents spoke Polish at home. She had scored down close to the borderline of mental defective in her early intelligence tests. No one had bothered to notice that she had managed to learn English since then, and that here was an alert if bruised intelligence. Chuck made a more than adequate chemist. He would never think up an experiment, but he could follow any formula and he was accurate.

They were broadcasting by then to other kids, trying to get them to rise and take their schools. Students who had never willingly spoke in class since the third grade made speeches and broadcast appeals. A daily newspaper was run off on the office mimeograph, and there was no shortage of articles and drawings and jokes and editorials. All of them were erupting opinions they wanted to share.

He kept trying to decide, day to day, if Corey was bright. He was no mushhead. Yet there were holes in Corey's mind. Corey was profoundly ignorant. In twelve years of school he had learned nothing about biology, physics, chemistry, music, literature, art, psychology, anthropology, or sociology. His history was a series of brightly lit countermyths, tableaux of great Indian leaders and peasant uprisings and guerrilla struggles, a Manichaean war stretching into the dim past. Corey had a sense of politics, of what made people move. He had a facility with public speaking. His record had enough nasty comments on it to keep him out of anyplace he might have wanted to go.

Billy made his first public speech about tracking and the school records. (His own had a note from the principal saying not to pass on information about his bad temper and therapy, because Franklin High needed the admission to a good school for their records.) At the end of his speech, it was voted to burn the dossiers. He was stunned and exalted before the fire.

It was still a school. Classes met most times of the day

and night. They found the library sadly lacking in texts
they could use. People proposed classes they wanted to
give or take. Lots came under the general heading of Who
Am I, Where Do I Come From, Where Are We Going?
They had learned nothing real in prefab history or civics
classes. Corey and Billy between them taught a course in
American History that got the kids pretty excited. Billy
found it sad and funny. He had never been interested, but
in his casual browsing and reading he had picked up a
smattering. Another subject that got people aroused—
though once again it was a case of pooling the few facts
that anyone knew—was Who Owns America? There was
also a course in local politics. Some of the kids knew a
little more about that. They had a chart going by the third
day that covered three boards of the room they were
using, filling in connections between the big local contrac-
tors and the steel companies and the city and county
governments and the unions and the Sons of Italy and the
Slovakian Businessmen's Association and the downtown
merchants. Then they trailed off. They found they still did
not know who owned obvious centers of power like the
banks. They did not know who owned the local paper. Or
the radio stations. They pooled what little they knew
about how to find out.

There were also courses in karate and self-defense. Billy
spent a fair amount of time in the gym practicing. He
could tell that the other guys were surprised. Already they
had forgotten that as a freshman he had been one of the
best on the scrub team. Because he did not strut and pose
around, they did not realize how strong he was. The girls
wanted to learn karate and self-defense too, but they complained that no one would teach them seriously. They said
the boys did not care if they learned or not, yet they had
much greater need.

He called what they did "courses," although they did
not look like anything that went on in school normally. The
first thing they did was to push the teacher's desk out of
the way and set up the chairs in a circle. In some rooms
they shoved the desks down the halls to build barricades
and everybody sat in a circle on the floor. Sometimes they
tried turning out the lights and talking in the dark to
break people of the habit of keeping their mouths shut or
worrying how others would judge what they said. They
knew nothing. Yet each had scraps in his head that others

maybe could use: questions, doubts, experiences, something seen on TV. They had to learn to give them to each other. What they were doing together was trying to learn how to learn.

Groups formed all the time that were just as eager to talk as the classes, but somehow in another direction. He called them T-groups and found them boring and silly, but Corey insisted they were functional. Corey said that people were finding out that what each of them had thought of as his personal problem that he must solve in his life, was not personal at all but a common problem. If he found others in a little group who had that same hang-up, he must begin to see that an individual solution was bullshit.

"If you find six other people confessing the same thing, you stop asking what you've done wrong. You stop feeling guilty about being such a stupid shit. You start asking how everybody got that way, and how to change the society that did it."

But Billy still considered the T-groups a form of titillation.

The fourth night, the police cordon outside was reinforced by busloads of tactical police, and they knew the crisis had come. "Four days and three nights to turn five hundred kids into a people," Corey said. They lay on the roof watching the police bring up a bulldozer and get ready to smash in through the south doors. It was eerie. The moon was risen and bright on them. The police did not move like men, because they were so encased in their weapons and paraphernalia. They carried side arms, cases for handcuffs on their left hips, a club for head knocking and ball breaking, a gas mask and extra rounds of ammunition. Some had devices on their backs for spraying gas. Others carried spray cans or grenades. They moved with the stiffness of men laden with gadgets and protected from any sense of what they do. Something that looked like a tank was drawn up.

They went downstairs. Corey stood in line for the mike. Everybody was trying to make ready for the assault. Some people were preparing to resist arrest passively, others hoped to make a stand. Wet cloths and jars of Vaseline were going around. Girls were taking earrings out of their ears to prevent the lobes being torn, and tucking their hair in to discourage being dragged by it.

Corey spoke briefly in his turn. "We've done our best to make this jail into a human place, living here together and communally. We belong to each other and we're a people now. We no longer belong to them or their rotten system. They can't hold us. We're water. Only if they can scare us and freeze us can they break us up. We're water and we can flow together. We're one tribe and we ought to be ready to leave this ugly place anyhow. We must move out and reach our brothers and sisters everywhere and call them out to join us.

"Soon we'll be together in another of their jails. Soon we'll be back out and free in the open again dancing together. We must not forget, we must not let them make us forget that we're people of one tribe, the first tribe of a new nation of the young and the free. Now they're coming and we must protect each other as well as we can. We belong to a new nation of the young and the free, and we're going to win!"

The police began hurling in tear gas canisters and grenades. Billy looked around quickly for Ginny, but he could not get to her, and then his eyes began to burn and he bent over choking. He would miss sleeping on the hard physics table. He would miss his crew. He would miss the rough meals in the lunchroom. He would miss the interminable meetings and speeches and hassles. It was all over, he supposed, but these had been by far the best days of his life.

How Joanna Accepts a Chain

FOR the second time that year, the pigs shipped Joanna back to her parents in Fort Dix, where her father called her names and her mother got drunk as usual and wept and shook her by the shoulders and hair clumsily. They shipped her back to the hopeless box of being Jill. Back to the creepy school and the prison of the base and the generals' sons who thought they were entitled to lay her because she had been around and her father was a flop—a permanent captain. Back to the world where people were numbers and little perches to defend and diseases. Back to the world where everything was known, and it all amounted to nothing more exciting than a laundry list.

The world of people grinding each other. Owning each other. Her mother drank gin. Her father ate shit. All god's children hated the nigger communist jew hippy bastards out there. The world of being excluded and exploited, or incorporated and exploited. You paid your life and you took your choice.

She was sent home from school one day for not wearing a bra. "But a bra makes my breasts stick out more," she said to the counselor. "I don't like my breasts to stick out." She knew the woman wanted to punch her but did not dare, not quite. She had a good time with the counselor, playing with the word "obscene." Joanna made a quick list of things she found obscene: powdering your face, wearing underwear that caused parts of the body to stick out or get squished in unnaturally, shaving under the arms or between the legs, dipping fingernails or toenails in paint. . . .

She didn't mind being sentenced to stay home for three days. She spent the time locked in her room rereading *Alice in Wonderland* and Sherlock Holmes stories and dancing to the radio. Sometimes she danced naked in front of the mirror, not to excite herself, because she did not find it exciting, but in order to study the movement of her limbs and muscles exactly. She improvised, then watched frowning and improved or discarded the step or gesture.

It depressed her that she could only define herself in negatives. She was not like her mother. She was not like her father. The conventional masculine and the conventional feminine were for shit. The primary business of base ladies was to talk about each other. What her mother knew could be contained in a greeting card and consisted of You're Supposed To's and Don't You Dare's. It could be summed up as, "Don't sit with your knees apart, Jill, you're a big girl now."

She did not want to be somebody else's wife or somebody else's mother. Or somebody else's servant or somebody else's secretary. Or somebody else's sex kitten or somebody else's keeper. She saw no women around who seemed to be anybody in themselves. They all wore some man's uniform. She wanted to be free, and free meant not confined, not forced to lie, not forced to pretend, not warped, not punished, not tortured.

They could always put her down by telling her she was only good at criticizing and didn't know what she wanted. But how could you know what you wanted if you had never seen it? Maybe it was only the made-up stories in books, in which people stood up straight and had feelings past nastiness and boredom and did things because they really wanted to. But if she was so filled with wanting, somewhere there must be something worth it. And she knew pretty much where to start looking. She imagined sometimes having the word FREE tattooed on her forehead, on her arms, on her back and belly. FREE, FREE, FREE.

They could coerce her and they could imprison her but they could not bribe her. They had nothing to tempt her with. The things she really wanted they did not have for sale. What did they offer her? On the one hand, they pressed her to "be like mommy." Little boys, be like daddy. Little girls, be like mommy. But if you raised your eyes from the wall-to-wall carpeting and looked, you had to shudder. It was the equivalent of a curse. Cut off your head, stunt your feelings, leap into a box and slam the lid tight. Spend the rest of your life charging your kids and your hubby for what you think you missed, sacrificing for them the self that never existed.

Or a girl could daydream about being a famous face.

She could dream about being photographed and stared at.
She could dream that her face or her boobs would sell ten
million cans of roach spray. She could dream that she
would lie on a pink cushion with her bush carefully
airbrushed out and millions of sad men would jerk off all
over the page in preference to having anything to do with
real hairy women.

Well, she was hairy Joanna and she didn't bother to
count the boys she had decided to fuck and never had she
pretended anything with any of them that she did not feel.
Now she was in her ascetic phase. Sex here was obscene.
She did not even touch herself. She was into discipline of
herself for her own uses. She would have liked to be
studying yoga or karate.

She went on attending school till finals. She was not
getting bad grades—not as well as she deserved, because
the teachers disliked her. That the work was easy when
she felt like doing it made her an even harder case to
them. The powers had her summer planned: a maximum-
surveillance camp for problem children. In the meantime
she did baby-sitting and snitched what coins she could and
ate a lot, putting on the weight she always lost when she
was free.

They had her seeing the school shrink, and she played
along. When he got too nosy about what happened when
she was on the loose, she told him horror stories about her
parents. He tried to find out what drugs she had tried and
about sex. She told him she had petted a lot. He said the
police matron said she was not a virgin. She talked about
police matrons so graphically, he got squeamish. She took
to rapping about her early childhood because that kept
him from pestering her about reality.

He was in his late thirties and wore a small, small
mustache no grander than his eyebrows. She imagined him
fingering it in the mirror. Did he ever do anything he
wanted to? He told her he had gone to school for twenty
years to be a shrink, and she understood that his guts had
been completely wrapped in cellophane. She doubted
whether he even knew that he was attracted to her, or
that he hated her in a dull itchy way. That was all a
manner of speaking. Correctly he letched on, hated, the
doll in his head. He had no sense that intersected with
hers, no means of apprehending who she was.

The third day of finals while her father was on maneu-

vers and her mother was out cold from the night before,
she left the house in the morning with her stash and her
sleepingbag, walked off the base, hitched a ride on the
highway and flew like a bird out of the bushes. By night-
fall she was coming out of the subway in Union Square,
heading south and east. At the fourth address she tried,
the guy was home and he said she could spread her bag on
the kitchen floor.

She kept all addresses in her head. A long time before
she had learned never to write down anything that mattered. What pulled her was getting out of the hate machine and getting to a place where people were gentle to
each other, didn't bug each other, shared what they had,
shared their food and their bodies and their music and
their space and their kicks. She would not grab at anybody
or let anybody fix hooks into her. Women mostly wanted
to take some man, turn him into a house and go sit in it.

She was scared of *them*, not of herself, not of being
alone or having to make it on the streets. She had gone
down into her psyche on acid and walked the pavements
peeled naked on mescaline, and she was not afraid except
of what the hate people could do to her.

They had tried to kill her. She was not particularly
afraid of physical pain. She had been beaten many times.
But they tried to make her ashamed. They tried to fill her
with disgust for being alive, for her masses of red kinky
hair they always wanted to cut off, for her soft and hard
body, for her simple ready sexuality, for her hard quick
mind, for her independence, for everything that was Joanna. They had tried to make her hate herself, and the worst
fear she had sometimes was that they had in part succeeded.

It was good to be in the scene. This was the world she
knew. In a sense it was all she knew; the base-hell and the
scene. She walked and walked the next afternoon in the
hot dusty June sun and dug everything—the free kids in
their colors, the posters, the headshops, the botanicas, the
joyerías, the boutiques, the Puerto Rican mothers on the
stoops, the ball games in the streets.

The second day she was sitting in Tompkins Square
Park when she picked up a guy. They had pirogi and
walked around. Then she went to his pad. He had shoul-
der-length wispy soft brown hair and a silky beard and
gentle hands. He made love to her rather languidly, while

her mind kept wandering to the pretty objects in the room. Still it was nice to have sex again. She took a bath in the kitchen and he washed her back. He told her that he was a film maker and if she waited till dark, he would show her the film he was working on.

So she waited and they ate pumpernickel bread and peaches and peanut butter and chocolate-covered graham crackers. He went out for a while, and she turned the pages of his books full of stills from movies and washed her hair and looked at the phone and tried to think if there was anyone she wanted to call. No one.

They turned on, and he pulled down black shades and set up the projector and started explaining. The film was full of out-of-focus shots of traffic and a child reaching for a ball in front of a fire and lots and lots of trees blowing their branches against blue skies and gray skies and night skies and the moon in the branches—and a girl with big breasts jumping rope. It all had something to do with the four elements and the Tao. He kept explaining and she watched it all patiently twice. Then they went to bed and she fell asleep and spent the night.

In the morning he went to work and she took another walk. He had made a date with her for later, but she knew she would not keep it. She had learned enough about his world to satisfy her mild curiosity. Handbills were up in the park saying that Shawn and The Coming Thing were giving a free concert that night.

She saw a girl she thought she knew sitting in the sun. It wasn't the same girl but they turned out to know a couple of people in common, so they traded stories and sat together. Joanna had loaded her sack with chocolate graham cookies and peaches, and Clare and she ate them. Clare told her Shawn only gave free concerts now and that he was beautiful and she would give anything, anything to shack up with him, just for one night.

Clare said the new head scene was called bread and it was cheap. Only the Indians had it. They used it together. They were a sort of cult, and they looked out for each other. Clare had had bread once. It wasn't like anything else. It didn't space you out. There was a lot of fake bread—everything from smack to speed—but you could only get real bread from the Indians. The Indians hung together; they lived in communes and danced naked and wore old clothes. They were not supposed to spend money.

Clare had been attracted to them, but it was really too
grim, with not being able to wear nice clothes. And
everything was meetings, meetings all the time.

Around suppertime, Joanna got hungry but Clare wasn't
interested in trying to hustle some food. Joanna arranged
to meet her at the park before the concert, and headed
back to the guy's pad where she had left her sleepingbag
the first night. The guy was home putting silicone on a
new pair of boots, and they talked for a while and then he
wanted to ball. He was older or else he acted older, and
he didn't move her. She said it was her period. He said
that was okay with him. She said he would make her sore.
She argued with him for a while. Finally she gave up and
sucked him off.

He told her a friend was coming on business and she
should go for a walk. She said she would be back later,
but she picked up her sack and her sleepingbag and made
sure she had her toothbrush and soap. She couldn't be so
uppity as to say she'd never come back, but she'd try
sleeping in a doorway first. So often she thought people
were okay, when it only turned out that they'd been too
busy to try to take anything from her.

As she hiked toward the park with her roll on her back,
she made little noises of displeasure and searched her
teeth for stray hairs. Old creep. She hadn't been using up
anything of his, sleeping on his kitchen floor. Hadn't even
been eating there. The body tax. To be obliged to have
sex with someone was about the only thing that could kill
it.

She wandered in the crowd till she found Clare. Then
they sat on the grass on her bag. Another group was
playing first as the twilight thickened, a hot June night
smelling of tar and rubber, smelling slightly green and
moist too under the trees, smelling of smoked dope and of
gunpowder from the firecrackers kids kept setting.

When Shawn came on she had a funny feeling. She
made Clare get up and wriggle closer to the stage.

"Isn't he beautiful!" Clare moaned. "Oh god, so beautiful!"

They were too close to the shell to sit but stood pressed
in the crowd. The sexual vibrations moved from swaying
hip to hip, from belly to buttocks. Sound like a medium
denser than air pulsed around them, sound in which they
stood and breathed and shuddered like undersea plants.

Hey jack-in-the-box,
prisoner in the dock,
boy on a string,
hey woman stuffed
baby just born
and already on something.

Look around and open your eyes
you can't help but see it
you don't even have to try.
Ashes on the wind, ashes, ashes.
Their world has gone
out of its mind.

See how rich the old men grow.
So sleek, what do they eat?
See how fat the old men grow.
We are their meat.

Look around, you're not blind
you can't help but see it
you don't even have to try.
Ashes on the wind, ashes, ashes.
Their world has gone
out of its mind.

The board of directors votes a raise.
The general cracks a joke.
Somewhere they're burning children
and the wind smells like smoke.

"Oh god!" Clare groaned against her.

"Hey?" Joanna poked her in the ribs. "Guess what?" At first she had not been sure. She never paid much attention to the hero pictures girls collected. Mostly at concerts she hadn't been close enough to see if singers had two heads or three. Who cared? But craning her head up at the shell she could see him well enough. Clare was moaning, cupping her belly.

"Hey? I know him, Clare. I met him."

"You're stoned."

"No, I'm telling you. I didn't know who he was. I mean, I said I was Joanna and he said he was Shawn, but

I never thought twice. It was in a crash pad on C, and who'd expect him there? Then the pigs arrived and busted us all. It was last year when I was sixteen, late in the summer."

"How do you know it was him?"

"I can see him with my own eyes. He's not hard to recognize from last year. He looks thinner maybe."

"Maybe that was when he ran away from the Nineteenth Year. Did you really talk to him? Did he speak to you?"

"Sure." She looked at him standing with feet spread, guitar held across his crotch, head thrown back. "I screwed him."

Clare hit her in the arm. "Stop trying to put me on."

"Don't get excited. We slept together while we were both in that pad. Two or three days, I don't remember."

"Oh, my god." Clare thought for a while, poked her again. "So if you really know him, we can go see him afterward."

"Shit, Clare, he wouldn't remember me. Somebody he balled a couple of times last year."

"Why not, if it really happened? You remember him."

"Yeah, but I remember everything about that because the pigs really worked me over. They broke one of my teeth. See this one? It's capped."

"Was that the last time you ran away before this?"

"Christ, no, you think I'm a Sunday tourist? Twice since then. But that was the worst beating I ever had, except for one time in the Women's House of Detention. Then the screws beat me till I started bleeding, you know, as if I was having a period."

"Maybe you can't have babies now."

"Well, who wants to? I'd be glad for that. But they wouldn't do me the favor." Joanna touched her hard belly.

"I'd like a baby, if I could keep it. I have lots of ideas about how to bring it up, but they don't like to let you keep a baby if you're on your own. Which is a fat laugh. I hardly ever talked to my father in my whole life, except when I flunked something. I'd love to have a baby, if they wouldn't take it away from me."

> I met an ulcer
> coming down the street

with a briefcase and a belly
and a tie
that said tweet tweet
like a dying canary
in a coal mine.

Why do you hate me?
Why do you hate
what I do?
I don't do it,
I won't ever do it,
to you.

I met a plastic petunia
pushing a baby carriage
piled with bits of glass.
She offered me a bite,
I said, no thankful,
and her great dane
bit my ass.

Why do you hate me?
Why do you hate
what I do?
I don't do it,
I won't ever do it,
to you.

I met a general with stars and bars
driving his tank.
He said, my boy come here, come here.
Lie down in front.
I want to test the brakes.
I said no dice
and he called me Queer.

Why do you hate me?
Why do you hate
what I do?
I don't do it,
I won't ever do it,
to you.

Back behind them, people had started dancing in a rough circle. "Hey, Clare. Let's go back and join them. I want to dance. It's been so long, so long."

But Clare was moaning and swaying and grinding her hips.

Joanna nudged her harder. "I want to dance. Come on!"

She couldn't get through to Clare, so she edged away by herself. Later on she'd find Clare or she wouldn't. Anyhow, she didn't want Clare pushing her to make a fool of herself with Shawn.

Girls were strange. They thought getting fucked by somebody famous would electrify them. Somehow a white light would shine into their cunts and suddenly their lives would have meaning. The god would touch them and bring them into the sunshine. Then everybody would see who they were: secret princesses.

Shawn had been all right but only half there, like somebody stoned. He was angry and raw and kept his thoughts locked in. He was like a dozen other boys, except for being better looking. She remembered that his eyes were a deep dark startling blue. He had used his tall lean athletic body well and he had a big prick. But the sex had been nothing special. His prick might be a yard long, but his mind was someplace else. His voice was unmistakable and cut through the electric flak. Big, powerful and golden it rose. But she couldn't remember his speaking voice. Mostly he had mumbled. He was a man like a dozen others who had entered but not touched her. Scratch my back and I'll scratch yours. She never pretended except when the powers had her entrapped.

After her arrest, the cops had questioned her a long time trying to establish who she had been having sex with, and she remembered now that they had asked again and again about Shawn. She denied everything. She didn't care if the doctor reported sperm in her. She went on denying. If anything had happened, it must have been when she was asleep and how could she know? That was all she would say and they could not crack her. She didn't care whether they sent her to jail or home. Probably they'd been out to get an extra charge on him. She was glad she had not talked. He had his own problems. The radio didn't play his records any more. He was blackballed.

She pushed her way into the circle of dancers. First

there was a rim of people watching. Then a slow circle moving. She could see now that kids came into the center to dance usually by ones but sometimes in couples or threes. When they came into the center, they would throw off their clothes and one of the people who seemed to stay there would gather the clothes into a pile out of the way. The kids seemed stoned as they danced, in intense and almost palpable vision.

> I had a woman,
> I had a son.
> They took them away,
> they made them run.
> Now I have everybody,
> everybody, everybody
> and no one.

One girl thin in her nakedness as a garden rake began to scream and fell to her knees. One of the regulars, a dark skinny guy with glossy black hair, came and squatted beside her talking. He helped her up and moved with her for a while and then she returned to the larger circle and resumed the slower dance around and around.

The nakedness had a strange quality to it. Every so often when there was a crowd in the park milling around and something was happening and people were turned on, some guy would take his clothes off. But this was different. She felt that the dancers did not have a sense of being looked at. That was not primary. Yet people were watching each other, watching the dancing carefully. Often in crowds if some girl got stoned and took off her clothes, she would be mobbed. It would turn ugly, with men swarming to feel her up. But people were respectful here. There was a discipline underlying everything. She could feel a response in the outer circle when somebody danced well, inventively, passionately. When a dancer finished he would find his clothes, dress and step back into the circle. Or he might fall to the ground and lie there until one of the attendants could come to him. Then the kid would be raised up and helped to dress. When he was together, he would return to the outer circle and the slower dance.

It was an image of something in her blood. There were things that all the kids who were not nailed down yet

wanted, even if they could not say. Certain things they
groped for, though no one had seen them. Something
beyond the tight consumption unit of the husband/wife/-
kiddies box of inducing neuroses. Some form of commune. Some form of social bond not based on buying or
selling or being bought or sold. This grave dancing naked
in the circle was one such image, something groped
toward in a hundred other botched contexts.

She felt a sharp urge to throw off her clothes and dance
in the center. She was a good dancer and proud of it. She
loved to move well on the music, feeling herself borne in
it and swimming with the beat. But something held her
back. She had a feeling that this was all a ritual, and she
did not want to appear a fool. How she would like to stand
there naked burning like a torch with her wild hair flying
and the beat surging up her torso into her flinging arms,
while the circle slowly pivoted on her. It was a good ritual,
if that's what it was.

Then a heavy-set man pushed through the crowd into
the circle but did not take off his clothes. He stood there
flatfooted and slumping forward, with the circle spilling
around him and reforming, and motioned the dark boy
over, who came trotting. "Billy-O, what's up? Something in
the wind?"

Billy spoke into the dark boy's ear, then turned and
left, thrusting awkwardly through the dancers and into the
crowd.

The dark boy came into the center. "Cool the circle!
Cool the circle!" People stopped dancing in slowly subsid-
ing motion. The attendants went about to the dancers in
the center and talked them into stillness. Everyone got
dressed. The attendants and most of the dancers did not
dress cool or well but wore plain old clothes, jeans and
work pants and work shirts, male and female alike.

"The pigs." The murmur came around the circle.
"Massed on the edge of the park. Going to raid us. Pass it
on."

A meeting was going on in low voices in the circle.
Then everyone broke from it and began to circulate. They
worked in twos with packets of papers in their arms. A
pair looked at every person they came to carefully,
checked the face against a sheet of photographs and
passed out a flyer. As they worked toward her, two boys
stopped beside another wearing beads and a serape. They

whistled. He backed away, but the circle closed and held him. People on both sides held on to him, and he was stripped and tied with a rope and photographed again and left on the ground.

When they came to her, she felt briefly afraid. But they looked in her face and checked their photographs and handed her a map of the area. "We move out through B. Go south away from the precinct. We take the cops on that side of the park, break their barricades and move out. Escape routes through roofs and between buildings or through basements are marked on the map for emergency use." They passed on. In one corner of the map was a buffalo head, and on the top it said WE ARE THE PEOPLE OF THE NEW NATION OF THE YOUNG AND THE FREE.

The circle was dispersed. People were prying benches loose and breaking some of them up for the slats. People were digging rocks or bricks out of the earth, picking up whatever they could use as weapons. The pairs of Indians with their flyers and their photographs of plainclothesmen were moving through the larger crowd now, stopping to check people, warn them and move on. The crowd began to eddy in the park. There was a smell of fear and anger. She could see nothing, but people passed on that the cops had completely surrounded the park.

"Why is this happening?" she asked the guy next to her.

"They're trying to force us out of the Lower East Side, to break up the community. They'll go through and check IDs looking for runaways and evaders. A lot of guys come down here to escape the Nineteenth Year. If you're under twenty, they just haul you off."

Up on the shell Shawn could see something funny was happening. He announced his next number and asked what was coming down. The dark guy who had been in the circle leaped onto the stage and, putting his hand over the mike, spoke to Shawn. Shawn shook his head and grimaced. They argued for a couple of minutes. Then the dark guy took the mike.

"The police have the park surrounded. Don't speak to anyone except our warriors. Notice their armbands. Follow them. Do as they do. Follow the instructions on your flyers and we'll lead you out. Join the tribes and survive! We're the new nation of the young and the free. Come with us!"

He jumped down into the crowd, while Shawn stood

there rubbing his blond hair on end. "Shit!" he said. "We can't even play for you any more without them turning it into a trap. It feels like dirt." He threw his guitar down and walked off the stage.

Immediately she heard screaming, and people began to run and push and push back. Stuck in a press of people she was carried along, and all she could do was try to move with the crowd and keep her footing. If she went down, she would be trampled. Shots or firecrackers? cherry bombs or fire bombs? Everywhere people were screaming and shouting. Some cop had a bullhorn. The big heavy-set guy named Billy almost knocked her over passing through with a whole park bench for a battering ram, leading a charge of warriors.

She was moving in the right direction, east and south, but the crowd came to a halt. Behind her people kept shoving till she wanted to scream. She could smell the first nauseous whiffs of gas burning her eyes and swelling in her lungs. Her heart hurt and she was being crushed. Acid rose in her throat and subsided. "Gas! They're using gas!" people were shouting. "Hold the line! Hold the line!" Then a shudder, a massive recoil passed through the crowd, and she almost went down underfoot.

They began to move forward again. Moving fast now. It was harder than ever to keep her feet as she was pushed and shoved and knocked from the sides and buffeted from behind. As she felt the curb under her and lurched forward and pushed herself upright on the man ahead, she felt something slippery underfoot. Wet and slippery. Bits of board and metal in the street.

She ran, she ran. The crowd was looser now. She was crying as she ran, but she remembered not to rub her eyes. She had lost the flyer she had been clutching and her pack had been torn from her shoulders. The small of her back ached from an incidental blow. She had torn her leg on something sharp. She ran and ran, the pavement pounding on her soles. Cars were honking ahead, people yelling. The wail of sirens from every side. She passed overturned cars. Some of the warriors were dragging wastebaskets into the street and setting them afire.

"Split up and move out!" the word came from ahead. "They're waiting for us. Split up and move out!"

Turning she ran down a side street. Others were running beside her. A police car pulled up on C with its light flashing, and two mounted cops came charging down. Someone seized her by the arm and pulled her stumbling down a half flight of steps into the areaway of a tenement.

She pulled her arm free but seized his hand. Cold, cold hand. He ran in big strides dragging her clattering after him. He boosted her up a fence and yanked her into a corridor and then up the stairs inside, up to the roof. Then pushing her down against the chimney, he lay on his belly and looked over the edge. He watched for a long time muttering to himself and cursing. Then he rolled over onto his back.

"I'm over here," she said softly after a while. In the moonlight she poked at the gash in her leg. Her sandals were wet and dark with caked blood, as if she had stepped in a river of it. Her back ached and her eyes were raw and sore. She still felt as if she might throw up.

"Who?" He came slowly toward her, bent at the waist with his arms hanging forward like a chimpanzee. "Who?" He squatted before her and put out his hand to her face.

"Joanna."

"I don't know you. Do I?"

She laughed. "Guess not."

"Shouldn't have gone to take the mike. Should have been in front leading it. Got caught in the back. Mistake."

She turned his face into the moonlight and saw it was the boy with black hair. He was mumbling and rolling his head back and forth on hunched shoulders. He looked spent.

"Are you hurt?"

"I never get hurt."

"What's wrong? Did they beat you on the head?"

"Mistake. But got the people out. Better clubbed than arrested. That's our line."

"Did you get clubbed?" She held his face in her hands carefully. Big head. Coarse black hair. Heavy bones.

"No. No." He lurched forward against her, fell into her.

"Thank you for helping me get out of it." She took his head and shoulders in her lap, his face turned into her breasts and hiding there. He was breathing slowly, hoarsely. His mouth was open and his moist breath came and went on her breasts through the cotton of her shirt. Gradually he stirred and put his hand on her waist, sliding it up under the shirt. A big hand moving on her surely, in animal confidence, fingers knowing her. The hand walked upwards. "Oh." He sounded surprised at her breast. "Oh." Surprised that she was not wearing a bra? Surprised that she had breasts? His hand closed hard on one breast and then he unbuttoned her shirt and nosing his face between her breasts, subsided again.

Her cunt ached. Her body burned and itched with desire. She wanted him immediately. A hot cramp of wanting. Her breath came fast and she tried to sit very still.

"Joanna." His hand closed on her breast again. "Joanna there."

She was sure he was about to fall asleep while she sat shivering. She could not stand it. Pulling his head up she leaned forward and kissed his mouth. Slowly his lips opened and his tongue came gently and surely into her mouth. His tongue came twisting about hers, and again he moaned softly. For a long time their tongues enveloped each other as she lay otherwise inert across her with his hand still holding her breast.

She was terrified that he was going to stay that way. He seemed to have no urgency. He took what she gave him and enjoyed it, while she wanted, wanted. She ran her hands along his back, over his chest. She had never been aggressive before. She had always asked the man if he wanted to, if he hadn't asked her first, and then let him. If he was good he would excite her, and if he wasn't it would soon be over.

But she was burning. She was ashamed but she had to. She touched him through his loose ugly work pants. He was not erect. She wanted to weep. Then more shameless than before, she bent and unzipped his pants and took his penis into her mouth. Slowly he swelled into her mouth. Then stirring himself gently, he undressed her and laid her on her back, knelt between her thighs and pushed himself still not fully erect into her. Then moaning he gathered her up against him and began, and in a moment she began writhing and calling out. Because he felt so hot and naked in her. She felt him entering her quick. He was totally alive in her. With soft choking noises, he worked into her and they came. With a great loosening she came down to him. Then he lay in her still, but half beside her, and in a short while his hoarse loud breathing told her he had fallen asleep. She slept too on the cold hard roof in the acid moonlight with his prick still tucked into her, but when she awoke about four, he had slipped out and lay on his belly.

She woke him. "Shouldn't we get out of here?"

Groaning, cursing, he wriggled away from her. Then all of a sudden he woke himself up. "Yeah. Find the tribe." He got to his feet scowling and dressed himself with hurried, sloppy motions, wiping his prick on the tail of his shirt. She felt enormously embarrassed. She had seduced him, raped him almost.

"Look, I'll stay here. I can come down quietly a little later. Nobody will pay me any mind."

"What?" He glared at her. "What for? Don't you want to go with me?"

"Well, yes." She turned hot and cold and miserable. It was just beginning to be gray dawn as she trudged down the stairs behind him. He turned left and obediently, miserably, she followed.

In a couple of blocks he roused himself and began to question her. Where did she come from? Runaway? The first time? How old? Had she ever been busted?

"My name is Joanna," she finished.

"I remember your name." He gave her an odd squinted look. Then he sat down on a stoop and she stood before him, her hands twisting together. "I'm Corey."

"I saw you yesterday in the circle dance."

"I wasn't dancing. I was just watching out. It's a little edgy to have our thing in the park because of the danger of a bust . . . Did you dance?"

"On the edge."

"I guess I was too worried to notice anybody. Are you going to join us?"

"I don't know."

"You have red hair."

"You don't even know what I look like." She laughed, because she was miserable.

"Do you know what I look like?"

"Of course." But then she saw what he meant. She came closer and hesitantly put her hands on either side of his face and lifted it into the gray dirty light. His hair was thick and straight and coarse and black. He had a high slightly hooked nose and heavy high cheekbones and large strong black eyes that stared into hers, stared and stared

her dizzy. His face was sullen, morose and beautiful. He
was swarthy and skinny with big tendons in the hands that
lay on his knees. Then the hands moved out and took her
shoulders.

"Joanna." He gave her hair a tug and then he slipped
one hand up under her shirt and gently touched her breast
and then took it away. "I wish we could take our clothes
off." Then he grinned, his face opened up in a dazzling
smile at her, and he lifted her by his hands under her
armpits and got himself up. "I'm tired. So tired. And I
have a lot to do when we get there. I'll have to go running
around and talking my head off and I won't be able to be
with you. But you can get to know the people."

"Will we be together later?"

"I think so."

He walked on and she followed, and at every corner she
wanted to run away. She was afraid, afraid. She had lost
her sleepingbag and her identity all at once. She was Jill
the prisoner on the base and Joanna the runaway outside
who belonged to nobody. Here she was, following him like
a stray cat hoping for milk.

SHAWN woke on a cot and lay still. He had been gassed and the aftereffects made him think of his childhood. Once he had been given ether, and it had made him sick for several days. Sign he had noticed on Avenue A near the park in a storefront dentist's office: GAS ADMINISTERED HERE. Come to me, ye wretched of the earth.

Then clear as a hallucination, he remembered the voice of the woman who had lived over Denise, nagging her daughter: "Now stop that crying, Marilyn. You cry all day and all night. You'll cry your eyes out. Yes you will! You stop that. You know how the rain washes the dirt away? Well, if you keep on crying like that, you'll cry your eyes out and you won't have nothing but holes left in your face. You hear me, Marilyn? You hear your mother? You keep on crying like that all day and all night and people'll say, Look at that girl. Such beautiful blond hair and nothing but holes in her face—Ugh! That's right, you stop crying before it's too late. You listen to your mother."

As he had then, he imagined cutting off the woman's head. Like clipping off a dead flower with scissors. His mother's long aristocratic hands. Wave bye-bye, Mommy. Baby's going away. He had won his battle with them. His money was his own. His mother had gone back into analysis. His father spent longer hours in the law offices of his elegant firm. His father had summed it up: they felt guilty because they had allowed him to go on with his rock music, which clearly had ruined his life, corrupted him, thrown him with unsuitable people, given him the wrong contacts, the wrong values, the wrong reactions. All their social conditioning in vain. They blamed themselves for having been dazzled by the money. The golden showers of Zeus. They had kept thinking that, being a silly fad, it could not last, so why stop it prematurely? Soon it would end and in the meantime the cash came in discreetly and was put to work to reproduce itself. His parents felt guilty, and even that severed them from him, because they felt guilty for the wrong crimes.

He lay on the cot with his eyes closed, pretending sleep. Murmur of voices. Smell of bodies. Socks and sweat. It did not feel like brig except for that sense of bodies. In the riot one of the warriors had come and led him out, brought him to their commune. He had sat in stupor while people ran past bringing in the wounded and laying them down on tables or the floor. They tended their wounded themselves, except for very serious injuries: those, they carried off to hospitals with forged ID. He stared at the havoc: the bloody heads, the cuts and bruises, the broken arms and broken ribs. Girls whose long hair was matted with blood wept hysterically.

"I'm the one who should be hurt," he said to the warrior who guarded him. "I wanted to turn them on to their freedom before it's too late, and all I did was lead them into a trap. I'm responsible for this blood."

"The system's responsible." It was the guy named Billy who answered him, a big heavy-set fellow with glasses still taped on his nose, who seemed to be in charge. "Not you. Don't kid yourself. And we're responsible too. Sure. We could let the pigs round everybody up. We forced a confrontation. But that means we got most of our people out. Better a sore head for a week than eighteen months a slave."

As the night ground on, a new tension rose because their leader, Corey, had not come in. After a certain point in their retreat, nobody had seen him. Billy was clearly irritated by the worrying. He strode back and forth clumping his boots and barked at them. "He's okay. You're wasting your time fretting and carrying on. He'll come in without a scratch. Who's cutting bandages? Who's monitoring police radio? None of this dependency shit. We know what to do."

Billy was not really fat, not in a soft sense. He was big-boned and thick-bodied and built like an ox with a slumped-forward belly and legs like pillars. His hair was short and looked as if he cut it with the blades of a fan. He had regular features, but he scowled too much and smiled rarely. He had a dozen nervous twitches and jiggles, and he was always scratching himself and sticking his neck forward like a turkey. His body fit him like a badly cut suit. It grated on Shawn to watch him move.

But clearly Billy was strong and enjoyed great prestige among the warriors. They told stories about his feats while he pretended not to notice. "Did you see old Billy pick up that bench and go charging through the cops? Shit, if he hadn't done it, we'd be standing there yet waiting for the wind to change. They went flying through the air. Jesus, do they wear the hardware! When a pig hits the street it sounds like a car running into a lamppost. Crash, man. Did you see old Billy scatter that line? Wham, and the cops are sailing through the air wondering what hit them."

"Hey, Billy." A kid with a bloody bandage on his head and a thick drawl. "Aren't you never scared out there?"

Billy snorted. "You're only scared of what you don't expect. I'm too mean to get scared. I get mad."

"You know, he's not shitting you. I seen him pick up a whole one of them metal barrels full of burning trash, and he throw it right at a cop car, and bang! it bust the windshield."

When Shawn made motions to leave, they sat him down again. When he said he was tired, a warrior assigned to guard him had taken him upstairs and almost tucked him in. "Corey say to take care of you."

Now he lay on the cot. Sun streamed in windows across the front of the loft, but otherwise the air was wan porridge. A girl was scrubbing dark footprints. Kids were still sleeping in the bunks and spread in rows on the linoleum. He did not want to move. He could consider himself rescued or made prisoner.

When he had been given his dishonorable-and-psychiatric discharge, he had thought at first of looking for Denise. When he started to search, he could not go on. He was somebody else. He had wanted a simple thing, to make her as comfortable as she made him. That simple thing had been blown to fragments. They had taken his easiness and given him angers. How could he resume something whose virtue had lain in its gentle ease—his ready-made family? In brig he had learned: frustration, rage, brutality, compulsion, oppression, fear and degradation. The taste of shit and blood. He had also learned that such was normality, the status quo, for most people crawling on the earth. Now he lay like a sick man on a cot, waiting.

A shadow stood over him. Weight plumped on the cot. Somebody sat down against his outside leg.

"Morning." Voice familiar.

He opened his eyes and looked at Corey, who gave back a black serious stare of inquiry. "Well, what do you want from me?" Shawn pulled himself up and sat against the wall, drawing up his long legs against his chest.

Corey sat cross-legged on the cot, facing him. "Your life." He smiled broadly and held out his hands, palms up.

"And my money?"

"That, too, would help."

Though Corey was dressed and he was in his briefs sweaty from the concert, he was not fazed. It took more than a little skin to make him uneasy. "Are you going to tell me I need you? You plural. Your wild Indians."

"We'll be stronger with you along. And you'll be stronger if you join us."

"I'm a rock musician. I'm no street fighter. I'd rather turn people on than harangue them."

"Turn them on to what?"

"To themselves. To each other."

"Where does that happen? Where's a big neutral space for dropping out and digging each other?"

Shawn folded his arms. "Look, I'm sorry about last night. I have to be more careful not to lead people into traps. Maybe what I have to do is buy an old movie theater where people aren't so vulnerable as in the park."

Corey tapped his arm lightly. "Whatever do you think you can buy or rent or borrow that is outside this society? The only outside is the other side: with us fighting."

"You aren't everybody. It isn't a case of with you or alone."

"Do you know another collective that works for you?"

A collective of three: but the powers had broken that. "The group did. The Coming Thing."

"And it came and went." Corey smiled engagingly. "Now you play with hired musicians, and it sounds it."

"Yeah. I'm not working enough to keep a group together."

"You're blackballed now."

Shawn shrugged. "That's mainly the top-forty-type stations. That wasn't our league after the beginning anyhow. That isn't what I want to do right now." Though he was beginning to sense that he had no idea at all what he wanted. He was flopping. "I don't feel persecuted, if that's what you mean. But Frodo and Shep and I were friends.

Even then we'd fight. If you aren't close, you start out fighting."

"We're into something past all that. Past couples. Past the nuclear family that works so well as a hotbed for breeding neuroses. Past boyscout troops and clubs and teams and parties and unions. We're a tribe."

"Yeah, sure, McLuhan says we're all tribal. I guess because we eat each other."

"Look, you have a great talent to move people, but where are you moving them to? You don't want to be a commodity. You want to give your music away free. But it turns out that nothing is free, on their terms. You can't free people all alone with a turn-on like a magic wand. You're not free yourself."

"Maybe I am. You're calling me to be a servant. Join another army. I didn't like the first one."

"Not free. Just alone. They're still using you. The only way you can stop that is by fighting them. Break down the alienation they've imposed on you. Join us. Then they can persecute you, but they can't use you any more."

He believed nothing. But here he was. It was a place, anyhow. He was tired of ricocheting. The quality of his life had been crude and grainy and mean for a while. Since his discharge, he had been living out of hotel and motel rooms. The trouble was that he could not find any place he wanted to be. Nothing that had suited before fit now. He was not easy in the company of other musicians. He was a bad example, somebody who had fucked up his career, fucked up not even over drugs, which was traditional, but over an office manager. He could not get a group together and hold it together. The audience would scream for the old songs, but he felt wrong doing them. Without the sound of The Coming Thing, they felt botched. He wanted to sing the new songs that carried what he was thinking about. But they were strange to the audience. He had to do everything with his voice and his sex. He had to do it all on his performance.

It was not working. He did not like failing. Corey was sitting there waiting and waiting, afraid to push harder, afraid he had not spoken well enough. Shawn clasped his hands over the dirty cloth at his belly and thought: heads or tails. No tails. He could not go back anyplace he had been. They had closed his doors and taken away the landscapes where he had felt good. Heads. Indian heads.

"There's nothing to get but my instruments and my amps—what didn't get destroyed in the riot. And a change of clothes and my straight-edge razor. Got to have my straight-edge razor."

Corey waived the sodium pentothal test for Shawn. Billy showed his annoyance. He said Corey was highhanded and elitist and that such a decision must be made by the whole council. The council was called, and Corey won as Shawn waited upstairs. Corey charmed them into letting Shawn through. The test was to keep out infiltrators, Corey explained. One of their best warriors had turned out to be a police fink, and he had caused their first commune to be busted and those who escaped had had to leave Chicago. However, as if to prove to Corey that his position derived solely from the will of the group, the council refused to exempt Corey's new girl, Joanna, and she had to take the test. Corey was furious and let it show. He disappeared and did not come back for a whole day and night.

Shawn saw Joanna for the first time that evening. He felt sorry for her, a lanky redheaded girl who seemed to wait stolidly, and yet he was sure she was afraid. He felt involved, because he was sure that if Corey had not pushed him through, she would not be obliged to take the test. Then Corey had run out on her, gone off to suffer his dark mood, abandoned her as if to show them they could not punish him through her.

When Shawn went over and took her hand, she gave him a shy smile. "I didn't think you would remember me."

"Why not?" Remember her. He did think that he had seen her, but god knew where. At the riot? No. Longer ago. Well, it did not matter and probably she would give him a clue.

She laughed brusquely. She had an odd voice, metallic and husky, that caught in her throat. "Well, it's been a year, and it was only those couple of days. I didn't know who you were."

"Sure you did. Just me. Right?"

She squeezed his hand and dropped it. "I really didn't think you'd remember. By the way I'm ... with Corey now." She seemed at a loss for the right euphemism. She gave him another smile as shy as the first but warmer. Then she went out with two warriors to the test.

Corey turned up the next afternoon. He came directly

to Joanna and grabbed her against him in a bear hug. "Are you all right? Come on. Come on." He led her away dragging by the hand without looking at anybody else. When he reappeared, he was in a sunny mood.

Most Indians spent their days and evenings out organizing among the kids. Even peddling the bread was a means of connecting people to the group. Basically there were four activities: organizing, defense and intelligence, activities that made for group solidarity, and food gathering and housekeeping.

The lowest level of involvement was contact—kids who looked to the Indians for leadership in street actions and protection in time of raids or dragnets. Then there were those who had taken bread, danced and considered themselves part of the people. Then there were members of a tribe who had passed the truth test. Tribes lived in a commune and were not supposed to use money. The means of living belonged to the group, which fed and clothed its members.

What they called organizing was largely rapping with kids about their situation, helping them to articulate demands, helping them to get actions started or to protect themselves against street harassment, to recruit them if they could. They tried to reach the dropouts, the evaders and runaways on the Lower East Side, but they also talked to kids in school. They had contacts in eight high schools and one junior high, and they expected soon to have more. Most of the underground papers in the schools were at least sympathetic to the Indians. Some of the organizers were trying to reach kids in the various city corps, although that was riskier and more difficult. Every day they ran off wall newspapers for the neighborhood, and printed leaflets.

To be a member of the warriors, a militia composed of both men and woman, a kid had to prove his loyalty, his willingness to follow orders and his guts. He might be told to steal a piece of machinery, chemicals, a truck. Two boys were sent to penetrate Bellevue and bring out an Indian under observation there.

The task had to be one for which the need was clear. Assignments were made in council. The kid being tested could argue and invent options, but if he refused, he would never be a warrior. Why did the kids want to be warriors? Prestige. People needed such strange paste to

stick them together. Some of these rituals struck him as
silly as those of the summer camps of his childhood, but
he kept his amusement to himself. Billy was the war chief:
he had invented the warriors. He makes good machines,
Shawn thought, with an edge of respectful distaste. He
found Billy opaque.

That night he sat in his first council. Everyone in the
commune took part, and anyone could initiate business.
People spoke one by one going around the sprawly circle.
You could pass, but if you passed too often or someone
thought you were holding back, he would chide you and
urge you to speak out. The process was slow and Shawn
found it tedious. Many were inarticulate and grappled
painfully to get some half-formed idea out. Those who
had strong opinions tended to soften them. "Well, I don't
know, but it seems to me ... I think we could kick it
around something like this. . . ."

Side by side with that style was developing another—
more militant, more "political," with its own jargon. It
seemed to come most naturally to the warriors. They were
harder and fiercer in speaking their opinions, as if the
jargon insulated them. They were always "fighting our
bourgeois violence hang-ups," "locating the cutting edge,"
"exploiting the contradictions of imperialism."

He passed the slow time examining the girls in the
circle, trying to guess who they might belong to, looking
for the bodies in the rough work clothes. That night for
sure he wanted to get laid. As he sat cross-legged his prick
was slightly swollen. He was coming back from the dead.
Really it was a drag how they dressed. Fine for scrubbing
the floor and hauling bags of potatoes, but it was a pig in
a poke trying to read the body through the loose denim
and khaki.

When the council finally ended, most of the Indians
took bread. He was curious but not willing to take the risk
that night. Suppose it cooled him off. Often when he was
high he wanted nothing but to listen to the patterns in his
head. Then dancing began. He asked a blonde standing
near to dance, and she stared at him. Then she laughed
and told him he would first dance with everyone. She told
him they always danced together after council, except in
an action crisis. People were to dance for a better understanding of decisions. They were supposed to dance out

any ruptures or quarrels. It was another way of being together, of expressing the tribe and each other.

"But suppose I want to express myself to you." He leaned close.

She would not flirt back. "Wait. Wait and see. Learn the language first." She skipped away into the big circle that had formed.

They played oil drums and paint cans and gongs and tambourines and a couple of guitars—neither in tune. It was raw. He would have to improve matters. Some kids shook rattles and clacked bells as they danced. Others squatted at the side rapt in making music. A short dark woman with an oil drum set the rhythm. Inside that rhythm the others improvised as they saw fit. The result was cacophony. Though sometimes they came together strangely into chance measures, mostly they hurt his ears.

He joined the slow shuffling outer circle. Sometimes people would do the same thing, pass along gestures, or steps, sometimes they would just shuffle along doing a kind of grapevine. At times they would hold hands and at times they would jog or whirl along without touching. Most were concentrating on what was happening inside the circle, but some were indrawn and pulled into their muscles, and after a while he understood that they were preparing their dances. Soon they would step into the center.

A girl or boy would step from the circle and take off the rough work clothes and drop them. Sometimes he would stop to paint himself. Sometimes she would not. Some spent ten minutes slowly drawing designs on their bodies. Sometimes a couple would stop and painstakingly paint each other. Some people stopped only to draw a line or two or a symbol or to write a word across their chests. Some just threw off their clothes and started to dance.

Mostly, early in the dance, they danced alone. But often enough, couples danced. Sometimes boys danced with boys and girls with girls. Occasionally groups of three or four would form. Some of the dancing was passionate, some comic, some competitive and muscular, some consciously graceful or expressive, some overtly sexual. Two guys were teasing each other, mocking, leaping higher and higher and making fierce grimaces and chopping gestures— a danced-out samurai duel. A girl was spinning in trance, spinning, spinning till she fell and lay on the floor, and another girl squatted to take care of her and eventually to lead her to resume a place in the outer circle. Sometimes after they had danced, people would dress again, but often they did not—especially if they had painted their bodies with care. The music pounded on. Bodies expressed the music's rhythms and their own.

The woman with the oil can was not bad. He watched her for a while. Strange-looking. Such a fat body and such thin arms. Like an insect. Then he realized she was pregnant. Yes, that explained the awkwardness as she leaned over her own belly toward the can. Pregnant. He did not know why that little fact kept tweaking at him. There were no children here, any more than in any other group of kids dancing. But if she was so pregnant and still in the group, they must mean to raise the baby. Maybe they really would be a tribe. But he must fight the Indians' latent puritanism, which made them play such crude instruments and restricted the décor to a couple of red and blue gels laid over two light bulbs. They had to understand that being ashamed of what's beautiful was a conditioning as repressive as any of the other programming—economic and social—that they fought.

If a woman was dancing alone and a man wanted to dance with her, he would approach slowly. Shawn understood as he watched that if a dancer was in trance or vision or working out a pattern of her own, she did not want anyone to relate to her. So the guy might watch and then drop back and dance alone, or dance an invitation to someone else to join him. Equally, a woman would step out of the circle and approach with the same caution, waiting to see if she was accepted.

Some of the couples danced a flirtation, danced a display to each other. Sometimes their dance ended with their walking through the circle and climbing to the dormitory, where only a dim bulb burned or seeking some private corner. People noticed or did not notice. It was accepted. It was one way of ending the dance. One couple danced rubbing against each other, a slow rubbing of belly against belly, breasts against chest, a short hairy bearlike warrior with a bandage on his head and a girl with cropped brown hair slightly taller than he, with long muscular legs. In the dim light he was not sure, and then he was sure, that the warrior had entered her. They continued their slow dance interminably swaying and writhing, and the fucking was part of the dance. For a long time he watched them until they eased apart and returned to the circle.

He saw that the rough clothes and the nakedness were part of the way the group assimilated their sexuality. That what they were to turn on to in each other had its origin in the tension between the working self with its lack of allurement, the men and the women working together in the kitchens and the lab, fighting together in the streets, and the dancing body, naked and precisely sexual. The body itself gave out its message: I want, I am, see me. They were not objects. They did not use clothes to broadcast their sexuality. The body, the dance, did that. Shawn danced smiling and approved. People turning under the feeble, the ridiculous, the puny wattage of a couple of bulbs screened with one red and one blue gel, dancing to the half-witted bang and clatter of crude instruments awkwardly played, still were glorious. They were naked in a new sense, or a very old one. Long ago people had of course taken off their utilitarian furs and skins to dance. Dancing is the art of the body. It wants to be bare. Yes. He understood the strength of dancing naked, and he was firmly convinced that they had never yet seen anything such as he would show them. Learn the language first, the girl had told him, but she did not know how quickly he began to speak in certain tongues.

Slowly he took off his clothes. He stepped over to the paints and considered. Then he dipped his fingers first in the blue and then in the red and painted a tangle of vines over his body. They would appear mainly black. He moved to the rhythm and found a song, one of his old songs that would lift on it. His voice could penetrate brick walls with amplification, but without it he could still fill a good-sized room.

> Shady baby,
> let the sun shine on your skin.
> Baby, baby, warm you up again.
> Gonna come back tomorrow
> be sure you let me in.
> Yeah, I'm coming back tomorrow
> make sure that I get in.

The dark and very pregnant woman on the oil can had picked up on him already. Yes, she was with him. Good drummer. Get her a decent set of drums and watch her go. Yes, he would form a group out of nothing, if necessary, but she would be with him. Open the doors of your body, drummer lady, and let out the baby, ripe and squalling. He wanted a flesh and blood baby, smelly and insistent and ready to grow into a child that would be his too. For the rest, he just kept on above the general clang and crunch of the random instruments.

> Throw open the doors of your body,
> open the windows,
> pull up all those blinds.
> I am the sun baby,
> I am the sun oh baby baby
> watch me rise and shine.
> I'm gonna warm you,
> love you, love you
> till you feel
> oh yeah, till you feel so fine!

Two girls started at once in the circle. The first paused at the paints, looking at him, seeing him, and then began carefully to paint a sinuous design over her body. The second saw that and came directly to him, throwing off her clothes in a straggled heap. So even here, a little competition. Grinning he came to meet her.

He stopped singing to keep his breath for the dance. The rhythm quickened and they circled each other feinting and tempting. She had a long braid thrown over one shoulder. She was pear-shaped and cuddly and frisked her round ass at him. Circling they teased each other. Her small breasts shimmered as she arched back and raised her hands high, high over her head.

He waited and then reached forward, took her firmly by the hips, lifted her high up in an arc and then brought her down slowly on his prick, slowly, slowly. He could feel the sexual vibrations back from the circle. Tensing his muscles, holding her firmly, carefully suspended and impaled, he moved half time against the increasing tempo, turning them slowly in the center of the moving outer circle, making a public ritual. Embarrassed, she leaned her head forward hiding in his shoulder, but her hips and firm ass responded. He could not tell if she came or only acted out coming, but it did not matter in ritual. As he came, he let his breath out in a loud high cry. Thinking how in concert he had cried so hundreds of times and the girls would shriek back—an orgasm of the ears. As he started to slide out, he lifted her high and gently in the air again and swung her around completely, then slowly let her down on her feet. Quickly she ran out of the center to the waiting circle.

He looked around for the other girl. She was stepping in place alone watching and did not come forward. She looked rather frightened. He came directly to her and invited her forward, and reluctantly she came with him. Gracefully, sensually he danced with her, keeping back, and she began to relax, though if he came too near, her brown eyes would widen with worry. He smiled at her, shaking his head. Even *he* couldn't do that twice in a row, and besides he did not wish to. She had prepared herself carefully, and he would wait for her. He would spend the night with her, he decided. She was plump the way he liked, and he liked too that she had stopped to make herself ready.

He danced well with her. He did not mean to do anything spectacular again that night. He liked to turn people on, and the outer circle were supposed to dig the solos. He had justified their eyes. She was good and responsive, and often she would inject an idea of her own and he would pick up on it. He did not have any intention of becoming a warrior, but the dance was his natural place. He looked around covertly and saw that many were still watching, and their glances were mostly friendly. Then his gaze brushed Billy's, and before he could control himself he had looked away from that intense stare of disgust. The big war chief leaned against one whitewashed wall, never joining the dance but watching always. A concentrated hostility in his eyes like electricity.

While he was pausing, Corey came and signaled that he wanted to dance. He had been dancing for an hour most of the time monotonously with Joanna, the two of them in close absorption. Occasionally they would hold each other close. Then Corey would dance alone, sometimes in joy, sometimes in frantic pain. His almost hairless body was thin, with the bones starting through the dark skin. His penis was flaccid and disregarded, never quite erect, never fully limp. He was not graceful. His movements were hurried and jerky, or slow and sullen. But his dancing was wildly expressive. He danced in god's eyes—in good or bad agony. He danced his visions. When he danced with Joanna he expressed inturned dependency, low-key sensuality—clutching the still center of his being.

Corey sought him out to dance, with steps and gestures wild but open. Corey was selecting him and dancing his affection openly. Corey, this dark skinny saint, was choosing him his brother. He could have picked up Corey in his arms and carried him.

Shawn wanted to go back to his girl. He was careful to throw her a glance from time to time so that she would know that he was meaning to return to her. She nodded at him with a strange smile, as if she tasted something bitter and sweet, and she waited. He could not refuse Corey. It was a ritual of pledged affection. In boyish admiration Corey had selected him and carried him off to make him a member of the tribe, to make him brother. He half suspected Corey had brought the Indians to his concert in the park not only because he expected the cops to come down on the kids, but because Corey had wanted him with the Indians. Or maybe began to decide to recruit him as he watched the concert?

When Corey had leaped on to the stage he had almost pushed him off. Something in Corey's face had troubled him. Violence. Black tension, seething and cold. He had thought, a nut, and got ready to punch him. But Corey had spoken gently and tamed him into handing over the mike. Had spoken of the situation, had said, "We must" and never "I want." We must, you and I, to save the kids. And the mike had jumped out of his hands.

It was a long time since he had had a friend. Since the days of the solid group. Frodo was in the Seventh Army Band. Shep was assigned to the Parks Department in Philly. Shep wanted to get married, but couldn't wangle permission. Wanted to marry old Melanie Clinton, who was teaching tennis in the parks to somewhat underprivileged children. He had seen her in Philly just after he got discharged and screwed her in the Porsche just before he sold that object. She still had no breasts. She was wooden and greedy and waspish. She had been a better lay at eleven—a better woman. It had depressed him. He felt he was smudging his own past. After that only groupies and a reporter who was supposed to be doing a story on why he had freaked out.

So he danced with Corey, remembering old unfriends and lost friends. Remembering how affection evaporated and left flabby memories. How the familiarity of old gestures irritated. Corey had chosen him friend and brother. As Corey's skinny body hard and coppery with the big tendons and bones straining against the taut skin, vibrated and leaped before him, he moved forward and embraced him, hugged him close. The feel of their bodies touching was strange and a little chilling. Corey hugged him back, and that ended their dancing.

As the dance was gradually breaking up, he went upstairs with his plump girl. Her hair was straight and caramel-colored, and she kept herself clean. She smelled like soap and tea. Her nails were short and scrubbed and her toes were little pillows. He sucked them as she giggled with delight. She had freckles on her shoulders and even lightly scattered on her big soft breasts. Her name was Ginny and she had been in the Indians from the first. She wanted to please and she wanted to be pleased and she was alert to small wishes in his body. She liked to fuck for a long time gently nibbling his neck. Her body delighted him: soft and springy, and between the lush breasts and lush hips a true marked waist he could squeeze.

She was waiting to see if he wanted her to go. "Sleep with me. Not much room in the cot, but how much room do we need, Ginny?"

So they settled down to snuggling and soft talk. He was full of questions. He felt, in a way, he was taking the tribe to bed with him. He had always been that way, saying to himself, this is my first black girl, my first Japanese, my first Italian, my first girl from the mountains, my first Chicana, my first Romanian ... Always imagining he could taste in her flesh the experience of being in some other skin. Denise had been the same, his pursuit of the ordinary, which in itself was exotic to him.

Ginny had run away from home to join the Indians, before they really were the Indians yet. No, she had not hesitated. Her parents did not love her; how could she miss them? She missed her younger sister. She would like to steal her away. There had been too many mouths to feed for her parents to pay much attention to the ones in the middle, especially girls.

There was a kind of shame when she spoke about herself. Her eyes were a light brown, the color of maple sugar, and he would have to keep making her look at him, because their gaze would drop away. She wanted to know about him. Then the eyes remained on his face. He found himself telling about his past two years in a soft deliberate way that left in the failures and the vacillations and the anger. She listened carefully and touched him.

He got up to piss. As he walked between the rows of bunks, something made him turn and in the almost dark strain till his eyes accustomed. Joanna astride Corey in a bunk. They had a blanket pinned up to give privacy, but he could see in from the end of the bunk. It was a fierce total act quickly over and all the time they cried to each other. It was like birds fucking, like sparrows. Quick and fierce and uttering sharp cries. He pissed and returned to his cot and the snuggle of Ginny's sprawled flesh, his head turning in toward her shoulder. He remembered Joanna now, though she had been different with him. But that fierceness: her nails in his back. Hot sweaty fumbling in her sleepingbag. He wondered if she had told Corey.

For a little time his money had been his. Shawn was amused at how it fied him. A couple of months—time that had brought him little pleasure. What had he done with it? Hired musicians, tried to give free concerts. Now he had turned it over. What the group had was used by decision of the group for the good of the group. Everything was mumbled over and haggled out until everyone had chewed and swallowed the decision. No leader derived his position from anything other than the feeling of others that his ideas were worth listening to, that he cared for them and that they cared for him.

What Shawn could do was express for them, move them, make their feelings real and articulate. He had been given his people. If he could not take their ways and rituals with seriousness, what had he ever cared for that he could not con a little, could not tease and play with? He had found a way to be healed again in his music. It was the *we*-sense of his old group expanded, the only *we* he had ever found, except sometimes in bed.

They bought a large, run-down farm in New Jersey, a wooden house nobody had occupied for ten years, a decrepit barn and various enigmatic sheds half caved in. Most of the land was in thick second-growth woods and scrubby brush and bushy pastures. A stream ran through it, coming down from a low mountain on the north. The first day with the first truckload, they discovered poison ivy and blueberries. They moved people out in the truck as secretly as possible. The purchasing squad consisted of the oldest and straightest-looking, who bought quietly in scattered towns.

The priorities were digging latrines, putting up a tent city, building an electrified fence and putting in crops that could still make it that year. Ginny, who was in charge of planting, made lists from books on vegetable farming and ordered the seeds and directed their sowing according to the book, without in some cases having any notion what she was trying to grow: beets, collard, kale, lettuce, spinach, turnips, lima beans, eggplant, peppers, sweet potatoes, cucumbers, melons, green beans, swiss chard, soybeans, squash and corn.

"What's collard?" a girl asked.

"It's a kind of cabbage," Ginny said firmly, and nobody thought any different for weeks.

Billy formed a crew, mostly from kids he had trained, to get a lab set up. They took over the building that had been a chicken house until the kids raising chickens complained. Then they put up a tent with a cement floor for temporary use and began excavating for the underground lab Billy had argued for. He said repeatedly that the electrified fence was just plain silly as protection, that they must give him more money and a lot more labor to make the farm secure. But few wanted to spend the effort yet.

They had left a skeleton crew on in the communes to recruit and organize. It was summer, and Corey argued that the communes would fill up in a matter of weeks. Some kids could not get used to farm work. Moze and Chuck and Greek Steve went back to the city after two weeks. They did not like the emphasis on physical labor, and they missed the street action, the tang on the nerves of danger. Billy defended their choice, saying warriors must not soften.

They had lots of injuries and sunburn and wasted effort. Most of the kids had little experience using tools, and they mashed their fingers and split their thumbs. But they were not afraid here, never afraid, and for most of them that was new and beautiful. They had been living in a drone of anxiety since they could remember. In dreams they were back in school and afraid. In dreams they were on the

streets, and if they were not too stoned to feel, they were
afraid. Here they were alone with each other in their own
fields. It was easy to be good at something, if only at
digging holes, and the holes had to be dug.

Shawn dug postholes and mended fence and learned to
do rough carpentry and simple wiring. He invented a new
kind of chair that nobody liked but himself. Working in
the fields, working on construction, he grew brown and
muscular and healthy. The work felt good because they
decided together what must be done and how they must
do it. It was rational. It was for each other.

He never forgot in some corner of his mind how fragile
it was: they had set up a kibbutz in New Jersey and all
the sane joy that they had was in secret. In the center of
the empire it was illegal to want to live in a human way.
But he knew he had passed some simple point. Never
would he take to the streets because it was proven to him
that millions of children were dying of starvation in Latin
America to make certain corporations and very specific
men with very specific family names even grosser and
wealthier, that peasants were forced off their land in
Venezuela and shot down in the mines of Bolivia so that
the fourteenth largest corporation in the world could become the thirteenth largest ... it was all sick, it was all
evil, it did not touch him. But he would pick up a gun to
defend his farm.

He would not join the warriors. Something in him was
set on edge by them. But he got Corey to teach him how
to use a rifle. He knew that if he had been sent off to fight
someplace instead of put to work for the Youth Services
Bureau, he would not have liked shooting peasants, but he
would doubtless have killed them as directed. Yet he had
not killed to protect his small family. Violence is the
property of the state. The state is the mechanism by which
those who own everything get us to obey them. To become human, he had to take back the will he had given
up. It was a quiet change. He did not talk about it. He
knew that Corey saw it in him.

Similarly, he saw in plump shy Ginny a sense of herself.
She fluttered less to please. Even if she made up answers
to questions she did not know, she did know more about
the planting than anyone else. She liked herself better. She
felt she was someone real. She no longer wanted to be
Joanna, who seemed so tough and sure of herself and sure

of her style, and who had someone to love her. She no
longer wanted to be Carole, who was thin and a warrior.
She no longer wanted to be Sylvie, who was blond and
always had somebody to sleep with. She no longer wanted
to be pictures in magazines or girls in advertisements. She
wanted to be Ginny well.

Intense exclusive couplings like Corey and Joanna were
rare in the group, and he did not form one. He tended to
choose new girls and show them off. If he came back to
Ginny every couple of weeks, it was in part because she
was growing such a sense of herself that he had to feel
connected to her, in the group. She talked oftener in
meetings. She spoke bluntly and simply, with an occasional homely example, and then shut up. Often the others,
accustomed to the male warrior style, just did not hear.
But some were learning to listen.

The one person who never danced was Billy. Sometimes
he walked out at the close of council. Other nights he sat
against a wall taking bread and watching with set face.
People tended to leave a gap in the outer circle before
him. Shawn felt sure Billy hated the dancing. He felt Billy
came close to hating him, and stayed out of his way. He
did not dislike the big awkward war chief, but his life
looked barren. Often he would become aware that Billy
no longer saw the dancing, that he had withdrawn into an
isolated high.

Shawn seldom took bread when he wanted to dance. He
did not need that total concentration. He wanted to stay
detached enough to dig his own performance and those
around him. Often he took it when he was going to sing.
He was better on it: he could drive himself harder for
longer. It made him feel as if he came to an intense point.
He wanted to push forward on a beam of light. He
became the beam, the laser. Everything else fell away.

He had persuaded the tribe to relax their ban on the
artificial, pointing out that they used electric lights and
tools. Now he had his Fender and a loose group of musicians so that the music was not quite so tincan-naïve.
The drummer, Dolores, was too pregnant to play but she
shook a tambourine, and soon she would be his drummer
again. That puritanism against the arts he had to fight
quietly but steadily. Music was his oxygen. "When people
are starving, how can you blow your horn?" "Because
people are starving, I must not leave off blowing my

horn." There were no people so primitive or poor they did
not practice arts: except a thoroughly exploited, colonial-
ized, proletarianized people—thoroughly robbed.

Shawn left the farm only when they needed him to
perform. As soon as the closed truck entered the city, he
felt his muscles tighten. The communes were full again,
even though the police had found one and broken it up.
Corey had to go back and forth. But when he was on the
farm, often they worked together.

Sometimes they worked in an easy silence. Sometimes
Corey talked from the inside of what he was trying to do.
Trouble and decisions. Here trouble had faces and Shawn
could speak to it, but outside was noise to him.

The sun was hot. They were stripped to the waist up on
the roof of the house, laying new shingles. Corey was not
allowed to work among the crops because he could not
learn to tell a weed from a plant. He would forget where
he was and step on the rows. The sky was glassy blue. The
roof under them burned their knees. The water in the
canteen was warm in his mouth as he stopped to drink.

"First I saw that child labor had become child consumption. That our role was to eat shit to make the
system grind on. That we were set up in a scene where we
couldn't do anything real with ourselves or each other,
penned into scenes where what we did together was spend
money and learn to treat each other as objects—dating
scenes. I saw that to survive we had to stop wanting their
things and only want what we could give each other. That
the system makes us useless to it and to each other until
we've gone through all the grades they set up, and then
they use us for fodder, for all the functions they don't
want to pay money for, and then they're ready to fix us
into our slots to keep running twice as fast in the same
rut, chasing mirages. You can't become a man at twenty-
two if you haven't been allowed to grow into a man."

"So that's why the rule that no one keeps money, and
no one spends money except the group."

"Because you can't cut down and withdraw a little. You
feel poor then. You feel like you're broke in the supermarket. You get into hustles, and then they have you."

Corey knelt banging unevenly at the shingles. Though
they worked side by side, it was easy to tell the work
Corey had done from his. It would be better if he worked
alone and Corey just sat and talked to him, but Corey

would be offended if he said so. Corey squatted with his collarbones poking out and his ribs showing in his sides and his face open in a big grin. He made passes at the nails and missed them, knocking them in crooked. Shawn would have to do half the work over. Corey stood up to stretch, flapped his skinny arms and almost lost his balance, laughed happily and sat down again, kicking his hammer off down the slide of roof. Shawn grabbed for it and caught it.

"The societies kids naturally form are tribal. Gangs, clubs, packs. But we're herded into schools and terrified into behaving. Taught how we're supposed to pretend to be, taught to parrot all kinds of nonsense at the flick of a switch, taught to keep our heads down and our elbows in and shut off our minds and shut off our sex. We learn we can't even piss when we have to. Raise your hand and ask the teacher for a pass. What kid isn't humiliated by that? What kid isn't scared the teacher won't let him go? And the teacher has the right to make the kid sit there hurting in his bladder until he pees all over himself. That's slavery. That's how we learn to be plastic and dumb."

"I went to a very permissive school," Shawn said. "Yet here I am. My grade school was too much better than the outside."

"We learn to be stupid. That the day is divided into periods, and nothing in any period has anything to do with anything else. One fourth divided by one half is what, sonny boy? Dayton is the capital of Chicago. A verb is an action word. Gravity is what makes things fall. Say it back right. Say the right words, and draw pictures in the margins of people shooting each other."

"Did you ever kill anyone?"

"Not personally. But we have. It's the same thing. We have to start over. We have to start while there are still human people left. Kids have a chance. We aren't mortgaged yet. We have to get all the kids out who are still alive and keep them alive. People who still have eyes will pick up on the way to live. The others can go on trying to make their crazy machine work on each other. But the young won't go into their system to be ground to hamburger any more, and gradually it will slow down and come to a halt. And people will walk away and learn to live again."

He put his hand on Corey's shoulder, smooth and bony

and hot to the touch. He could feel the pulse. "I don't believe those who have hold of the riches of the world, including our bodies, are going to let go. But I don't have any better ideas." He believed in nothing beyond the moment, but the moment was good. Corey wanted more from him, searching with his black stare. Shawn felt vaguely pressed on and picked up the hammer.

In August Corey went out to Chicago, and thirty more Indians followed him back to the farm. He was already talking about starting one on the West Coast. While he was gone, the dark woman Dolores who played the drums gave birth to their first baby, who was named in council Leaf.

"IF you had bothered with nineteenth-century history, you'd know that this whole farm business is a throwback. Brook Farm—utopian cranks off in the woods to start the good society, and at each other's throats in six months."

"We aren't giving up on our organizing. This is just one of our bases. Don't you see what it does for the kids— letting them get their heads together?" Corey flung himself down in the high grass and sprawled there waiting for Billy to lie beside him.

"Sure. A regular summer camp and 4-H Club training program. Sound minds in sound bodies. Maybe our melons will win a prize at the county fair. If they don't wise up and bust us all first."

"It's a lot less likely here than at the city communes. We've taken good precautions against a raid. With the warning system and the tunnels, they wouldn't find a soul aboveground who can't wave a solid ID in their faces." Again Corey motioned him to lie in the rippling grass, giving him a broad lazy smile. He wore only a pair of dirty wash pants cut off at the knees, and his body had tanned a coppery brown.

Billy felt sweaty and uncomfortable standing, but if he lay down it would be hard to get the confrontation he wanted. Corey was always slipping through his hands. He would come to meet Billy agreeing, partly agreeing, turning everything off obliquely, turning concrete objections into abstract agreements and turning general criticisms into reasonable and loving accounts of minute details. The gentle runaround. Corey could not let him disagree. He felt smothered and handled and yet somehow not touched. Shifting from foot to foot he felt like a big hot sweaty fool, and finally he got down on his haunches and pulled loose blades of the tall grass between his fingers. Fingers stained with chemicals. Still a freaky specialist.

Corey was staring with wide eyes up into the sky. "First, our people make themselves real here. When they leave, they're stronger. Some may not be able to take the strain in the streets, but they would have broken anyhow. Here they can be useful."

"Some of my boys find it harder to take farm life. They miss the action. They didn't join up to plant potatoes. They want to take on the man."

"Well, we're doing that. But we have to try to be self-sufficient. We have to show what we mean. We have to give people something good to feel loyalty to."

"People can feel loyal to each other if they're fighting together. Unity that people get through struggling is worth ten times as much as what they get handed to them on a plate."

"Creating something better is struggling, too. We need to keep it up on both fronts: making real, visible alternatives, and confronting the system."

He would seize Corey, and Corey would change shape and color. Stay! Stand! "So we set up a summer camp in the Jersey hills for wayward adolescents. The man can let us get away with that. What would it matter to General Motors if we set up twenty? The kids aren't causing any trouble here."

"But they're all the way out of the system. That's the biggest trouble we can make."

"Don't kid yourself. There's nothing political about squash and beans."

"Don't kid yourself, Billy. Food is the basic stuff of politics."

"Only where people are hungry. There's more food to be looted from a big supermarket than we can raise here."

"That's an idea." Corey sat up on one elbow. "Exemplary action. In some suburb. Shopping plaza situation—like Franklin, remember? We'll bring that up in council." Corey's eyes were crinkled up with excitement. He scratched his chest with excess energy. "INDIANS RAID SUPERMARKET. Wow! I dig that. That's beautiful. Free food *now!* Give some of it away nearby, someplace where they need it. Big Robin Hood scene. It's lovely, lovely. I'm going on the first one. Soon as possible."

Billy felt numbed. First it had not been a suggestion. Second, if it had been, that would no longer matter. He had learned, in fact, never to tell Corey his strategic, even his tactical ideas, because Corey would just naturally co-opt them. Corey would present them to council as his—

just naturally. Because Corey did not differentiate between where he personally stopped and the Indians started. He wanted to present an idea as groovy, to get it across, so he took it over and dressed it up in his best rhetoric, thus somehow transforming it completely. Corey acted as if he truly could not, did not, need not distinguish between the I and the we, yet he was only one man, and maybe his ego was as sore as Billy's. Yes, it was there, throbbing away.

"Anyhow, what I'm trying to say is just this: Maybe a healthy army of barefoot kids who know how to pick tomatoes isn't a good fighting corps. My warriors belong on the streets."

"So keep some of them on the streets." Corey grimaced. "But we have to gather all the tribes. Everybody can't make it on the streets. We have to grow or we perish."

"I'm not saying we should scrap the farm. But too much effort's going into it. We don't need it that bad. We do need the warriors. They're the core of our power."

"The tribe is the core. The whole tribe."

"You can prance around all night beating on cans and turning red in the face and having fits, but if we can't defend our people, we can't lead them out of the system." Corey did not pay enough heed to their reality, their vulnerability. He was hung up on symbols. "Without the warriors, we're just a mob of silly kids ready to be herded up."

"Right. We have to protect our people."

"How? Corey, how?"

"By growing. By building up the tribes. The warriors too."

"Right," he said, but didn't change. Like Corey's absurd catering to Shawn. Shawn wasn't even a warrior. He had never gone through his initiation, and Corey defended that openly. Said that Shawn was a shaman, not a warrior, and they needed shamans. Needed his obscene strutting and showing off. All they needed from Shawn as far as he could see was Shawn's money, his name and his talent at getting kids excited. Billy was sure there was some cheap efficient chemical means to the same target. Yet Corey treated Shawn with the same deference he used toward Billy, absolutely the same. Besides that, Corey hung around with Shawn; he would pick Shawn out to work with.

He had tried to talk to Corey about Shawn. He had used a phrase Corey had picked up with delight, but not as he had meant it. He had called Shawn "post-scarcity man." Corey grabbed that phrase as if he had meant Shawn was some sort of ideal they ought to strive toward. Jesus! He had meant that Shawn acted as if they were already in post-scarcity, whereas they were in the belly of the beast fighting their way out. There was only the potentiality for post-scarcity, but people were hungry and deprived and destroyed. He meant that Shawn had never known scarcity himself. Corey had answered him with a smile, that neither had they, after all. Of course Billy hadn't—not physical scarcity—but he had known emotional starvation and intellectual deprivation, and he had taken care to comprehend the power structure and economic web of the world they lived in. And imagine Corey saying he had never known scarcity. Billy had seen the shack Corey had grown up in: a peeling wooden box stuck up on cement blocks. Not even a lawn, just a shack stuck up lopsided out of the mud.

Corey didn't have a father, his mother worked. Early he had been shunted into the lowest track. Even if there had been no Nineteenth Year of Servitude, what would he have had to look forward to? The Army? Trying to get hired in the mills? A dishwasher's job or a job in the car wash in the shopping plaza? Jail, if they had caught him in the one job he had held. Sometimes Billy felt years older than Corey.

If they hadn't started the Indians, he, Billy, would be at Cal Tech, but where would Corey be? Corey didn't understand that the titillating prestige he had enjoyed as a dealer in high school was just a way of keeping him quiet until he went into the cheap labor pool with the other discardable slobs. The only sector of the economy where post-scarcity reigned was the labor market, where there was no lack at all of Coreys ready to do whatever it was not yet economical to have a machine do better. Then his only contact with Shawn would have been to fill the tank of his sports car and wipe his windshield. Corey thought he was saving everybody else, but never noticed the despair yawning before him.

"What's wrong?" Corey leaned on bent elbow, tickling Billy's arm with blades of grass. "Tell me what's eating you."

"What's *really* going to happen to us? Don't you think about it? Don't you wake up at night and feel you have to know?"

"We're going to make the revolution. We have no other choice."

He yanked the grass out of Corey's hand and scattered it. "*Look* at me, Corey. We're going to make a revolution in the United States, in the center of the empire. With bubble gum? We're going to blow up the Pentagon and bring the troops home?"

"If nobody would go to work at the Pentagon, if nobody would go into the Army, they couldn't crush us. We can't break their machine—they have enough firepower to blow up the world ten times. But we can get the people out."

"Corey! No rhetoric, Corey! Look at me. I think we'll die in a skirmish long before the real revolution."

"We win, or the world ends. There's no use being defeatist. Despair is the worst vice for a revolutionary. We can win."

He wanted to take Corey by the shoulders and shake him. To hurt him into response. He raised his hand, but he could not touch Corey. Could not touch him. "Don't call me defeatist. I'm looking with my eyes open. I'm ready to die in that skirmish. I don't think we can win in the fat homeland. Do you think so, Corey? I think all we can do is help the people out there fighting for their freedom. Are you ready to die?"

"You have to want to win, Billy. People come to us for a better life, not a good death."

"I'm asking about what you think will happen!" He turned away, resting his cheek against the ground. His eyes closed for a moment. He felt weak and huge, then his anger came back. "I'm going back to the city. I want to fight the enemy, not pretend they've gone away."

"What about the lab?"

"The boys can turn out bread and anything else we need. I'm not in the mood to work in it anyhow. I'm tired of cooking."

Corey grimaced with worry, but his voice was soft and pushed at agreement. "Sure it'd be good to have someone strong back on the Lower East Side. Things are moving fast. Also, we need somebody good in Chicago. The shit has really been coming down on the kids there. And things

are uptight in L.A. It's good to move around and keep
your hand in, keep an eye on how things are shaping. . . .
What about Ginny?"

"What about her?" Billy hunched into his shoulders.

"She's doing a good job here. I've never seen her so
together."

"What's that got to do with me?"

Corey sat up. "Well, because she loves you. Naturally, I
think she'd want to go with you."

"What for? She's always got Shawn."

"She hasn't got Shawn. You know. She just screws him
sometimes. That's not anything."

Shawn the prick and his nocturnal games. He debased
the girls by his strutting, but none of them could see that.
Nobody cared except him. Of course, Ginny didn't mean
anything to Shawn. That didn't keep him away from her.
Didn't keep her away from him. "Don't see what it has to
do with me."

"Don't you believe she loves you?"

"If she doesn't have sex with me, she has it with somebody else."

"That's not what I mean." Corey shrugged. "You don't
sleep with other girls that often, do you?"

Billy shrugged back, scowling. After all, Corey knew he
didn't dance, although he ignored it. Often he had tried to
push Corey for a confrontation over the dancing, but
never succeeded. It was too popular to make an issue in
council. He knew he would lose. To strut around in the
circle stark naked: the idea that anyone could conceive he
would do that made him furious. He wasn't a smooth
talker like Shawn. Oh, he'd gone to bed with other girls a
few times, especially after some street action when everybody would be making a fuss after him and some girl
would decide she was interested. Like Carole, who was a
good warrior, with tight discipline and never lost her cool:
but how embarrassing to have her suddenly want that.
Only with Ginny sex was easy; only with Ginny he did not
feel awkward. He was used to her and she made it
comfortable. She admired him in a different way from the
others. After all, she had come to him before he'd become
some kind of freaky hero.

He was intensely annoyed with Corey for talking about
it. He didn't talk to Corey about his private relationship
with Joanna. Why should he drag Ginny off to New York

with him? That's how Corey acted. Joanna was very ambitious, he could feel that in her. She wanted people to look at her, to admire her, to pay attention to her too. But she couldn't get into anything, because Corey was always having to run here and there, and he just dragged her along like his baggage. If he didn't know where she was for ten minutes, he would start asking people frantically. He seemed scared shitless she would vanish.

When Joanna spoke up, people would notice her with surprise as a person rather than as an emanation of Corey. They'd say with shock, Joanna really is bright, you know? Joanna has ideas of her own. Then Corey's voice would ring out, Joanna? Joanna? and she would go running. She sat in on meetings as Corey's woman, because Corey needed her there. She wanted to be there in her own right, but she never had a chance to prove that right. And Corey could see nothing.

Then Corey dared sit in judgment on him because he would not say he loved Ginny and drag her off with him away from her job. He did not know if he loved her or not. Probably he could not love anyone. There was too much anger in him. But he knew he would not gobble her up to feed his esteem and smother his loneliness. So he scowled at Corey and kept his face shut. In the warriors men and women were equal and fought as equals or they went down, and there was no messing around when they were under battle discipline.

Corey made a sad face and shut up about Ginny. "When do you want to go?"

"Soon."

"Be careful, you know. We can't afford to lose you. Our chief thrust now has to be organizing. We're not ready for too much confrontation. We should never fight when we can't win. We should never move into the streets when we know the injuries will be all ours."

"We have a lot to learn about street tactics. We won't learn it digging potatoes and sewing pants." Billy raised his big fist. "Fighting is what takes people across the line. Then they're ours. Otherwise we're just bullshit."

"What brings people across the line is what we offer them that they can't find out there."

"Kids that come in because they think it's groovy to take off their clothes—we haven't changed them, we haven't got to them. Somebody else will offer them a new game, and off they'll go. One kick is like another. The new one wins."

"Joanna! Hey, over here." Corey sprang to his feet. She was plodding down the hill with a basket of gooseberries, sweaty and red-faced with her carroty hair tangled over her shoulders.

"I have to take these into the kitchen before they get bruised. Let go, I'm dying of thirst." She tried to push Corey away as he hugged her. "I'm dying for a cold bath."

"Come on, we'll take a shower together." He pulled the basket from her and started downhill. The conversation was over. Billy remained squatting in the grass. Then he got slowly up. Maybe he had wanted Corey to talk him out of going. He knew only that he felt cheated.

The bread had no effect that night. He could not get high, could not rise off the ground where he sat into the distant cold ring of liquid stars above them. The drums pestered him like mosquitoes. He was invisible sitting against a tree in the vague flicker of firelight. Invisible to all of them drunk with their bodies and their sensuality.

He did not mind the mystics, the solitaries, the seekers who spun on the wheel at the beating heart of the music. They were only after what he was after when he took bread. They could not see him or anyone else. They were solitary and pure in their burning, and their flesh was an instrument. Like dervishes. They shared nothing he could not reach. The vision hardened them. He approved, though that was not his way.

It was the others who danced on his head, those who used the ritual to move each other, to finagle what they wanted, to strut and preen and rub lasciviously in the firelight. The painted bodies wavered like flames. They were so sure. They could tease and mock and wriggle their breasts and buttocks and poke their dicks in the air without shame. Without shame or clumsiness they summoned everyone to look at them.

Rage grew in him. It was a lewd nightmare danced on his head. They ignored him sitting alone, or if they looked, they smiled or waved or felt sorry. Dared to pity him as he saw them in his clarity.

Even Ginny forgot to glance at him when she was in the center. There she was mocking him with her wriggling body. And Corey could say obscenely that she loved him.

There was Corey leaping about, shaking himself like a puppy dog with Shawn, imitating the combat Shawn had never yet been tried in—tried and found wanting. He ground his teeth. Joanna was dancing with one of his warriors, Big Ned, almost dancing circles around him. Dancing to be watched, showing off. He shut his eyes.

Middle-class brats having fun and confusing their games with changes in the real world. The government had for the moment chosen repression, but the liberal mode would come in again, and all that fun and games would be co-opted. Sex was the hottest commodity. You'd have the whole population fucking like rabbits at every bus stop, and so what? The Roman emperors had been fond of orgies. They'd all rather fuck than think, fuck than fight. Easy! In the morning he would talk to his men one by one and see how many were fed up and willing to return to the city. How many would follow him. How many were ready at last for some action.

As soon as he was back in the city, he knew he was right. Running away was nowhere. To stay in there close to the enemy. Now every day he had his face rubbed in what he was fighting, who he was fighting, why he was fighting.

He found the atmosphere slack in the communes, but the opportunity for change wide open. Let Corey stay in the country. He would run a tight ship for a change. Time for the warriors to shape up: drill and weapons practice, discipline, political education. Anyone who could not keep up the pace should be jolted out. He had made enough excuses about what the warriors were not ready for. Maybe the farms would have a use, of stripping off the soft queasy layers and leaving only the unyielding core for him to work on.

He looked through the potential cadre with a harder eye than he had ever used. He had to choose well. He studied the warriors who had followed him from the farm, the few who had already come back to the city before him, the new recruits. Carefully he chose his lieutenant, Matty, solid, strong, politically hard. He was sick to death of the mushiness. All the soft democratic mumblings of the council did was to concentrate power in Corey's hands. Corey pretended to a false equality. He pretended there was no leadership, that he was not a leader; with the other half of him, he pretended that he was the tribe.

Billy could remember when in fact there had been no leadership: when they had taken the school, the first time. But patterns developed. Now there was merely unconscious leadership, irresponsible leadership, leadership with the left hand and out of the side of the mouth, leadership through charm and manipulation.

Well, Corey had for the moment abandoned the city to him. Corey was bored with New York. He would not remain fascinated by the farm forever, but in the meantime the city was Billy's, and here he was going to develop the kind of model the rest of the tribes could emulate. Responsible leadership, practicing criticism and self-criticism, would relate to the mass of the tribes and the kids they were trying to organize in a conscious, political way. A cadre responsible to itself with discipline and a clear sense of priorities. Why fight the farm? He would simply make it irrelevant. He would not deny he was being elitist: he would be clearly and responsibly a leader and create an apparatus that would produce others, thus making himself finally and truly unnecessary.

He loved and hated the city. It was the city of empire. Yes, he was locked in combat with it the way the old radicals of Israel, the prophets, had gone railing to Babylon. Whore, cesspool, golden sepulcher. Corey felt nothing of that. He was never anyplace. He was always wandering around the map of his brain. The chemistry of real places could not get through to him. He would sit on the subway humming and babbling to himself as if he were jogging along a country lane in the back of an open truck. Shawn: what was his natural landscape? The cinematic floodlit pools of youthcult: an eternal wave coming in on an antiseptic beach, high midnight on the Strip, strobe-spastic boutiques. The carbonized freeways of the brain. Los Angeles: city that was nothing but a slot machine dispensing plastic toys. Nothing was visible there but a whole people dying of consumption. Here you could see the pillars of the empire.

Pillars of the empire. It had been stinking hot for a week. He had been killing himself every day. Wednesday at noon he smelled a wind stirring the fetid air of the Lower East Side. There was a vein of lead in the mugginess. Green and gray shimmered in the sky. He told his new right hand, Matty, "I'm going off to inspect the ass of the ruling class." He had to scowl to get off alone. As soon as he came out of the subway at Thirty-fourth, his stride lengthened, his pace quickened. How clean it was! A light fog of poisonous smoke hung in the air here too, but of course no one in the glass houses was smelling it.

Buildings where corporations live. Prettier, as the time and money defined pretty, than anything else built. They could even afford to "waste" a little of the golden footage in plantings, cement plazas, arcades, once in a billionaire's while a fountain or a reflecting pool. Nothing went on for miles that was humanly useful. Somewhere out in the empire people were mining tin and pumping oil and growing soybeans and making rubber. Here was the accounting and administering, the finaglings of how to turn labor into profit, the edifice of words and lies and images created, the selling of what no one needed into what everyone must want, the high-level bribery, the stock-option plans and the media bamboozles.

The Garden of Mammon, full of glass headstones glaring in the sun. The earth is my shit heap, I shall not want, say the ruling class. They were gutting the earth as fast as ever they could, their vast factories pissing into it, scooping out the elements and the minerals and leaving only a poisoned desert for the billions who would inherit the plundered craters from which everything profitable had been extracted and consumed. After them, around them, the big famine, the final hunger.

Corey would be wondering what to do with these strange aquariums built for paper. But Billy understood that that was not his problem. He would not live on to being human. He was a weapon, forged in a society that had discovered that great profit could accrue to some people (those who counted, those who counted each other) by sending the young of the powerless off to be killed killing far larger numbers of peasants here and there who wanted to control their own lands and their own lives. Because every time a bomb exploded, every anti-personnel weapon that sent its hundreds of particles tearing through the soft tissues of soft bodies, every helicopter that was shot down with its crew, every plane hit with a missile: brrrring, brrrring, on the great cash register in the home-land bank. It was all profit. It would have to be replaced.

It was the perfect form of fantastically expensive and forced consumption, paid for by taxes.

He walked and walked. Now he was among their dwellings. The wind was rising down the long avenues. Lava-like clouds were piling up beyond the East River. How comfortable they made themselves! How jolly and cozy it must be in there, knowing rats were chewing babies just three miles north on 110th Street and that two miles south on Fourteenth Street girls were selling themselves for supper and a fix for their pimp.

Did that consciousness titillate them? Or was part of owning the world never to think of all that? Did they laugh at the fools they robbed, who were fool enough to admire them and vote them into office so they could arrange things more conveniently for their enterprises?

He felt silly asking those questions. They thought they were the real people. The people they ate were just fodder. It was like asking a diner to weep for the fish on his plate. No, it did not do to be concerned with them. He watched the limousines glide by, the exotic cars, the exotic dogs. He carried over his shoulder a sack of grenades, still invisible, and tossed them right and left to bloom like Johnny Appleseed planting his trees.

He must remember that it did not matter if the lady walking that fuzzy orange beast was softhearted and spent boring hours at meetings she thought worthy and worried about the starving natives of some other place. She was dressed in the skins of natives. He must not concern himself with the inside of her head.

Let him live long enough to kill a few of his enemies: the enemies of most of humankind. Let him live long enough to forge a weapon that would kill more. Born twisted, born warped, born in the center of the empire, he could only pride himself that they had not succeeded in using him. They had come close. But he had escaped them and turned. For the society, the system was mad: it caused the people in it to go slowly mad. They could not care for each other. They could only hate and fear and compete and fantasize; they could only rub against each other and try to use each other and suck on their own anxieties.

He would never live to be human. Nobody like him or these people could imagine what it might be like to be human, in a society people ran for the common good instead of the plunder of the few. Dimly, like a blind man imagining the sun, he could call up fancies of a person who was strong, unafraid, social, generous, gentle, ready. The brother. He could almost imagine. Tenderness swept his body. Someday there would be people. But that coming would not be gentle. It would sprout from struggle and death. Someday there would be human people.

The skies opened up and the rain fell down, straight down hard upon his body. His shirt was plastered to his sides. Water ran in streams down the sidewalk over his shoes. People scuttled under canopies and sent out doormen to whistle at cabs. He was alone in the embrace of the water. He raised his arms into the torrent. How good it felt! Good to be alive for a moment, even as a weapon! Let it all come down.

KIDS had broken tribal rules before. The error was discussed in council until they all agreed on a verdict. The person might be required to fast in solitude for a few days to clear his head and body of what had been eating him. He might be barred from the dance for a couple of weeks. He might even be expelled from the group. But Chuck was the first warrior to commit something that everyone saw as serious. He was caught selling bread at high prices and keeping the money.

Chuck had only stayed on the farm a few weeks before returning to the commune on Spring Street, so the council to judge him would meet there—his commune plus representatives from others. Corey would have been glad to avoid this council in the name of tribal democracy, but he knew the situation was important. Almost he had persuaded himself that he had to go to L.A. immediately instead. He knew it was from squeamishness that he wanted to stay out. He had to be there to make sure everyone understood the implications of what Chuck had done, that the political message of the situation was clear. A contingent from the farm drove in. He rode in the back of the closed truck with his head in Joanna's lap and said nothing.

He had wanted Shawn to come.

Shawn had leaned on the new bench in the dining hall, still holding a plane in his hand. "No, man. Sometimes you're blind. Willfully blind. I can't sit in on the trial of one of Billy's warriors. I'm not a warrior, I never bothered to become one, and I never will. All we need is for them to start talking about the elite country types trying to control their councils."

Everybody always had such good reasons for not wanting to stick their fingers in the fire. Never that it would hurt, of course. "You think I shouldn't go?"

"You have to. You're a warrior. I'm not."

"Don't feel that way. You're respected."

"Not by Billy's boys. That's fine with me. I'm not big on judging people, anyhow. It's not my scene."

Do you think it's mine? he wanted to ask, but swallowed it. Don't push too hard on people. He had wanted Shawn with him. It wasn't the same as needing Joanna there, but it was strong. Shawn made a balance in him. Shawn held him to the light side of himself, just as Joanna held him steady and sane. She kept him from sliding into his withdrawn inner blackness; she kept him from cracking, from splintering. Shawn gave him an opening to others. With Shawn he could play in a good way. With Shawn he could talk bluntly about what happened. He did not have to put on a performance, to convince and act out and demonstrate.

Shawn had not followed out of belief. Sometimes he was afraid he did not know why Shawn had followed. But with Joanna and with Shawn he could open his doubts, and that kept him able to move and change and roll with the punches. That was the major thing: not to get hung on being right, not to let himself go rigid.

They left the truck several blocks away and walked to the meeting. It was a hot September night, and the air felt like mud, an element twice as heavy as the air of the farm.

"How dirty it is," Joanna said softly as they walked.

To look at the garbage of casual living all over the streets, bottles and cans and newspapers and broken chairs and banana peels and pizza boxes, had to make you feel that being human was a mean low thing. City people were like pets trapped in a cage with their own shit. Shawn had talked about the use of shit to make you feel defiled, to break you down to self-loathing in brig.

"Hey, the air's like spaghetti!" Corey shouted. Everyone felt dispirited. He had to rouse them. He pantomimed fighting his way through a forest of wet spaghetti. Clown, he went lunging over the sidewalk offering himself to their stares and laughter. At the top of his raucous voice he sang:

> "I am an Indian, wild and mean,
> The reddest thing you ever seen!
> How! How! How! How! Now!"

All six of them joined hands and went dancing up the
street with Ned, the husky AWOL with the fatback in his
voice, at the head of the line whipping it around, and little
Ben on the end almost flying. When they came to the
commune, they shushed at once. But Corey thought they
brought a little wave of energy—positive good energy—
with them. The room was packed already.

At first when somebody had done something that bothered people, they held gentle family sessions, everyone
talking about why they were upset and the person respond-
ing and usually trying hard to understand. But somehow,
slowly, a court emerged. Maybe their society had got
them so used to thinking in terms of blame and punishment and using power to put down, that they had carried
some of that over. He liked the old way of gentle sessions
better. But they encountered little gentleness in the streets.

First the witnesses against Chuck spoke. Rumors had
come to the commune that the Indians would sell bread to
anyone now, but that their price had gone up. The rumors
were so persistent that Matty, who was head of security in
August, set out to run them down. Being head of security
meant you handled intelligence for a month. Corey had
been strong on that. "Function corrupts," he had said till
he got the idea across. "We don't turn anybody into a gun
or into a shovel or into a stove or into a desk or into an
account book."

Matty had found that the peddler was Chuck, but he
had watched him for two weeks longer. He wanted to
understand what Chuck was doing. He then discovered
that Chuck had opened a bank account in his own name
and that he was buying a car, a three-year-old Ford
convertible he kept in a garage in the Village.

Chuck rose to defend himself. Corey had known him
since high school, and he felt sick. Chuck had been in the
first assault on Franklin High. He had been beaten in the
first bust. He was a solid-looking boy with a brown
moustache, a deep voice and an ingratiating smile. "Look
here, I been with the Indians since the beginning, and I've
pulled my share and then some. Everybody here who
knows me knows that. I risked my skin as much as
anybody, and I'm not boasting, just telling the truth. But a
man has needs. I've always had a car. I like to drive. I like
to move around. I can't ask permission every time I want
to wipe my ass, I'm not a kid. I had a job caddying in

high school and I always had money in my pocket that I earned.

"Look, I see some girl and I want to take her out. I'm not going to try to convert her first. You got to have some money to spend on a girl. I want to take her to the movies or for pizza. Girls like you to have a car. It's nothing serious. Maybe I just want to pick her up and drive around and lay her. It doesn't do you any harm. The girls in the commune are fine. But when I'm on the street and I see a chick I want, I got to go after her. I don't want to organize her. Maybe I don't even want to see her again.

"I'm risking my ass peddling bread. The Mafia don't like us none, and if they get one of us, they cut him up or bust his guts open. They killed Sandy and we think they killed Eileen. They don't like us selling so cheap. I never held back a penny of the regular price. I turned that over fair and square. But what I could get above that was my own hustle, and I can't see what skin it is off anybody else's back. I just want to feel like a man sometimes and have a good time. That's only human. Why pretend to be some kind of crazy monks?"

Sitting on the floor beside Joanna with her knee against his, Corey could feel that she was unmoved by Chuck. She sat there rigid and condemning, and he wondered at her intransigence. The smell of his own early adolescence was in his nostrils. Maybe he had traded those needs in on others—Joanna and playing chief. She would laugh at his squeamishness. She would tell him, I'd make a tougher chief than you do. He answered her, But I'm not a war chief, Billy is.

Almost all tribes made that distinction, and he thought it a good one. It was too much to ask that the same human being be held responsible for protecting and nurturing and preserving the ways of his people, and for leading them into wars. For instance, Chief Joseph of the Nez Percé was thought of by many as a great general because he had shepherded his people on such a long skillful retreat, but he had never led them in battle.

Aw, poor slob. Why had Chuck followed them at all if he understood so little? How many kids were as untouched inside? Fifteen years of programing, and he thought he could shake them alive in a few months of communal living. Poor bastard, Chuck could never see how dangerous he was to the group. It was a re-education problem, but they had little way of handling the exchange of political ideas. After all, kids came in mistrusting words, hating their programing, sick of the processing of school, ready to puke at the old coercive rhetoric of Buy and Die. There were almost no tools available in the tribe to communicate political values, but only to embody them. Which worked, sort of. Sort of. To be left with exemplary action because they could not talk to each other properly, made him feel like banging his head on the floor.

Corey rose. "If you disagree with the rules, Chuck, the place to disagree is in the council, not in the streets, not when you think you're off where none of us can see you. The enemy has guns and tanks and planes and submarines. The enemy has chemical and biological and nuclear weapons. The enemy is ready to use gases that choke and blind us and prisons to break our souls and clubs to break our bodies. He's ready to use shotguns and dogs. The only weapons we have are our bodies and our lives. The only weapon we have is our solidarity. The only weapon we have is our trust in each other.

"There's only one thing we can deny the man who owns everything: ourselves. He owns the streets and the sky-scrapers and the water that comes out of the tap and the gas we burn. He owns the music we make and the cigarettes we smoke. He takes away our minds in his schoolrooms. Then he sells us back our dreams and charges us our lives. He reaches into our pants and manipulates our wants and sells us images to feed those desires, so we will want and want and want. So we will become men defined by owning things made of pasteboard. The man taught you to take women like tissues and wipe yourself in them and throw them away.

"You don't need to go out of the tribe to know you're a man. Here you can be yourself, and women don't ask more of you—or less of you, Chuck—than that you be yourself. For real. Nobody gets caught. Nobody gets stuck. There is no marriage, because we are all married to each other. We are each other's family. Children belong to the tribe, and we are free to love each other as we can.

"Yet you chose to travel back into the man's bad dream. You took the promises of the system and cuddled them inside you, and you would not throw them out." Part of him was listening to himself and watching the faces . . . no, not watching. Feeling into. A sense that came back, like judging temperature, so that he knew he was in touch. The heat of attention. Part of him was steering his speech where it had to go. "You came with us and lived with us and yet you did not belong in us. You want to be a part-time Indian and a part-time warrior and a consumer the rest of the time, a slave the rest of the time. But we live outside their law and inside our own. You cannot have what we have—the tribal thing, and what the man sells—the capitalist consumer thing. To play both sides is betrayal. To play both sides is treason."

He looked around as he sat down, and he saw that the faces were still with him. The faces were against Chuck standing lonely in the middle, turning to his accusers as they spoke. They spoke for exile, and the sense of the group was to vomit out Chuck, to expel him at once. Corey knew expulsion was important, for what Chuck had done was the one absolutely rotting action. They could not contain in their body the dreams of success and merchandise and commodity sex that inhabited Chuck like demons.

Billy rose. Corey thought, he is going to speak against expulsion. Protect his warrior. He hoped someone else besides him would rise to oppose Billy, but he began to put together a speech in his head. In a way, such a crisis could be used for that political education they were always lacking, to articulate to the tribe in that very moment of making their collective decision some of the bases of such decisions. Then the judging itself—the expelling of the person from the tribe—was not purely punitive but contained the seeds of learning and growing for the collective. Then Billy knocked the rough framework of his speech out of his head.

"Expulsion? What kind of fools are we? Are we playing children's games? Chuck broke the rules, so we won't play with him any more. He cheated and lied and bartered with our enemies, so we will let him go and do as he pleases all of the time on their side. What kind of fools are we? It's our lives we're playing with.

"This man is a warrior. This man has taken the oath to obey the group with his life. He knows our defenses. He knows where our communes are and who is in them. He knows where the farm is set up in New Jersey and where the West Coast farm is. Finally, he knows the formula for bread. He can go and manufacture it for the Syndicate tomorrow. He has shown already he thinks of it as something to sell to the highest bidder. He thinks of himself as something to sell to the highest bidder. If we let him go, we have only our own destruction to look forward to.

"I trained him and I trusted him. When we are on the streets fighting the man, when we're moving into a new neighborhood or a new city, it's our lives that are on the line. I trusted him and you trusted him, and we were wrong. We were dead wrong. He turned on us. He sold us. He sold us for cheap pickups and pizza and a flashy car.

"We are not playing children's games. He sold *us*. We cannot expel him—turn him loose—and survive."

Billy moved to the center of the circle. There he stood, big and slightly hunched, with his fingers at the front of his belt. He faced Chuck. He stared at him till Chuck squirmed. Then he turned slowly around and looked at the circle. He held out his oversized hand and turned the thumb down. "Death."

"Death," Matty said.

"Death," Billy's warriors repeated one by one. "Death." "Death." "Death."

Corey saw that he had been outflanked. Private caucus. The more-militant-than-thou warriors. God damn them. The mood of the meeting was thick and ugly. Never, never could he do what had to be done, never was he close enough to sense moods and changes, never did he spend enough time feeling people out and giving them a sense of their place and their value. Never enough time, never. He stood to argue for imprisonment. Chuck could be detained on the farm. They could try to re-educate him. After all, they had time. Perhaps it was everyone's fault that Chuck had been left with the inside of his head full of ugly nonsense, while no one had noticed and no one had cared.

Matty answered, "Who among us wants to be a jailer? We came out of the system to make ourselves and others free. If we haven't won him to us in all the time he's been here, if he's been hiding what he really wanted all this time, what does re-education mean? He fooled us once, so he can do it again. How can we trust him? And who wants to be his jailer?"

"Who wants to be his murderer?" Carole asked: hard-edged Carole of the warriors. Maybe she had slept with Chuck. Or maybe she just hated what they were doing.

"We'll draw lots," Matty said. "It's like security. Nobody should have to do it, but as long as we're in the belly of a sick society, everybody has to eat some shit."

"It has to be done at the farm," Harley the street fighter said. "It's too dangerous here."

Chuck was staring from one to another, his eyes just pulling from face to face in dumb fury. "You're all crazy bastards. You know that? Crazy bastards! I didn't do anything you all don't want to do. That's why you want to get rid of me. Don't you see I'm willing to go? I'll walk out that door and wash my hands of the lot of you. I don't need your old bread to make a living. I can get a job any time. Shit, I can promise I won't bother with it. And Billy, he's lying, because he knows I never could work good in the lab. All I ever done was break glass. I don't know the formula for water, let alone bread."

"You're an evader," Matty said. "What wouldn't you tell to stay out of jail?"

"So I'll go to your farm. What do you want out of me?"

"You just said you didn't want to stay with us," Billy said. He got to his feet. "Why should you want to stay on the farm? What's new that's going to keep you honest? We'll draw lots."

The momentum had escaped Corey, and he had to regather it. A dangerous feel to the room. It was necessary to do something to heal the collective. The will of the caucus must be healed into the will of the body. Further, a bad task must not fall on someone who might be broken by it. Finally, his political instincts told him he must stay on top of decisions. Regain control. Corey stood. "No. I'll perform any sentence of the council. I accept the judgment of the tribe and stand ready to carry it out." Had to, had to. Heal the breach.

By vote of council, the death sentence was confirmed and Corey was mandated to carry it out that night. Chuck was bound and Ben went for the truck. Corey wanted to leave fast. "We won't stay for the dancing." It would turn his stomach.

"We don't dance after council any more," Matty said. "Cadre have criticism, self-criticism. Dancing is for after we've won."

The trip back was black and silent, a long tunnel under a mountain. Joanna held his head in her lap and stroked his forehead. He had an urge to draw away from her. He would not let himself withdraw. She was his strength. But he could not speak to her. He could only lie in his blackness as the miles slipped under them.

The guards let them in. It was late and most of the tribe asleep. But Shawn was sitting up with Ginny and Ben's little sister Ruth and three of the farm warriors, awaiting them. He looked at Ruthie waiting, and for an instant he loved her better than anyone, clearer than anyone. And knew he could not communicate it out of his trouble. She was little as a comma and dark, and she spent most of her time with the chickens. She danced by herself singing words you had to stand near her to hear:

> I used not to live anywhere.
> I used not to live anywhere.
> I used not to have hands.
> Now I live here.
> I used not to have a face.
> Now I see me.
> There used to be others.
> They used to be tall.
> They used to be mean.
> Now I see you.

Ginny stepped forward, her hands clutched. "We didn't know if you'd be back tonight, but we thought we'd wait. Billy didn't come?"

Corey made a brief report. The others filled in. Bound Chuck lay like a bag of laundry. Corey could not look at him.

"I'm worried about Billy," Ginny said. "He's getting harder. Things are building up in him."

"Things build up for all of us. And power corrupts," Corey said bleakly. He wished Ginny would shut up.

"Is it corrupting you?"

"Corey isn't interested in power," Joanna said fiercely. "All he cares about night and day is the group." And me, her eyes said sideways.

"The group isn't power?" She had such a way of looking at him sometimes. It made him remember, but he always pushed it away. He did not want to connect this Ginny with that one. They were comrades now. But her look sometimes pushed on his forehead like a pointed finger.

"Better do it on the hill. Take him up to the cabin. Nobody's there now," one of the warriors said, and all three left quickly. Corey got his .22 from storage.

"You're going to kill him? Have you gone crazy?" Ginny stood arms akimbo.

I met a monster walking up the hill. His name was Corey and he grinned and grinned and his hands ran blood. The executioner's shame. He told Joanna to untie Chuck's feet and told Chuck to get up. Chuck shook his head. He would not move.

"Why are you going through with this? Just because they've gone mad fighting doesn't mean we have to. Why?"

Joanna repeated the argument to her from the council meeting. Ginny frowned. She sat on a bench, looking down. Corey prodded Chuck with the rifle till he got up.

Joanna said, "Corey, he wants the gag taken out."

"No."

"Why not?" Joanna shook back her curly hair. "It must be nauseating to have something in your mouth."

"It must be nauseating to have a nice conversation with the man you're about to shoot."

"Maybe he has something to say."

"Sure he has: Don't do it; I want to live. Hurry up. Unless, of course, you don't want to come with me. Maybe it disgusts you."

"Of course it does. But I won't let you go up there alone."

"And you, Shawn. Still sitting this one out? Still see it as none of your business?"

Shawn winced. "All right. What I love best is your forgiving disposition."

"Listen!" Ginny stood up. "We can't let him go, because supposedly he would sell the formula for bread. Okay, we stop selling bread. We give it away."

Shawn sat down. "Why not? We want to cut people out of the money system. What better way?"

"Because the council decided. If you two felt so strongly, why the hell wouldn't you come along? We can't set ourselves against the decision. We can't start creating factions. Billy uses the money that comes in from bread for buying guns. He's into weapons training with the warriors. The time to fight the decision was at the council, not afterwards because you don't like it."

Ginny spoke a few words to Chuck and walked out. They started for the cabin. Corey wanted to send the others away from him and to keep them, to tax them for failing him in some murky way he could not define. They stumped up the hill on the path, tripping over rocks, lashed with branches. He hated the broad back of Chuck stumbling ahead. Wanted to drive the rifle in. The flashlight streamed ahead of them, swinging as Shawn walked. Insects fluttered through the beam.

He could no longer remember why it had been important to assume the will of the council in his person. Symbolic leadership materlializing in concrete act: concrete dirty painful act. Heal the group. Fight schisms. Now he mistrusted his judgment. Long scramble up the hill. They were all panting. The dampness of sweat disgusted him under his clothes.

Shawn went into the cabin and lit a Coleman lantern, which hissed loudly. No electricity up here. Water from a spring fifty yards away—the spring that became the stream running down through the farm. It was a dull night. He could see no stars. The wind was soft and tired. It must be three. He did not own a watch. At demonstrations, he borrowed one. He saw Joanna and Shawn retie Chuck's legs and then they came out to him. He had dropped his rifle and left it on the ground in the path of yellow light from the cabin door. Cabin they had built for people to be alone with their heads. He still believed in fasting and vision. Would what they were about to do pollute the air?

"We should dig the hole first," Shawn said. A shovel leaned by the door, and Joanna picked it up over her shoulder.

"A hole by any other name. Why don't we dig the grave here, where he can supervise?"

"Come on, Corey." She touched his arm. "It has to be away from the cabin." She spoke very softly.

False delicacy. They were about to kill Chuck, but they must not discuss it loudly in front of him. That way it would hurt less, no? "Why don't we ask him where he'd like to be?"

Joanna let go. "All right, I'll do it." She plunged blindly through the underbrush. Shawn chased her with a flash-

light. Corey followed sullenly. Joanna and Shawn finally
agreed on a spot, and Shawn began to dig. It was slow
work. Finally he said, "Come on, you dig for a while,
chief."

Corey took the shovel and worked savagely. "How
handy that there's a shovel here. It's for burying garbage,
you know."

"Look, we didn't vote to kill him."

"Yes, you did, Joanna baby."

"Just to make it unanimous. Everybody raised his
hand."

"Everybody except me."

"But you were waiting for the verdict. You said you'd
carry it out. That's why you didn't vote."

"How do you know why I didn't vote? Did you ask
me?"

Joanna bit her lip, turning to and fro. "Did you want
me not to vote? Think how that would have looked."

"Think how Chuck's going to look soon."

Shawn yanked the shovel from him and finished the
hole. Corey did not want to kill anybody, not even for his
best ideas. He blamed himself because he had not thought
of an alternative. That meant they had not cared enough
to invent a way that Chuck could live. Yet he was being
sentimental. Chuck was a dangerous slob. The wind had
stiffened. The sky looked thinner as they trudged back to
the cabin.

"It'll be light soon. So we can see what we're doing."
The rifle lay in front of the cabin. He had hoped somehow
it would have been stolen. He had hoped that Chuck would
have escaped, but he lay bound on the canvas cot. The
supports were two x's. Almost he hated the boy now,
although he still pitied him and his plastic desires, pitied
his awkward assertions that they all shared his itches,
pitied his naïve hustler's self-conning. Corey sat down on a
rock. Yes, it was getting lighter. Gray seeped through the
air.

Joanna was standing in front of him. Her hands dug
into the mass of her tangled hair. It was not red yet. "It
has to be done soon. It will upset people to know we're
here."

"By all means, let's everybody pretend nothing is happening." Corey heard himself and felt shame, but he could

not stop. Bitterness rode him. He was rubbing himself into it, and he could not stop.

She looked at him, stepped close, her eyes narrow and hard. "Do you want me to do it? Is that it?"

"Of course not." But he was fascinated. A pit. He did not know if he were more fascinated by the idea because that proved she would kill the boy for him, or because then he would not have to. It made him dizzy.

"I don't believe you." After a minute she went and picked up the gun. She held it gingerly but did not offer it to him.

"God damn it, what is going on?" Shawn came over.

"Corey can't do it."

He did not move. He did not know if it were true or not. He had the feeling he could, if he chose, rise and do it and be done. Still he did not. He was waiting for something else.

"Oh shit," Shawn said softly.

They stood there. The gray wind very slightly moved Joanna's hair. Shawn took the gun from her. He shook Corey by the shoulder roughly. "Come on, we have to carry him out."

"Untie his legs. He'll walk."

"I'm not going to shoot a man running from me. Why should he walk out? Come on." Shawn pulled him to his feet.

Shawn took Chuck's shoulders and he took Chuck's legs. Chuck stared at him over the gag and mumbled something. They sat him up against a tree and Corey took the gag from his mouth. Wet with spittle.

Chuck made a sour face and felt his lips with his tongue. "Are you going to shoot me?"

He was looking at Corey, but Shawn answered, "Yes." He got the rifle and fumbled with it, finding the safety catch. "Is it loaded?"

Corey nodded. He wanted to run away but could not.

"Why are *you* doing it? *He* can't. Corey! Let me go, Corey. I knew you couldn't do it to me. You don't have to tell anyone. I'll go away, you can trust me, you know that. Corey!"

Shawn stood about ten feet from him and raised the rifle, squinting, grimacing. Still he missed the first shot. Chuck screamed and tried to roll away. Shawn stepped close and shot into him, shot into his neck and head. The shots came quickly and horribly loud. He shot until the rifle clicked empty. Then he threw it down.

Joanna took two steps forward, staring. The blood ran out of Chuck in a pool that looked black on the gray leaves. Then she turned away and vomited. Corey felt his gorge rise and fall back. He took a deep breath. Still the blood ran out of the boy. He saw Sandy again. Killed by a shotgun blast. Mechanically and remotely, he made his body work. He got to his feet and walked over to Chuck and examined him carefully. "He's still bleeding."

"I guess he will for a while," Shawn said. "Come on, we have to carry him to the hole. I wish we hadn't made it so far away."

When they lifted him, blood ran in torrents from his mouth and Corey almost dropped him. They carried him between them. Joanna stayed in the clearing. Then she called, "Corey! Corey! Wait!" And came thrashing after them.

They put him down in the hole. His legs were crumpled and Corey knelt and straightened them. The legs were still warm and he was not sure Chuck really was dead. Then he looked at the head and away. He took the shovel and threw dirt down on him. Dirt hit the face. Dirt fell on the open eyes. The open mouth. He bent and shoveled, bent and shoveled, until there was no more hole but a small mound. Then they scattered leaves on top. It still looked like a grave.

"You're both bloody," Joanna said. She looked down at herself, turning round and round. "Is there blood on me?"

"Why would there be?" Shawn asked. He turned and led the way to the spring. Shawn knelt and washed himself in the cold water, and Corey did the same. Cold fresh water tightening his skin. Corey felt that they had come through, but that he was the only one who saw that. Shawn took off his splattered shirt and rolled it into a ball. Then he shoved it under a rock. He went shivering back to the cabin and took the blanket off the bed, and after they had dried themselves, he wrapped himself in the blanket.

Outside, he picked up the rifle and handed it to Corey. "It's yours, isn't it?"

"Do you want it?"

"Oh, sure. Listen, you know we can't tell them who did it."

"Why not? You did it," Joanna said sourly. "He couldn't."

"You know why not. It's done and it doesn't matter which of us. But it will matter if they find out it was me."

Corey shook himself. "We acted together. No one will ask. Let them think the easiest thing."

They went down the hill silently, Corey first, Joanna second, Shawn last. Corey carried the rifle, still warm in his hand. Joanna had the flashlight. When they got to the farmhouse, he put the gun back in the storage room. Nobody was up.

"Good night," he said to Shawn and touched his arm. When he and Joanna had gone to bed, they did not make love. Neither of them moved to do it.

He forgave himself for not shooting Chuck, but he saw that Joanna did not. She could not see yet why that had worked. Because he felt enough steel in himself that he could say in the privacy of his head that if neither of them had stepped forward, he would have done it—and that the proof of the fact that his weakness had function was that Shawn had stepped forward.

Out of the dark, Joanna said, "You know, I made it with Shawn once."

Why did he feel so cold? "Yeah? At the dance? I don't remember."

"Of course not. Last year, before I met you."

"How come you never mentioned it?"

"Well, I never gave you a list, did I? You never told me everybody you went to bed with. You never even told me Ginny used to be your regular girl."

"That was in high school, before the Indians. Before anything. And it didn't mean shit."

"Well, this was a long time ago, and it didn't mean anything either. I didn't even know who he was."

"So why do you tell me now, Joanna?"

"I thought of it. That's all."

"Have you ever gone with him again?"

"Here? Don't be silly."

"Why should I care? We don't own each other."

"Of course we don't," Joanna said, and rolled over away from him.

"Do you want to?"

"Want to what?"

"Go to bed with him again."

"Oh, I don't know. I never thought of it."

"No? Shawn goes to bed with everybody."

"But I don't. Not any more. Do I?"

She was punishing him, but he could not accuse her, because he could not say how. He could not explain to her that he had not failed that night. Her sharp behind stuck into his stomach. She went to sleep.

THE rendezvous was in Bear Mountain State Park. They pulled the car off the road, camouflaged it and hauled in the provisions on the hiking trail to the site agreed on in the negotiations: Corey, Shawn, Carole—who was on the farm recuperating from a bad beating—Big Ned and Joanna. Nobody was at the meeting place. They built a fire and sat around waiting, and after a while Ned and Shawn began to speculate that they had stopped hiking too soon. Then they saw they were surrounded.

Joanna went stiff with fear when she saw the kids. Immediately she was ashamed. Unconscious prejudice. After all, people were scared of the Indians often enough. But the skinny, skinny bodies standing just into the firelight holding clubs and chunks of rusted metal and knives and two with guns, froze her. Black impassive faces and pitiful, emaciated bodies dressed in rags and a few too-big coats.

The tall boy carrying one of the rifles, Marcus, came forward and examined the packages of food, holding the gun on them all the while. "Okay," he said. "Search them."

They were lined up and searched and their weapons taken. Ned started to object, but Corey signaled for him to submit. Then with Marcus still holding the gun on them, the black kids fell on the food. Wrappings went flying. With a knife, a boy who looked twelve called Tiger divvied up the salamis into sections, and then they were gone, skins and all, gone. Like tossing bread into a school of hungry fish. A swirl of dark bodies and rags, and then nothing. Her mouth twitched, but she was too scared to smile.

"Bring me food," Marcus commanded, and a couple of the kids scurried up with chunks of bread and cheese and raw hotdog. Within minutes everything was eaten and the boys sat on their heels staring at them across the flames. "Is that all you brought?"

"That's all we brought this time. There were only us to

carry it, after all," Corey said with a big easy grin. "How to get you more food is one of the things we have to talk about. But we did bring blankets in the green pack."

So they all sat around the fire, and the parley commenced. It was tense enough. Some of the older boys kept eying Joanna and Carole, and their chief asked outright if the women had been brought for their use.

Corey explained that they were warriors, too, and part of the negotiating delegation. Some of the kids sniggered, but the moment passed. Normally Joanna would have pushed into that breach, because she was increasingly aware of how disregarded women were in parleys and councils. But tonight she wanted to stay invisible. Corey could give an imitation of ease, and tonight that was fine with her. Even Shawn looked cowed.

The kids had been in a summer camp for underprivileged children when Harlem was shelled, and they had fled the camp into the Catskills. They had had a hard time. They had known nothing of how to live outdoors, and they had had to learn. Food was their biggest problem, and medicines second. They had learned to hunt and trap: they ate squirrels and birds and dogs and occasionally a deer. They raided campsites and cars. They lived assuming they would be shot on sight. They became fast-moving nomads. They counted five days' journey north, south and west as their territory. Winter was the worst time. Though they tried to give the impression they were so tough nothing could scare them, five boys had died the winter before, and clearly more would die this winter if they faced the same prospects of overexposure and starvation. They had tried to make clothing out of hides of animals they caught, but they did not know how to preserve the hides. The skins rotted and stank and fell apart, or they dried brittle and tore. Corey told them to try soaking the hides in piss. (Later she would ask him why he had said that, and he would say he did not know. He would change the subject.)

Corey was making his pitch for why the boys should think of themselves as Indians, but they were not interested in hearing him out. "Solidarity, shit. What we want is food," their chief Marcus said.

"But the only reason for the food is because we're allies. We don't give charity."

"You give whatever we tell you to, Whitey, if you want to get out of here. You're hostages, dig?"

"We don't give hostages. We're all expendable. You think the tribe would have sent us otherwise?" Corey smiled and smiled. "You can kill us. Then try and find any other natural allies. We're trying to help, because we want you occupying this territory. But we don't want you starving to death doing it. We don't want you occupying territory defensively. You should be in a position to conduct guerrilla warfare—to raid and retreat and raid again, at your choice. Your band should be growing, not dying off. You should be recruiting kids to join you. Otherwise you're accomplishing nothing here." He was on his feet now and they were watching him and listening. Mesmerization. She had thought they might prove immune. Just once, she thought secretly, she'd like to see him work on a person or a group and the object of his manipulation just sit there and yawn, with the words sliding off like drops of oil.

"This should be territory you occupy not to hide on, but to control. Both a field mouse and a mountain lion occupy territory. The one does it defensively, and the other offensively. Dig?"

Oh, they were all going to be mountain lions tonight. She was scared and bored too. All the fencing. Quibbling over semantics. The kids wanted food, and Corey wanted to arrange for them to have it. But he wanted some sort of agreement with them that they were henceforward Indians; he wanted lines of communication and alliance set up. She thought half of it was that he wanted to be able to say to people that there were black Indians. Words. Shawn was as bored as she was. "Oh, to die and be eaten in the Catskills, under a harvest moon," he murmured in her ear. "Poor kids, all they have is hating whites, and Corey's damned if he's not going to steal that away, too. Does it ever come over you in the middle of one of these half-assed trips, to wonder why you're here? But after all, you'd be with Corey anyhow."

(Yet the next day on bread it came back to her differently. Not all of her had been bored. Or scared. She went into vision and danced away from Corey. She turned on him in anger and forced him back, to leave her alone with her vision for once. She danced into that small fire. She danced that they had taken her away with them, only her. The others had been left to depart in safety but had not been able to stop the boys from stealing her: see, see, she said to them, to Corey, the black Indians of the Catskills have stolen me away and they are real savages, not like you: they are real savages. By a small fire they raped her, each and all. She became their queen and their slave. She did not belong to anyone, not even the tall leader, Marcus. She made it with all of them, anyplace, by the side of the trail, by a creek running over flat rocks, by the evening fire. But she was as tough and as good a hunter and as good on raids. She felt herself growing hard and lean and wooden with hunger and cold. She felt herself turning into a fox. She was happy.)

The negotiations were drawing to a close. The moon was behind a mountain and her legs were numb under her with cold, while her face was parched with the heat of the bonfire. The boys were not to be Indians, but they were to be cohorts of the Indians, allies: a complicated nonsensical treaty was arranged, such as was dear to Corey's heart, plus a few practical arrangements in the real world for food drops and medicine and warm clothing worked out.

They stood in the clearing saying good-by with stiff solemnity. Nobody smiled, nobody touched anybody. Corey had started to suggest dancing after the treaty, but Joanna had said loudly, "No! It's much too cold." He was crazy sometimes.

After they had put out the fire, Marcus stood on the ashes and spoke to them, his arms crossed. "If you come here to fool around with us and pull the wool over our eyes, don't go away thinking you fool us. We don't believe in nothing white. Nothing half white. We know each other. We know our territory here. This turf not a bad turf. We know how to die on it.

"We're into waiting, and we're into seeing if the food and medicines you made big promises about turn out to be just words, or if we can eat those words. But get one thing straight, you, Whitey. They are never going to take us. They are never going to bring us in. They are never going to put us in the can or in the cage or behind barbed wire, dig? We don't know about you. Sooner or later, we going to find out if you got balls or just big mouths. So have fun, Whitey. Maybe sometime we can see about parleying again."

Marcus waved them off from where he remained, hold-

ing his band drawn up—emaciated children standing at
attention around the ashes—until Joanna was no longer
able to look back and see anything. They returned stumbling through the black woods, twisting ankles and tripping over logs and treading in icy water. Finally they
came to the car and dug it out of the brush.

They always had to be traveling lately. "The only thing
that can save us is growth," Corey said, again and again.
He gave a lot of speeches. Half the time she knew what
he was going to say. When he found a good phrase, he did
not believe in letting it go to waste. He was trying to fight
factionalism and get the tribes into harder organizing.
"Better people who aren't quite Indians yet, then stan-
dards that keep people from ever joining." There were
groups calling themselves Indians in Portland, Oregon, and
Iowa City, Iowa, in Austin, Texas, and Milwaukee, Wis-
consin, and they had to be on the road more and more.

Too often the tribes seemed to be waiting for kids to
come to them. Too often they got quickly into local
confrontation that worked to seal them off from kids who
might be won over, but didn't yet see the whole point. She
noticed that Corey really did not trust the reports of other
travelers. He had to go and see for himself. If he heard
that things were bad, somewhere in himself he believed
that he could set them right. So even when he delegated
traveling, he tended to do it himself in the end anyhow.

Often they traveled in a loose band, taking some people
from each tribe along to the next to tighten the bonds, as
Corey called it. Always there were the three of them.
Shawn had stopped fighting Corey's pull. There had been
no discussion. As much fuss as Corey had made before
about wanting Shawn involved, about the need for Shawn
to step over the line and give himself fully, Corey never
rejoiced aloud in the change.

It came out of that night on the hill. Sometimes she
wanted to finger that sore. She would have thought Shawn
might withdraw. Perhaps because he had shot Chuck for
Corey, he could only make sense of that by coming even
closer. It rubbed on her. Corey had won out of weakness.
He had made Shawn assume responsibility, and now
Shawn was hooked. She was almost sorry.

Back on the farm, Joanna and Corey had their own
room. It had begun as a small meeting room that Corey
used for talking over problems and ideas with people one

or two or three at a time in his frenzied effort to keep track of developments, to keep close to everyone, to keep things in touch and moving. At first they spent the night there in sleepingbags when they just had to be alone. Then she had built what she called a couch, but it was really a three-quarter bed. She was proud of her handiwork. Corey couldn't drive a nail in straight. The room was still called the small conference room, but it was their room where they could be alone any time when Corey wasn't talking to someone. Others tended to hold their conversations elsewhere.

Demanding privacy, asserting their needs as a couple would never have gone over in the context of what Corey was always saying publicly. She was sure Corey had understood what she was doing, but had not helped or said anything. Only he would point out to Shawn with pride, "Isn't it a groovy bed? Joanna built it."

After all, he had to be alone with her. He needed to dump out his troubles and his agonies, needed to cuddle up and be loved together again if he was going to be any use to any of them. He was a big baby, always hanging on her, grabbing at her, rubbing his face in her breasts, singing songs to her knees and her cunt and her wild red hair.

"Look how high the hair grows on your belly. All that stiff carroty hair. How come it grows so far up?" He lay like a sea urchin, all angles and bones and huge luminous black eyes, twisted around her, prodding at her, peering. "Who ever heard of a girl with so much hair sprouting out of her muff? You're not a girl—you're an orange polar bear. You're made for fucking in a cold climate. You're what those black boys need to keep them warm in the Catskills when the snow comes down."

He lay on his back with his hands under his head and sang in his harsh wavering voice:

> "Joanna has a hairy cunt.
> It's the kind of cunt I want.
> I get on my knees and grunt
> for a touch of Jo-Jo's hairy cunt!"

He would drive her half crazy with hanging on her and teasing her. There was a greedy baby in him that wanted all her attention, all of the time, always. That could not bear for her to look aside, to turn her mind away, to take up a piece of work. That if they had to be separated for a day would invent a hundred ways to make sure her thoughts stayed with him—by picking a quarrel just before she went off to the far fields to harvest tomatoes, or just before the truck left for the city for provisions. That if she paid too much attention to anyone else would contrive to collapse suddenly and mysteriously ill, exhausted, seized by depression. That pushed her toward other people, but before she could make real contact, pulled her back.

She had her weapons. She made him laugh at his carefully acted-out agonies. She made him aware of manipulating his own moods, till he would sometimes stop and grin and say contritely, I'm trying to pick a fight, aren't I? He would stop himself, and he was obviously grateful to her for the discovery that sometimes he could just stop. She had allies: His own enormous will to be good. His will to be good for her, for himself, for everybody. He would tell her that she was making him human. She would say that they were giving birth to each other. They were bringing each other up right this time.

She had thought she was free when she was Joanna on the loose, but she had been a sleepwalker. Nothing had touched her, not even the brutal beatings, never the easy in-and-out sex. Now she was Joanna alive. She was good because she could help him and he needed her. By his need she measured her strength. And yet . . . if tomorrow he did not need her, if they were in fact growing each other up, what would she do then? Then who would Joanna be? He would still be Corey the leader, but who was she? She could still judge herself mainly in negatives, she could make lists of what she was not, starting with the fact that she was not a lush waster like her mother, that she was not closed and scared and squashed mean like her father. More than Corey, much more, she had stood alone, she had made it on the streets, she had had no one to turn to. When she fell, there had been no one to catch her. There had been no benevolent guide on her trips. "Now I have you."

"Now you have the tribe."

Yes, but how? She remembered Harley introducing a newcomer: "This is Ginny. She's in charge of planting.

Ned and Francine head canning. Anita's running a sheep project. This here is Joanna, Corey's girl."

Of course most of the girls were just names: "Nancy, Lena, Sue, Gloria, Hilary ..." They got stuck with all the inglorious daily jobs that made the place run. Unless a girl thrust herself forward insistently or forced herself into the warriors, she could spend her tribal life washing dishes and peeling potatoes and changing babies. A few men like Shawn disliked the sexual roles and consciously crossed over to help care for the babies. But the girls who did not push hard, found themselves quietly pushed down. Joanna herself was no nonentity. Indeed, everybody knew her not only on the farm but around the country: but they knew her as Harley had introduced her. "This here is Joanna, Corey's girl." She was brighter than Ginny, for instance: collards were a kind of cabbage, my eye.

After she had found out that Ginny used to be Corey's girl in high school (not from him of course), she had tried to get to know her. She had thought it would be easy to form a sort of dominant friendship with her, because Ginny was pliable. But Ginny bent and sprang back. She listened and asked questions, but she did not confide.

Joanna tried to get her to talk about the other men she had been involved with, to lead up to Corey, but Ginny was as blank as paper. She would say only that she no longer felt close to Billy, that he had gone away into something where she would not follow him.

About Shawn, she answered, "It's pretty, but it's like water. He's my friend. Shawn is changing every day— don't you see? A little piece of him is way back in something else, and another piece is someplace we haven't got to yet."

Ginny's way of turning off her curiosity. Then she looked straight at Joanna and said, "Someone's been telling you history, um? Well, that didn't mean a thing. I hated myself in those days, and Corey hated himself, so you wouldn't expect that we could mean much to each other."

"For me, that's what it was like before the Indians. I mean, fucking guys when I felt like it or when it was easier to do it than not to. Before Corey, I don't think it ever meant anything to me."

It was midmorning and they were standing on a slight rise that separated the rows of garden vegetables from the stubble of the harvested cornfield—a rise in which one of the security tunnels had been dug. Ginny frowned and turned from her. Made a slow circuit of the horizon. Turned back with her face calm and blank again. "I wasn't saying that Shawn or Billy meant nothing to me. Because you have an old-fashioned type of possessive relationship, you can't imagine you can care for a man without feeling stuck to him." Ginny spoke softly, but Joanna felt as if she had finally knocked on stone in the girl. "What happened with Billy was very important to me. He was the first person I ever met who dealt with my brain at all. He didn't want me to love him particularly, he didn't even particularly want to have sex with me. He wanted to be admired, but he had only learned to be admired for doing certain sort of inhuman things well. He wanted to be seen as a human being. I could understand, because that was what I wanted, too. But I was so crippled that I couldn't imagine anybody would have a reason to pay attention to me for myself."

"Girls are brought up to feel that way."

"Oh, yes. Well, my head was full of sand. I knew that the ideal girl is frigid—attractive and full of guile. She's an actress before anything. She pretends a certain response but feels nothing that she can't control. But I was tickled pink if a boy paid attention to me. I did everything but wag my tail. So I was an easy lay. And I despised myself."

"I wasn't into the guilt thing. I just sort of took the meaninglessness for granted until I met Corey."

"But to me that's the same old bag. Taking your meaning from outside. Saying, he loves me, so I'm real after all."

"I don't think that having a relationship here implies the things that marriage meant outside."

Ginny gave her that bland impermeable look. "I guess I do think so. Possession is possession. You think that because I don't live with one or the other of them and because I don't say that Billy or Shawn or anybody else is central in my life, that those are just casual lays. I think in a way I see where they are and what they're into clearer than anybody could who was involved in 'having' either of them."

Realizing they had come to an edge, they both drew back.

Still she recognized that Ginny had done important

work, and she had not. Joanna tried reorganizing the food-ordering procedures, but that brought her into conflict with the kitchen staff and she backed off. She had either to accept an area of responsibility and carry it through, or stay out. Something not staked out yet. Then she worked up an orientation course for newcomers.

She tried to give each new person a clear picture of where everything was and what everybody was up to on the farm, and a sense of how the project fitted into the over-all strategy of the tribes. She wanted each one to have a sense of possibilities, to have a fair chance of choosing work he or she would like, so the newcomer wouldn't get stuck digging holes or washing dishes because he was a new kid. At least people who arrived in the next month didn't think of her as just Corey's girl. She had a little following among them—they might come to her for information or advice or to rap. They listened to her ideas with the kind of attention they'd show to any of the accepted leaders.

Suppose she'd joined up with the Indians on her own because she'd been hanging around the Lower East Side that June. Surely she would have joined. She'd been attracted by the dancing and curious about the bread. Suppose she'd met Corey after she had already come into the tribe. Would she have been a warrior? An organizer? She imagined herself doing something really tough on her initiation: some act of exemplary and dangerous terrorism that everyone would admire. Of course they would have ended up together anyhow. Who else would put up with Corey, really? Who else could break through all his nonsense and touch him? No, they had to be together, but imagining that coming about in different ways was an interesting fantasy. She played with it when she was taking her turn on the kitchen work she hated. The one good thing about traveling was that she got out of it.

"Suppose we'd met the first time I ran away from home?"

"You'd have hated me." He made a crooked face. "I was awful!"

"But that's scary: that we could meet and not recognize each other." If they had met, would Joanna be different now? Would Corey? What did that mean?'

"You were the captain's daughter. I was a juvenile delinquent."

"I was not! I was a runaway." She squinted in the mirror, trying to make her face old. Where would the wrinkles be? She drew her face haggard and called him to look. Instead, he made his sinister half-breed villain faces. He would not interest himself in how she would look in thirty years.

In November they traveled out on Long Island. A tribe was occupying a colony of fancy beach houses—eight kids who seemed to have known each other for years. One of the houses belonged to the girl Gisele's parents, and it turned out they were there with at least tacit permission, although her family pretended not to know.

Joanna was quickly put off by the scene. The boys and girls, pretty and sleek and healthy and by no means uniform in their dress, reminded her of sea birds that shrieked and mewed along the beach and went diving to seize some scrap of garbage. They lived in one house at a time until they had broken everything in it and filled it with garbage—until nothing worked and everything was clogged and fouled. Then they abandoned that house and moved on to the next. They played cards and tried on clothes they found in the closets and watched television and chased each other around the dunes and played touch football. They had a supply of bread, though they did not manufacture it, but they used whatever they could find on the market, and they had a whole pharmacy of pills and powders. The communal dance was bluntly an orgy, and both Corey and she stayed out of it. It did not follow their council, because the group had little to decide. There was almost no work to apportion, besides minimal cooking and fetching provisions. They were the children of abundance turning plastic plenty into waste.

Corey watched it all for a couple of days before he began to try to talk to them. Joanna was plain disgusted. She found having to maintain any pretense that these were Indians more than she could manage.

Corey directed most of his arguments at Gisele, the girl who had started the group. She was a willowy tanned ash blonde with a neighing laugh, somehow an inordinate number of shining white teeth and the facility for looking straight through Joanna. He based his approach on trying to show Gisele how they had failed to stop consuming, and that that was the basis of their continuing class relationship. They were still wanting the same things; they had just found an easy way to get them for a while. They had dropped out of the service mechanism, but they were still firmly plugged into wanting and belonging to the same shiny things that the society had been using all along to manipulate them. They were not making their own culture. They were still plugged into the spectacle. They were not free. They were not yet Indians.

Gisele listened, claiming that they were twice as free because they could freely use the society to support themselves. It was a true guerrilla warfare situation, Gisele said, in that they were living off the countryside.

You have not yet broken your ties, Corey said back. Guerrilla warfare, nonsense: this is only a family quarrel. You are not working in a counter economy, you are not recruiting. You have not yet left home.

Joanna spent her time sitting out on the dock freezing in the jagged wind, wrapped in a blanket over her coat and watching the gray waves and the white birds. The fourth day in the afternoon, Corey came and plunked down beside her. He spat into the waves and spat again. "Shit."

She looked at him sideways. His face was soft and sullen and yet amused. Only a slit of black eye showed under lowered lashes. Lip thrust out. Slightly swollen. "My, my! What have you been doing with yourself?"

"So, she got me."

"Was there any doubt? Isn't that what we were waiting for? Can we leave these decadent little creeps now?"

So Corey for once gave up on a would-be tribe, and they left. They talked to the Suffolk County tribe that was making their bread for them, and discovered they didn't like the beach folk either: felt used and patronized. They cut off the bread supply to the beach and let them be. Corey was in a sluggish depression for two days. He finally told her what had happened. He had gone into the john to piss, not shutting the door because he never did. Gisele had followed him in and as he was finishing, she had helped herself to his prick. He had not been able to keep an erection, with her half seated upon the laundry hamper stuffed with used towels, and she had mocked him. That had made him angry enough to harden, and the act had been completed upon the lowered toilet seat. It was his opinion that that was where it belonged. As he left her, he had reached over and flushed the toilet to demonstrate his feeling.

"Oh, how can you be such a hypocrite? What else were we waiting for?"

"I was trying to get through to her. She had enough guts to drop part way out."

"So why didn't you go on trying to get through to her?"

"Because I'm not a machine. I don't like to feel used."

And he hated to be laughed at, she thought. It felt good to be back at the farm. It felt good to be among their own people. To see the dance as it was supposed to be, instead of a crude parody. Though the dancing could frustrate her at times. Often it was just a way for Corey and her to express affection: no different from couples dancing at a high school prom, in a way. Corey had a responsibility to the ritual at the same time, and had to be keeping an eye out for people whose visions frightened them, for hysterics and bad trips. He was good at calming. She suspected that he played around with hypnotism in inducing or turning off visions. She suggested as much, and he got angry and scornful. "Hypnotism! What kind of bunk is that? You're just not the visionary type, so you have to think there's some sort of hocus-pocus going on."

He would use a bead necklace or a feather to send them under, she was sure, and his calm voice to call them back. Sometimes he would dance alone, lost in a savage agony in-turned and burning. If she danced off then by herself, he would grow angry. Indeed, his dances were regarded with respect and people gave him room. She did not like them, but she kept her mind off that. Something violent and awkward and exhibitionistic made her want to turn away.

When she danced, she danced to a pattern that pleased her. She worked out steps that were graceful or sensual or amusing and then improvised against that pattern. But Corey would not let her improvise against him. Once in a while dancing with somebody else, she would really get going. Then she would feel a sense of continuity in being Joanna. How often she had danced alone in her room. For a while she had had ballet lessons, when her father had been assigned to Fifth Army Headquarters in Chicago. Though she had started out way behind the other girls, she was naturally well coordinated. But the teacher never made her a favorite. Madame LeBoeuf had said that there was something coarse in her movements. Too much earth. More fire, more air!

She was a much better dancer than Corey, but he wouldn't admit it. Sometimes when he was gone for the evening, she danced and danced. Even with Shawn: he was graceful and clever, and they improvised along a fine thread of connection. There were other good dancers, and those nights she would dance with all of them. Once in a while Corey would be in a calm laissez-faire mood, and then she could do the same while he was present.

Naturally, the sexual dimension was missing. He would say, "You can be with somebody else if you want to. We don't own each other." Sometimes when he was high or feeling his charisma, or conversely when he was depressed and wanting to prove himself, he would dance a lot with others, mostly girls, but also those mocking competitive prancing duels with other warriors. But always the time came when he turned and collapsed, pulling her to him from across the room, from whomever she was with or whatever she was into.

The other men liked to dance with her if they liked to dance, but it was an interval. It was nice but slightly artificial. Something in their manner said that when she used sensual gestures she was not quite fair, or that they would overlook them. She was unsexed for them. Corey was not quite unsexed. Sometimes away from her, he would go to bed with some girl. He would tell her deprecatingly. He told it that they came after him, and she believed it. Girls liked to flirt with him, girls liked to touch him. He was easy to touch. He was as simply sensual as a cat. He liked to be stroked. But then she would walk by, and he would nudge the girl off his lap and come loping after to tell her something. He was satisfied to try out his charm and get a response and quit. Many girls looked after him with a sour expression.

Sometimes she did get jealous of all the stir and fuss around him when they were traveling. Shawn knew that, and he would tease her:

> What a road show are Corey and Shawn.
> They like to turn the folks on.
> They razzle and dazzle
> and burn to a frazzle,
> while Joanna conceals a yawn.

Back on the farm this time, two weeks worth of new arrivals had come and settled in. She couldn't just start orienting somebody who'd been there for two weeks and had already made a small place for himself. Finally she had to see that she couldn't really make a case for the kids she had oriented doing a hell of a lot better than the ones she'd missed. It had been a make-work idea, a sappy scheme to create importance for herself. Corey must have been patronizing her politically to encourage her. Or he had simply refused to confront her on it. Or worse, he thought it did not really matter how she kept herself busy.

"Aw, come on," Shawn said. "It was a good idea. But with all this running around, you just can't do it. That doesn't mean it wasn't worth doing. Can you judge how the kids felt?"

Big Ned was from Fink's Bend. He was not exactly a runaway. A couple of times a year he wrote his parents a scrawly letter without a return address, and sometimes he would buy a gaudy postcard to send them from San Francisco or Seattle. This time, coming back from St. Louis, Big Ned was driving, and he drove them to Fink's Bend. "I just got to stop by and see how the folks are doing. We're safe with them. People, I just got to see if they're okay. They can't write to me anywheres. We won't stay but an hour or two. And I can drive all night to make up."

The river was pretty, the town was mean and the house was out back of town, as Ned had described it. It was a farmhouse without a farm, an unpainted two-story with a lean-to attached, and two tires in the yard full of dead petunias, while another tire for a swing hung from a horse chestnut. It was a couple of weeks past Christmas, but a tissue-paper wreath that one of Ned's sisters had made at school was still nailed on the door.

The gas stove had a heater in it, and they all sat in the crooked kitchen around a big table drinking coffee and eating eggs and fried potatoes that two of the girls had cooked. Mr. Howard, Ned's father, was a laid-off miner, ten years laid off. Joanna thought he was an old man until she looked at his eyes. Ned told them Mr. Howard was in his late forties. He was smaller than his son by more than a head. His eyes were a pale but glittery blue-gray always roaming over them all and asking questions about who and how and what they were that he was too hospitable and too polite to ask out loud. They were waiting for Ned's ma to come home. She was the only one with a regular job. She worked in a clothing factory moved into town to take advantage of the cheap non-union labor of the ex-miners' wives.

Mr. Howard had been out of Fink's Bend, mainly in the Army. He had come back with a metal plate in his knee and gone into the mines until the owners closed them down. Once again he had left, to go to Chicago for work. There he had been hired and laid off and mugged and his salary at the new job attached to pay for a TV he had bought for his hot furnished room, and the new company hadn't liked his salary being attached, so they'd fired him. After that, everybody had said he was too old.

Mrs. Howard had had to send him the money to come home.

He was answering Corey's questions one at a time, shaking his head as he talked and listening to his own tale as if wondering at it all. He told it as if he were sure there was a joke in it if only he listened. He watched them carefully for their reactions. He told it as if it must be a funny story, a shaggy-dog story, if only he knew how to look at it.

He wanted Ned to stick around a while. He kept saying Ned had to stay long enough to go hunting, and he'd see if his boy was still good for anything. See if he still knew how to use a gun. He poached, of course, and he hated the wardens.

Mrs. Howard arrived finally after dark, thin and wispy and gray and too excited by Ned to talk. Three kids were still at home, and Ned impressed them that they must not tell anyone that they were there.

After supper, Ned and his father and Shawn and Corey drank white lightning while Joanna sat in the kitchen with Ned's mother and the girls. They were shy of her and did not talk much. Ned asked his father a lot of questions about people he had known, and Corey asked about the town. After a while he came out to the kitchen and asked the kids lots of questions too. He had to loosen them up, but he teased them until they were giggling, and then he got them talking about the school and the kids there and their lives and the town.

They left the next morning early. Corey was silent for half the day, before he began to talk about Fink's Bend.

"It's a worked-out colony. The powers came in, they worked those mines and worked the men and got what there was to get, and then they cleared out. Leaving hunger and waste and a gutted land. I don't know how to deal with it. Maybe we depend on a certain amount of fat. Of course Ned isn't revolting against his parents. They didn't fuck up, they got fucked over. Like my old woman. But it's like we're irrelevant there. We can't tell Ned's family to come along and turn Indians. But they've been robbed. How can we give them back what they need?"

Ned said only, "It's a pretty place. You ought to see it in the spring. There's still a lot of room for hunting and fishing. It's good country, even if you can't do nothing with it."

"I don't know how to speak to the guys standing around the streets of that town. We've worked out our own language and our own way of being together, but somehow it doesn't include those robbed bastards, and it ought to. It's our fault that we can't. It's dangerous. The people who should be cheering us on all think we should be lined up against a wall and shot. But I know I can't make it with them. Maybe we just have to try to reach their kids and that has to be enough. But it doesn't feel like enough. It feels like failure."

So much time riding in the rut of a highway. So much time half awake, half asleep, with his heavy head on her shoulder and their legs cramped in back seats. So much time driving into the glare of headlights with a rock station turned loud till the whole car pounded. Dairy Queens and Howard Johnson's and Glass Houses and Savarins and Chicken Delights and McDonald's Hamburgers and Dad's Old Fashioned Root Beer stands. They were always constipated or belching and raw-stomached. Shawn and Big Ned could fart at will and had contests. Corey was broken out in pimples. He had picked up crabs somewhere, and now she had them too. They seemed to grow up in waves. She would itch frenetically. Then they would die away into a lull that would make her imagine she was rid of them. Then they would swarm again.

Yet at times it seemed to her that they ran back and forth across the countryside upon tracks. From commune to commune they rushed and imagined that they were reaching out. Every time they passed a school in session, she had a strong sense that that was where their caravan should be halting.

She tried to correct the maps in her head and tried to remember that they were only going from little group to little group across the country in scattered patches, and largely they were talking to themselves. Though their survival depended on building as big a base as possible, kids tended to become quickly uncomfortable with people outside the movement and not to want to deal with them. Their jargon and slogans isolated them. It was a drag to talk to people who did not share your assumptions: you had to start with ABC, practically. Older Indians often showed their contempt for new recruits, who soundeed too much like the society they had all just left. They hated what they had been, and kids who reminded them of their old selves.

Corey had a theoretical grasp of that narrowness and was always pushing the need to grow. Nevertheless, he would extrapolate from the tiniest scrap of contact to a roaring movement. Because of Marcus and his boys in the Catskills, he would talk about the Indians as a black movement as well as white. Actually, their only contact was the food-and-medicine drops monthly. Because they had some farms, he would talk of them as having gone to the countryside like Mao to build their peasant base. But no one on any of the farms ever talked to another farmer. They were farming in secrecy, as remote from the rest of the countryside as any gentleman farmer. Because Billy had trained a few warriors in small-weapons use, Corey would talk about the Indian army of urban guerrillas. Sometimes in listening she felt as if they were all manipulating words and symbols and imagining that somehow the symbols would convert themselves magically into real power at the instant of need.

Corey still talked a lot about the Indian resistance in the past, but that mythology meant little to most of the others. Most of the kids talked a great deal of Mao and Che and Lenin, and if they could make a comparison, no matter how farfetched, between something they were doing and some action of one of their heroes or some piece of history in China or Cuba, then they were suddenly more confident, they felt real.

"Despair is a revolutionary crime," Corey would tell her. "We must have a real will to power. We must break through our own impotence into real struggle." At times she felt as if that breakthrough was only a form of theater. They were always whipping each other into more-and-more-militant thrusts of rhetoric. Nobody dared seem less revolutionary than anybody else. Their language was all of armed struggle, while they had not one plane or tank or bomb.

She thought again and again of what Corey had said about Fink's Bend, and it seemed to her that in a way he was wrong: that they did have something to say to everybody. The desire to be free was an old native urge. Fink's Bend had been populated by people who had gone there to be free and independent. Everywhere the mechanisms for keeping people passively in their places were eroding. People were not getting back what they wanted for their sold labor. Taxes grew and services shrank. Prices rose and quality decayed. Everywhere people felt used and betrayed and coerced and cheated. Mostly they blamed each other or the blacks or the foreigners who kept making trouble for the U. S. Army in the various countries they happened to live in, or the kids who kept making noise and rocking the boat. Joanna kept thinking that somebody ought to be talking to them.

But somehow they were not getting any better at talking to people who were not yet Indians. They were getting louder and angrier and shriller. They were getting surer they knew the answers—all the answers. Councils tended to turn into sharp debates now between different sides gathered around leaders who could argue a position and put others down. The shyer, the less verbal, got less verbal still and finally kept their mouths shut. The louder got louder still. In some tribes the women might as well have stayed out of council, for they were ignored and afraid to speak.

There was fear everyplace. There was reason for fear everyplace. Wherever they went, they heard stories of arrests and beatings and raids and imprisonment.

SHAWN felt burnt out much of the time. The three of them were still together a lot, but they were separated more in their functions. He would set himself up with whoever he was playing with while Joanna went off to do her woman's thing and Corey rapped with the council. Joanna had her own style—tense, and yet somehow plain—but she didn't think so, or pretended not to. "I don't like you to listen. Eh, I sound like Corey." She made a monkey face.

Shawn said, "We all sound like Corey."

"Nobody sounds like you."

"Nobody looks like you."

She fluffed out her hair in mock coquettishness. "Do you look at me?"

They flirted that way, in intervals. They were so much together. Of course he and Corey flirted too, but in an easier way, all told. It was easier for Corey to demand affection and easier for him to express it. There wasn't even curiosity between Joanna and him, because what could happen had, long ago, and meant nothing. But he saw her and she saw him clearly. They were alert to small signals. Shawn always knew when she was bored or irritated or tired to exasperation. She could tell when he was about to become monolithically stubborn or to infuriate strange warriors by acting in ways that showed off his utter contempt for their virtues, his gentleness, his sensuality, his mockery.

They watched over each other and took care and tempered the rasp of circumstance. They were each other's road managers. Corey had to be more alert to the special conditions of every commune, every encampment, every council. He could not listen at them the way they listened at him and each other. They took care of him but he could not, on the road, take care of them. Corey kept pushing them to play larger and larger independent roles—within the context of what he was about.

"Corey's less dependent than he was?" Joanna said, trying out the words. It was snowing. They sat in a car with the heater and wipers going, waiting for a warrior to bring them formulas that Billy wanted to go into production in the lab at the farm. Some kind of cheap explosives. They felt uneasy but as Corey said, they couldn't oppose what had been decided by council, and who wanted to sound counter revolutionary?

Shawn drew on the steamed-up side window. He drew a Corey devil face with horns. "Nonsense. He's just completely assimilated us. We're extra selves."

Or they would reverse positions. Both Joanna and Shawn could do that, because they could switch their polarizations according to mood. Generally he had a strong sense of self and was seeking a sense of connection. Generally she had a strong sense of connection and was seeking a sense of herself. But they could switch.

He shared with her a mistrust of their roles. At times she accused Corey of using the aroused interest in women's liberation to sneak in his influence through her, Trojan-horse style. She would say the division of labor between them was the same old sexual division of labor—reproduced. Then she would change her mind and assert that only a woman could speak to women's problems, because a man could not help but be manipulative in any situation with women.

Whatever the rhetoric, in tribe after tribe women mostly ended up running the kitchen, taking care of housework and babies, running the mimeograph machine, serving as bodies in demonstrations they had not planned or directed, serving as runners carrying messages or equipment of whose purpose they were often kept ignorant, doing all the tedious daily tasks that made tribal life possible. The women who made it into more effective and interesting roles did not think of themselves as representing a constituency of downtrodden women, but hung out with the male warriors and acted as much like them as possible. Joanna never felt that she was in danger of behaving that way (like Carole for instance), but she felt something crooked in the heart of her new political role that she could not quite liberate.

"I'm not liberated!" she yelled at Corey.

"Nobody is till everybody is. How can you expect to be liberated in the middle of a vast prison?"

"Words, words! You just mix them around and make boxes with them to hold your head in. I ask something real, and you give me back an abstraction. Plastic Man!"

Shawn thought Joanna was a little off in thinking of it all as a man/woman thing. He thought it was beyond that, a whole way of relating in dominance or submission that was built into the sex roles, true enough, which was one reason he wouldn't fulfill them, but built also into other relationships—parent/child, teacher/student, employer/employee, doctor/patient. Whenever the balance of power was unequal, there was a driver and a driven. Power was the lethal vice, the turn-on with evil built into it, because it required a victim to manifest itself. Power implied subject and object. They needed some way to recognize (for everyone to recognize) that everybody was a subject. Corey and Joanna were still arguing in the back seat as Shawn drove.

"For instance if I disagree with you, I do it now. I don't stand up and argue with you in meetings. I say it to you afterward."

Corey shrugged broadly. "Well, I can listen better now. We don't have to use councils to talk to each other. We need to use councils to listen to everybody else. It would be irresponsible for you to use up council time on something we can do better on our own time."

"Because I'm your private property. That's why."

They sulked and scratched at each other and filled the car with the sulphurous fumes of their angers. They made up, curling into a ball. Black coarse hair, tangled carroty hair, their tough skinny bodies criss-crossed on a mattress into a porcupine of warm flesh and wild hair. They found each other in some dark underground knot of interlocked roots. Shawn sniffed around them. Different from anything he had known. Not for him. But it had an interesting atmosphere to it. He wondered what it would feel like to live so embedded in another.

And Shawn's own role? Why wasn't it altogether right? Better than it had been before the Indians. What he did was no longer ambiguous or commercial or sold out. Still, in the context there was something manipulative. He could remember how it had been when The Coming Thing had first got started, that sense of music being the most important event in the world, that sense of white-hot sexual joyous happening, of the world in flower. He had shared then a sense of making a new music with honesty and passion and abandon, of being the creative center of a pulsating universe.

He wasn't making a new music now. He was using what he had learned. Rather, it was being used. He had put himself and his music in the service of the revolution, but somehow there was no interaction. In itself his music had become less vital. He knew he was not as good. How could he be without a regular group, without a committed group of genuinely talented musicians to work with, without being able to close into himself and into them and build musical ideas? He said every day that that was no longer important, but part of him did not believe it.

Yet he knew that he fooled himself when he imagined being someplace with a good group of musicians really turned on again and making the music he wanted. Running away from the Indians would not bring him to musicians' heaven. The happiest time for The Coming Thing had been when there was the least gap between audience and performers. They hadn't been that wise musically in the early days, though they had listened to all the old blues records and country music and fifties and sixties rock, and they'd thought they were able to do anything under the yellow sun. They had had great energy and the conviction of being right and a desire to play their music and get laid by groupies in piles from one coast to the other.

But already before the hired systems analysts had come trekking to Washington with their mammoth tracking system in the sky, The Coming Thing had been losing that natural rapport with their audiences. As they gained musical sophistication, they had begun to lose some of their teenybopper audience, who turned from them to newer, harder-sell merchandise to gobble down like candy.

Cracks had begun to appear in their solidarity. Shep had wanted the accouterments he expected with his money: what had really got him pissed was being treated as a hippy instead of as a successful young entrepreneur. He wanted to marry his debutante and receive the social deference that should be his by virtue of birth and education and accomplishment and possessions, in spite of his hair hanging down in brown curls on his shoulders and transparent shirts and brocade pants and jewelry to his navel. Frodo had wanted fun and games, a never-failing supply of sexual victims. His sadism had flourished. His games had grown more elaborate, his rites had required more props.

What had Shawn wanted? After a certain point it had not mattered what he wanted. He knew that the world that had seemed to float on their best music required a revolution to come to pass. In so far as their music spoke urgently of joy and spontaneity and connection, it had been unconsciously but inevitably political. Their music spoke naturally of the world where the streets did belong to the people, where the grass was to sit on and to smoke and every child had hills to run on. The music called people to dance together loosely with their whole bodies.

The necessities of making a new world call for different behavior from what will be typical of that new world: he told himself such things every day, to produce in himself patience, to hold to some simulacrum of discipline, to keep his temper in check. But sometimes he wondered if the Indians were interested in making a world where he could play his music.

The media discovered them. First liberal magazines for intellectuals wrote studies about why they were not significant. The *Village Voice* had for some time covered their visible actions, usually with an ironic detached reporter sounding rather weary of it all. The hippest of the commercial mags, aimed at exploiting the teen market, assigned a woman who sounded sympathetic and who was also very careful to make it clear that they were totally incorrect, of course, even if they were personally groovy. Then an interpretive piece appeared in the Sunday magazine of the New York *Times* on how they were merely the newest embodiment of generational discontent such as readers were accustomed to accepting as inevitable, comprising a small minority of young people (polls cited). Their ideas were influenced by anthropology but little different from the last generation of disturbed students who had been handled competently, while the peculiar form of their tribal customs could be traced back to conceptions of the Noble Savage, James Fenimore Cooper, Mark Twain and other writers tamed by the schools into docility.

Esquire put Shawn's face on the cover in feathered headdress, and inside had a snotty article heavily laden with psychoanalytical insights. The author attacked the rock scene in general and claimed it had been only a matter of time before some manufactured sex hero took his power seriously and abused it, leading his mesmerized fans after him. The author depicted Shawn as a pampered teen-ager unable to adjust to adult authority, who had created a cult around himself of permanent adolescent irresponsibility.

If the Indians had read magazines, he would have been in trouble being set up as a leader. But they did not. Shawn found it all pretty funny. He had never felt so crushed by responsibility before in his life. Corey was not amused, but Joanna was. She memorized the juicy parts and recited them at what she felt were appropriate times when they were traveling. The gist of most articles was that the Indians were a violent, pseudo-fascist group of adolescent misfits, a band of bottle-throwing Peter Pans.

The brunt of the media attack on them, the "line" of explanation, however, was set by a group of ex-radicals and left-liberals comfortably housed in various universities. It was a real ulcerated hatred that seethed in the works they produced that analyzed the phenomena of the Indians. Men who had tenure in oak-shaded campuses where, amid the rhythmic yells from the football field and the songs of the glee club, institutes solved the problem of dispersing tularemia germs against enemy populations and invented models for counter-revolutionary game theory in Brazilian villages and chatted of megadeaths and genetic management, wrote about the violence of kids in the streets armed with bricks and bottles with thunderous denunciation and scathing indignation.

Some of the academic ex-radicals took the position that unrest among the youth would provoke fascism. They wrote about fascism as a dramatic change, a coup d'état, the Pentagon marching on the White House. None of them imagined that it could come in like the morning paper, that it would be just the same families maintaining themselves in power by slightly different means. No swastikas, no eagles other than the Bald Eagle rendered extinct through DDT: only the American Flag. No SS, no storm troopers, no blackshirts: only the regular police armed with tanks and gases and high explosives and training in "riot control." They did not see that black people and kids already lived their lives in a police state.

Sociologists and social psychologists got grants to study the Indians. They interviewed captured Indians in prisons

and stockades and juvenile concentration camps. Some of
the kids cooperated, hoping to shorten their time. Some
refused to speak. Some lied in beautiful arabesques of
absolute invention. A few of these inventions such as the
war dance passed into the scientific literature, into common
myth, and late in that winter Shawn found himself visiting
a tribe in Cleveland that had adopted it.

The most important attack on them was contained in a
book by a professor at Yale who had been active himself
in radical politics in his graduate-student days. When repression had come down on the movement of that time, he
had found his colleagues extremists and veered toward new
colleagues. He was still regarded as a radical by most
academics, but since he did not organize or agitate or take
part in any actions but only wrote acceptable scholarly
texts on the French Revolution, he remained inside the
pale.

His thesis was that poor child-rearing practices, a lack
of strict toilet training, the absence of the father from
most homes, and the decline of discipline in the early
grades of the schools had led to a total breakdown of
socialization practices. He called the street children the
new barbarians, equating their revolt with the End of
Morality. He compared them to the Huns, to the hordes
of Attila sweeping into the power vacuum of the declin-
ing Roman Empire. "The issue is freedom within discipline, within the orderly constraints of society. If we quail
before the attacks of these barbarian hordes, we will have
lost at once three hundred years of lawful decision-making
and two thousand years of common morality." He claimed
that the new illiteracy had produced a great degradation in
the capacity to think and even to feel, and that the children
who fled the system were benumbed and brutalized savages
—truly feral and subhuman.

In the meantime a Commission on Social Disruption
and Violence reported to the President their recommenda-
tions. Channeling came too late. All six-year-olds must be
tested to detect criminal tendencies; to determine their
future potential for criminal behavior; to locate those
children with delinquent character structures and prevent
the development of fullfledged adolescent deviants. A full
battery of predictive tests must be administered to all
six-year-olds, the psychiatrists and psychologists advised,
and the young hard core disruptive boys sent to special

camps for treatment. All adolescents should be required to produce a certificate of mental health before being allowed to enter society, fill jobs or assume responsibility.

Tabloids headlined TEEN GANGS HOLD PAINTED SEX ORGIES. On television, detective and police heroes tracked down young villains who belonged to tribes and seduced innocents with dangerous drugs. At the same time teen magazines pushed the buck look and the squaw look, with fringed shirts and beads and expensive deerskin moccasins and boots, with beaded headbands and feather hats that looked like run-over chickens dipped in paint pots, wampum belts, clay peace pipes, Deerslayer tunics for that huntress look, fur rugs for that Tribal Pow Wow, genuine (more or less) buffalo greatcoats for Shaggy Male Splendor, saddlebag purses and washable body paints that came in powder horns and little clay pots.

Rancid waves of commerce touched them from time to time. They would find kids who thought they were Indians tricked out in costumes from the local Bizarre Bazaar of their town's fattest department store, and would have a rocky time persuading them to strip down and start over in the oldest clothes they owned.

Corey: "Indians don't dress up like department-store dummies. Indians dress to be invisible. The red Indian wore deerskin because it ran past his door. Wear what you can make and replace. Make yourself a sack. You aren't selling yourself. Put on a bag and wear it with pride. Who you are you can't buy in a store. You have to make it together."

Shawn sang:

> We are in the belly of the whale
> and the whale is going down.
> Hold your peace,
> sit still and drown.
> If you want out
> you got to use a knife.
> We're in the big white whale.
> Prisoner, how much, how much
> do you want your life?
> Going down, dying
> going down.
> Everybody's like to drown.
> Blubber and steel,

smog and rubber.
You got to chop right out to freedom,
see your road and choose it,
take a knife and use it.
Cut your road to freedom if you can.
You got to kill Leviathan,
hey, prisoner, look up
before you can be
a man.

"That's a male chauvinist song," Joanna told him.

"Well, woman doesn't rhyme with much, does it now?"

"Who said people will only listen to jingles?"

"Shawn. He said, one good song is worth two dozen warriors throwing bottles at the National Guard."

"But he didn't dare say it in council."

"No, Joanna-love, because he didn't want two dozen warriors throwing bottles at him."

"Why not, if he wants so much to be a man? ... Shawn, don't you ever feel trapped?"

"Often enough. But it's orneriness and laziness, you know. We weren't brought up to do much of anything real."

"Am I doing anything real now?"

"What kind of stupid thing is that to ask? Yes, we're really fighting. We're really alive and soon we'll be really dead."

"It's just that trying to make change is so much of it pretending. Making images of what might be. Pretending we've already done things we've only begun to do, or don't even know how to begin on."

"But they lie more than we do. Propaganda was their invention to begin with: the way the people with power construct the world to prove they ought to have power, or that there's really no such thing as power, or that what really matters is burning witches or lynching blacks or hunting commies."

"But there's so much we pretend not to notice in each other. We pretend each other is better than he is. We pretend to think we're further along the road than we know. I want to be more me. I want to use more of me. ... I'm not wrong! He leans too hard and he gobbles me without seeing it. Then I bitch and go for his belly. Because everything stays in there between us."

"Loving is difficult, so I've been told. All this racketing around the country doesn't make it any easier."

"It has to loosen, somehow. I have to open it up. But a scared bitch in me keeps saying that I can't bear to lose him, so don't rock the boat. I take those fears out on him too. This is the only good thing I've ever had. I never loved anybody before—I hardly even fooled myself. Oh, of course, back when I was little, I loved my parents, I loved them a lot. But that's so far gone, so buried by now. But I thought I was naturally cold, and I thought everything people said about relationships was a lot of nonsense to hide that they were scared to be alone. Maybe it's a taste, maybe it's a habit. Maybe now I'm scared to be alone too." She twisted her fingers in her kinky hair and her light-brown eyes looked no place while she frowned like a child. "Do you love anybody?"

"Yes. Corey and you."

"Both of us separately or both of us together?"

"Separately. Together, you're a closed corporation."

"But you love him better?"

"Don't whine. Don't pull at things."

"Pulling at things is something every good revolutionary has to do—no?"

"Not everything the same way, hopefully. Pulling at a blade of grass is different from pulling on a doorknob."

"I'll find out."

"Nobody finds out anything by making tests to do it."

He watched her go away hands clasped behind her back whistling and shuffling her feet. Prickly Joanna. What was love anyhow? A doing. A habit. A set of aches. A context. The name of a box for putting people in. Tomorrow night, back to the farm and maybe plump Ginny in the night. Unless there was somebody new who would . . .

No. Ginny. Too long between. She never talked to him about how she felt about him. She kept a certain amount of space around her. Not coldly, but because she was building a sense of herself. She was making herself slowly and firmly. It was as if she came out to meet him, pleased to see him, but quietly shut the door behind. She was reluctant to talk about Billy with him, because they did not get along. But she would talk obliquely. She would say she thought she could love anyone if only she looked at him closely enough. The determining factor was a real desire to be loved—not to imagine oneself loved in some idealized way, but to be loved in the flesh day to day, with the lover alive and a separate person and continuing to exist even when you found it inconvenient.

She was not quite as plump as she had been the first time they had gone upstairs together and she had taken him sweetly into her fullness. There were still bouncy soft piles of her, but the piles were firmer.

Tomorrow night on the farm he would find her in the dance, and she would paint herself gravely and come to him, and they would go to her cabin or his, and she would be clean and bountiful and smell like tea and soap. He would stretch out with her and play and be at ease. Very simply they were friends. Very simply it was good together. And the tribe rolled around them and included them, and, of its need, let them come together or draw apart into their tasks. They did not need a structure to meet inside. He did not have to borrow or buy or steal a house to be with her. The best part of what he had had with Denise he could touch with Ginny.

All except for Stevie. There were three babies at the farm now, and he liked that and he wanted them quickly to reach the stage when he could talk to them and play with them beyond tossing and tickling and making noises. He would take on baby-tending tasks without the self-righteous, assisting-women's-liberation attitude of the other few men who were willing. He dug kids. But he wanted them to stop crawling and mewling and dripping and sit up and be ready to take things in. Then he might just revolt against all his traveling and singing and turning people on. He thought he might be nursery-school teacher for a couple of years. That would suit him just fine.

He wanted to take the elements of music apart and put it back together right with the very young children. That was where he would find his alternate society. He thought that one of his greatest strengths was that he remembered so exactly what it had felt like to be a child.

It was early spring and time for plowing and planting when they got back. They had been gone since the middle of February. The farm smelled wet and pale green and earthy, with a streak of manure. Mud puddles and tracked hallways. The air felt volatile. Everyone looked solid. People always looked healthier to him on the farm than anyplace else. The reason was simple enough: they got out a lot, they worked hard, they were not anxious or afraid. Most people look good when they feel like that. He ate with the second shift for supper in the dining room smelling of lamb stew and fresh-baked biscuits. People mingled with them, greeting and asking after friends in other tribes and telling anecdotes of the past month.

Council was mainly reports and felt endless. Shawn was sick of meetings. He felt that he had passed the month in a mumbly twilight meeting. Joanna seemed to spend especially long on her report. She took it seriously. He stifled yawns and twitched and waited the time out. There was Ginny, round as a rabbit, giving him a little warm smile across the circle. To husk her out of her coarse clothes like an ear of sweet yellow corn and nibble her down. On to the dance, come on. Finally.

He never enjoyed dancing as much in other places. This was home ground. He took just a little bread to hone his traveling fatigue. It always turned him up a couple of notches, like a guitar put back in tune. Then he moved out into the ease of it, striding in the rhythm of the turning circle. The circle began with a casual shuffle, people just getting ready to loosen up, letting the rhythms soak through them. For maybe forty minutes he followed the circle, watching the dances develop in the center, before he shucked and moved in.

Little Ruthie, flat body tough as a root, came to dance with him. Their dance was playful and calisthenic. He would never touch her sexually, and she trusted him not to. Even more than her brother Ben, she had been hurt early in some way she could not put into words, frightened into wood that had only slowly turned into living sapling on the farm. Perhaps he would recruit her away from her chickens to his nursery school. Maybe she could bear to grow up gradually with the smallest children. She would leave him soon and dance off into trance, singing to herself. Now her dark urchin eyes gleamed at him. She leaped and beat her hands on her hard belly and thighs, making a counter rhythm. Her hands made a flat drumming. She kicked up her heels and leaped toward his head.

Sylvie came out, and for a long time they improvised together. She teased him, while he turned it into gesture. He flattered her, he bent his tall body over her and pivoted around her, but he would not come closer than polite dancing distance. At first she had been one of the girls that attracted him most, with her air of elegance

even in the day's work clothes, her air of wearing them
with a difference—a few stitches taken in the right places,
a different way of draping the cloth. What had pulled him
at first made him indifferent now. She was not much
changed. Probably she could still go back. She could fit
out there. That was not interesting any longer. He liked
signs of growth, even stress marks of change. She was still
counting points for being wanted. He had been a good
match for her when he had come. He had danced to make
the circle watch. To force recognition.

He dropped back into the circle to rest on its currents,
watched pattern and signal and trance. When he finally
stepped out again, he sought Ginny with his eyes and
asked her to come to him. Her eyes smiled back at him,
but she made a little gesture of sorry. A serious coupling?
But she could indicate that dancing. She danced with no
one tonight. Probably her damned period. He would dance
a while, then step into the circle beside her and wait for a
chance to draw her out. He still wanted to spend the night
with her, he wanted to talk if nothing else, to lie beside
her talking softly in the dark, and he needed a gentle way
to convey that.

Corey had been dancing all over the inner circle, starting groups of three and four and five, inclusive, pouring
over, wanting to gather everybody to him in a loose gag-
gle. Joanna had been shuffling along stiffly in the outer
circle. Now she stepped from the circle, stripped her
clothes into a neat pile and painted herself deliberately but
minimally. Then she came toward Shawn. She did not
pause in the imperative wait to see if she were accepted,
but came directly. Why did he feel cold and even a little
naked? They had danced dozens of times. After all, she
knew he would dance with her. After all, nothing. Her
face was stiffened by an awkward smile.

She moved awkwardly for her. She seemed to be choosing every small gesture, all her muscles locked tight.
"What's wrong?" he muttered.

She did not answer. She moved close as if she meant to
speak, but nothing came out of her mouth twisted up in
that stiff smile. He understood all at once then and spent
the next ten minutes pretending to himself that he did not.
She loosened up and moved more easily but with that
deliberation. She danced provocation, invitation, all with
the strained intentness of decision. He could not move

back from her. He could no longer pretend he did not understand. There was too much connection between them for him to get away with that. Her hair swung against his chest. The hair of her orange bush lightly brushed his thigh. He felt charged and helpless. He felt the circle around them and he felt naked. "Why?" he muttered to her.

"Have to. To break through it. You know."

"I can't."

She moved back a little and eyed him. "Oh, yes, you can." She was smiling that strange determined smile.

He could not turn his eyes from her. He wanted to look at Corey—for help, advice—but he was afraid to look anyplace. Her decision burned at him. "Not here. Not with him here."

Her eyes held him, showing fear. "Think how bad it will be for me with anyone else."

He could not look away from her. He felt divided from his body, hugely naked. He took her hand and pulled her to stillness. "Get your clothes."

They picked up their clothes, passing through the circle. He did not look at anyone, only at her back walking before him. They dressed. Then she followed him through the cold muddy night to his cabin.

No one was there yet. He lifted the flap on his bunk and they crawled in. Sat down cross-legged at opposite ends. She kicked off her boots. Her feet were bare inside, with the soles black from dancing.

"We don't have to now, you know," he said. Almost whispering. The room was very quiet. Faintly they could hear the dance. "You made your point walking out with me. Everybody will think the thing, anyhow."

"Everybody but us. And Corey. We'll know."

"Listen, it's an act of desperation tonight—"

"I didn't come here to talk." She took off her clothes in the cramped space of the bunk.

He got out to strip. Stood looking a minute at the fallen blanket. Still had a strong desire to hightail out of there. Could not leave her. If there ever had been a time when he felt less like balling, he could not remember it.

They did not look at each other, but between them yanked back the covers and crawled into the narrow bunk. The sheets were cold and coarse. She put her arms tight around him and buried her face in his shoulder.

They lay facing side by side. His prick hardened against her belly, but neither of them could move. A little spasm of tears ran from her hidden face across his arm. It seemed to him they lay for dreadful hours pressed front to front, her heart beating into him, her hair tickling his nose, her arms clasping him in frozen rage. His arm began to ache under her until he began to want to laugh or sneeze or do somersaults.

Finally he did laugh and rolled her around the bed roughly, swung her on her back and buried his face between her thighs. Ay, the same Joanna, she was none too clean. She smelled like low tide on the mud flats. But she felt good enough, and her frozen languor broke. She began to make wet noises and wriggle against him and reach for his prick. When she felt more than ready, he swung around and climbed on. He held himself back and went slow and easy into her. It was hard for him to believe that they had done this before. He had never made it with Joanna, no, only with a strange fierce teen-ager who was hiding out—almost as much from him as from the forces of repression.

If everything up to now that had happened between them since she stepped into the ring to challenge him had been awkward, desperate, abortive, just plain clumsy, their bodies actually fixed together seemed suddenly right. They both relaxed. She opened her eyes and smiled at him and sniffled her nose clear. He felt she had been right, maybe not in terms of Corey because who was he to judge that, but at least in terms of the two of them, that this was both natural and good. This was the natural expression of their caring. What they were doing had nothing in common with his own set of sexual tastes and predilections and explorations and habits: he would never have picked out Joanna except in desperate indifference. No, this was more friend than sex object, more saying than having.

He wanted the fucking to be long and easy, a conversation rather than an explosion. He wanted to move permanently beyond shame and embarrassment and awkwardness with her. She came quickly and shallowly and seemed ready to quit. He would not. She had borrowed him to work out a problem of her own, but now the dialogue was between them.

Was he competing? Was he trying to make his wide mark, in the old way? Maybe, maybe. But having her there, he could not let her go back again with as little impression as the first time they had tumbled together. He had a feeling that if what happened was not strong, not substantial, if it did not happen out to her toes and down to her bones, that she would turn on it. He did not want to be used. If she went back to Corey after having really been with him, she might go back with less defensiveness, with less sense of being in the wrong.

After she had come, she wanted to slip away, to wait him out, and he had to fight her stubbornly. She was not sensual. She did not melt into her sexuality. She did not easily open into cycles of more. She did not soften. He had to wrestle and wield and batter her into another cycle. She remained always aware and mistrustful under him, a little dubious. Even as she came fully at last, she cried out, "No! No!" and he could not convince himself she accepted the orgasm as more than a trick he was playing on her.

He was aware as he slept that she dozed fitfully and lay awake most of the night. The bunk was narrow. Their bodies kept bumping and jarring. In the morning very early she crawled out.

"Will you be okay?" he asked from where he lay.

"Sure. Go back to sleep."

He got up annoyed, feeling grumpy and cheated of sleep. He had a great unwillingness to deal with people. He did not get out of his bunk till everyone else was dressed and gone. Therefore he missed breakfast and did without and felt grumpier. He had signed up for fence-walking detail to be out in the air, looking forward to a good hike. But sloughing through the mud exhausted him, and he felt cold and hungry and bored with his thoughts. From wanting to avoid everybody, he passed into feeling as if he were in exile. They would be talking about him, and here he was acting as if he were ashamed to face up. Corey would imagine he had run away. Joanna would think he was acting like a weakling. All morning the only people he saw were half a mile away, except for strange cars passing on the gravel road. He made fence repairs efficiently but without enjoyment. He came in for lunch sullen and bored with himself.

Corey and Joanna were eating together across the room. He sat down quickly where he was. The soup was thin and peppery, as if the cook had tried to make up for a shortage of meat with an excess of seasoning. It sloshed

in his empty stomach. People greeted him and went on
arguing about whether it was possible to turn being in jail
into a useful experience. He could not tell if he was being
excluded or if he was excluding himself because of his
silence and sullen face. He felt stupid with paranoia. What
he wanted to do was to stare at Corey and Joanna, but he
was afraid to be caught watching. He stole quick glances.
Corey shoveling in soup, bent slurping over the bowl.
Joanna sponging her bowl with bread. What did he expect
to see? After all, they were together. That was what
mattered.

But had he doubted that? What he had to know was
Corey's attitude toward him. He did not see them get up.
He only caught a last glimpse as they left the dining room
by the door nearest their table. All afternoon he could not
control his bad fantasies.

He got back early for supper and was one of the first to
sit down. Ginny came in just after. She waved but did not
smile and went on to sit at another table. He was furious.
It was, after all, her damn fault. If she knew how much
he had wanted to spend the night with her, she would stop
looking so superior and stolid. It would be a golden
pleasure to pummel her for half an hour.

Corey came in with Joanna behind and immediately sat
down across from him. Joanna squeezed on the bench
beside Corey and gave him a look that said, I don't know.
She looked tired but scrubbed. Her hair was still damp
from washing. He felt she had been washing off her trans-
gression and was immediately annoyed with himself. After
all, she had needed a bath.

Little Ruthie was passing on her way to find a late seat,
when Corey reached out and caught her by the arm and
made everyone slide over to fit her in. He put his arm
around her and gave her a hug, and she returned a special
sweet shy smile. She was tiny and she sat down tiny,
coming up to Corey's armpit. Corey leaned over to speak
to her and she giggled and replied softly into her plate.

Shawn was shocked. Then annoyed with himself again.
She could not be younger than some of the groupies he
had laid.

"Don't look so startled, Shawn," Corey grinned at him.
"There's more than one way to spend a night. Don't you
know that yet? Maybe not. Beautiful Ruthie, what kind of
a piece of chicken do you crave? Do you want a dark

piece or a light piece? You should have a little dark piece, like yourself."

"A wing."

"To fly on. Don't you think Ruthie could fly? Two wings for a little bird."

Corey ate heartily and gestured with a drumstick and sucked on the bones. He laughed and waved the drumstick and made jokes and dominated the table in both directions. He saw the wishbone in Joanna's breast and took it away. "Who wants to fight wishes with me? Shawn? Come on."

He insisted on making a big production, lining them up both standing one foot on the bench and matching arms over the table. Everyone stopped to watch. Shawn was out of sorts at the spectacle and exhausted with trying to figure out what Corey was up to. The bone was greasy and hard to break, but he was angry and with a violent twist of his wrist he broke off the center piece.

"Shawn wins again! Okay, what did you wish, Champ?"

"If he tells you, he won't get it," Ruthie said.

"If he tells me, maybe he will."

Shawn slid back into his place on the bench. "I wished I knew what was going on in your head."

"That was a silly waste for a good clean wish. Think how easy it is to find that out by asking."

"Suppose I ask?"

"What's going on in my head? Chicken. Ruthie with wings on flying to and fro around the barn. More chicken. Maybe more potatoes and gravy. Ruthie with wings on sitting in a tree. Joanna says she defines herself in negations. She says women are taught to define themselves in negations. She says she has added a new negation. Ruthie with wings on chasing butterflies in the old apple orchard. Ruthie knows about butterflies. She says the first ones that come are called Common Blues, and they're small and the color of clear sky. She says, if you catch them the dust from their wings comes off in your hands and they can't fly. She doesn't believe in catching them."

So went supper. Afterward there were meetings of various work committees. When Shawn left the house for his cabin and bed, Corey was still up arguing with Big Ned and Harley and New John, while Joanna nodded half asleep in a chair.

The next day it rained: He spent most of the day

playing music with a couple of the guys and Dolores. Corey and Joanna were in their room whenever he walked by. And the next day. And the next. The fourth day of the rain, Corey went off with a pack on his back to the cabin on the hill for fasting and meditation. Shawn felt like going back to bed when he heard that.

He went in search of Joanna and found her in the laundry. "What's happening?"

She was wearing a sweater of Corey's, old and bald at the elbows, big and shapeless on her. "I'm washing, can't you see?"

"What's happening with Corey?"

"Nothing! I don't know." She knotted her hands in the sweater. Her face was flat with depression.

"Can't you talk to me?"

"He's trying. What more can I say? No, I don't want to talk."

"I want to know what's going on."

"He's not mad at you, if that's what you're worried about."

"Is he mad at you?"

"That would be against all his principles. Wouldn't it?"

"Are you being sarcastic?"

"Aren't you being cynical? I told you, he's trying to accept it. He feels he will, but he's having a reaction. So he's gone up on the hill to try to work it through."

"What kind of a reaction?"

"An unhappy reaction, what the hell do you think?"

"Now don't walk back and forth over me in boots, Joanna. What kind of reaction were you trying to produce?"

"I just couldn't take the absolute dependency. I just wanted to be my own person in the tribe. I just wanted not to be gobbled."

"Maybe it'll work out yet, Jo. He hasn't done any of the really bad things he might have. He isn't trying to make us feel guilty or disloyal. He isn't running round playing martyr."

"No . . . Maybe it's worse."

"How?"

"Leave me alone!"

"Remember how he went and hid in the streets when you were being tested? He came back."

"It's just that he can't help it!" She turned away to the line of dripping clothes.

"It all seems so damn unnecessary."

"I knew it would be better to do it at the dance. It would have been open and ritual. I think waiting for me all night was the worst part for him."

"But he's spent the night with other girls."

"Yes. Isn't it silly? Now let me wash. Go away and let me alone till he's back. Okay?"

How long would Corey have stayed on the hill? They never found out. He did not come down the next day. The next night Shawn was lying in his cot dozing but not totally out. He awoke at the first noise and sat up. Four A.M. It was the warning bell going off. He shouted to wake the others and grabbed his trousers, stepped into his boots and buttoned himself as he ran into the air. He stuck his head in the cabins he passed, shouting to wake the sleepers, and went on. He found Joanna already dressed and running from the house.

She yelled, "It's some kind of raid. The sentry called in. We've got to get everybody into the tunnels."

"Not everybody. We haven't built enough new ones. One armed group should fall back toward the mountain. We should never concentrate all our people in one spot."

"So how shall we divide people up?"

"Send people to the tunnels as long as there's room, but start good warriors and people with lots of experience falling back along the trail."

"We've got to get Corey."

"We'll pick him up as we move out. I'll see you on the mountain."

No way to tell how many people were up by now or into the tunnels, in the general chaos. On the other hand, most of the Indians were used to passing orders and making decisions and clearing out in extreme confusion, in street fighting and raid situations, and none of the running around was aimless.

Big Ned came racing toward him. "Taking some warriors in the truck. Going to try to go out by the south gate. If we can get through we'll warn the city communes to disperse. We'll meet you with transport on Beaver Road, where the old logging trail comes down."

"No, by the ravine. You can park hidden there. Try and get through."

The call came from the north gate that cars were breaking through the fence. Then they cut off the warning system. Shawn passed the word to seal the tunnels. Word got passed back to him that everybody not inside should take to the woods and fields and move out. He began jogging toward the hill, turning everybody around who was still heading toward the tunnels. He ran into Ginny carrying one of the babies, Sarah Jean.

"What the hell are you doing running around with her? Why aren't you in a tunnel by now?"

"Joanna's underground with the other two, but I had to go back for this one. I'll have to carry her up top."

"I can manage. Give her over."

But Sarah Jean wakened to find herself joggled and cold and let out a piercing wail. Ginny took her back. "Just help me tie this scarf into a sling so my hands are free. We better get out of here."

They trotted slowly. He would not leave Ginny and could not make her move any faster. Cars were pulling up to the farmhouse. More headlights on the drive. He did not turn around again. Sarah Jean was crying, but her cries were muffled by the scarf and Ginny's body. Their progress was a slow trot, slower as they began to climb. He kept imagining slinging the baby in the scarf over one shoulder and Ginny over the other and leaping up the mountain like Superman.

The orders were to disperse and make their way over the countryside to one of the other roads. From caution and convenience there was always an old car or two parked in each of the fields that bordered on a usable road. Only a handful of Indians were scattered along the hill trail climbing, then, since most of them who hadn't made it into one of the tunnels had faded across the fields and into the brush. Halfway up, they had to stop for Ginny to catch her breath. She had a stitch in her side. In a small clearing they sat down on a rock.

He could not see much. Searchlights and spotlights moved here and there below. They could hear the loud mumble of a PA system broadcasting some demand or appeal, but they could not make out the words. Occasionally they heard a shot, and a couple of times a flare went off. A series of dull bangs sounded. Not until they had started to climb again did they hear the sharp erratic crackle of rifle fire and pause to look at each other. Orders had been to escape and to avoid confrontation. But somewhere down in the fields, there was fighting.

"I haven't been here since the night we took Chuck up," Shawn mumbled.

"That's why I didn't like Corey coming up here to fast. He always has visions, anyhow. I've never seen anything else scare him the way he can scare himself."

"You think it's my fault."

"I think there is always more than one way to do what you think you have to do."

"You mean, like Joanna you think it would have been better to do it in the dance?"

Ginny laughed shortly, coughed. She was out of breath from climbing. "Did you think that? No. Myself, you know I'd be tickled if you never did that again. But you could've talked it over with him first. If Joanna had told him what she was going to do, do you think he would have said boo?"

"Shhh. What's that?" They froze. A small animal rattling the bare branches of a bush. They went on. He pushed Ginny up the steep inclines with a hand braced in the small of her back, or he shoved her up by the buttocks. He put his hands on her more than he had to, but she ignored it. "Ginny, don't you see, Joanna couldn't talk to him first. The whole point was to act independently, not with his permission beforehand."

"Mmmm. Takes two to be dependent. She could have launched her liberation by letting go her tight hold on him, too."

"Women are the hardest juries for women."

"I guess I'm a hard jury all the way around. I've known Corey such a long time. She made a mistake in the way she did it. Hurting him wasn't what she had to do."

Probably because he was so tired. Yes, must control his reactions. Yet he was hurt and angry. He wanted to take out his anger on her and throw her down and jump on her. Judging, judging him. His voice came out high and ironic and rather stagy: "Don't you think it's strange. We're running for our lives. There's a battle going on down below. Maybe it's all over for us. Our home is gone. Maybe our tribe is destroyed. And we're analyzing the subtleties of a love affair."

"Well, you've caught me alone, haven't you? You've been giving me those Absolve-me glances for days. I'm telling you, Joanna privatized their thing even more than he did. She wanted him so badly. You overlook that." She wrinkled her nose at him and shifted the baby to take its weight differently.

"I haven't been asking you to absolve me. I guess I don't think I need absolution. I've been asking you to talk to me. I guess I think friends should discuss differences, instead of presuming to sit in judgment on each other."

"All you want is your nightly bone."

"How do you know what I want? Do you ask me?"

"Do you ask yourself?"

He took hold of her by the arm and turned her to him. Sarah Jean immediately started wailing again. "Would you please not haul at me? I'm tired already, and I just don't feel like being touched."

"By me."

"All right, by you. I don't feel that close to you."

He felt muffled in his own anger and helplessness. He really wanted to shake the daylights out of her. He also wanted to scream at the top of his lungs that he loved her. He thought she would walk away with a shrug. It seemed meaningless to say that while they pushed up the mountain trying to save what they could, while their friends were in danger scattered through the night. What did he mean by it anyhow? It was a thing you were supposed to say to a woman; it was supposed to make things good between you.

When they came to the top, the Coleman lantern flickered in the cabin. Ben shouted when he saw them. His little sister Ruthie was cutting off the slices of cheese for Corey and handing him a canteen of water as he squatted beside the lantern eating. "Where's Joanna?" He leaped to his feet.

"Down in one of the tunnels," Ginny answered. "Tunnel D, with the babies. She's all right."

"What are you doing with that baby up here?"

"I didn't get back in time. They had to seal the tunnel."

"They should have waited for you with a baby, damn it. Ben and Ruthie came running up to warn me. Brought some food along. But why didn't Joanna come on up with you? Was she on nursery duty?"

"No, Sylvie was. I just happened to check the nursery

when the alarm sounded. Nobody was there. I don't know if Sylvie panicked, or if she went off duty without getting someone to take her place, or what. But I got Joanna and we did what we could."

"Hey!" someone shouted from the path. Corey blew out the lantern. He took up one of the rifles and Shawn took the other, and they waited. Two more warriors stumbled into the clearing, one of them, Jim, without a coat, with only pajama tops tucked into his pants. Jim's teeth were chattering and Corey told him to wrap himself in the blanket from the cot.

"Should we wait for more stragglers or move out?" Shawn put the question. "Ned was going to try to get out by the south gate with the truck and meet us by the ravine on Beaver Road."

"What's the point running away till we see what they're up to?" Corey relit the lantern, paced back and forth. His cheeks were hollowed with the stubble of several days, and he looked gaunt and a little mad. "It doesn't sound good. A raid in the middle of the night sounds like they knew for sure we're here. But if they stick around too long, we might have to make a diversionary attack to get the people out of the tunnels."

Jim got to his feet. "We fell back only as far as the first woods. We waited there to cover the retreat of the others if it turned out to be needed. We lay down in cover to watch. We saw the pigs attacking one of the tunnels with tear gas. We saw the kids come out choking and fainting. After that, we beat it up the hill because we figured we couldn't help them any more and we better try to get up and pass the news along."

"Which tunnel?"

"A. The one by the chicken house."

"What happened? It wasn't sealed yet?"

"Corey, they came straight at it, as if they knew it was there. We were too far to tell for sure. Maybe they saw somebody trying to get in. Anyhow, they cleaned it right out."

"If they start searching the woods, we're cooked," Shawn said.

Corey shrugged. "Do they have dogs?"

"We've all left tracks in the mud all the way up."

Corey scratched the stubble on his face. "Let's send a

scout down to the road to see if Ned got through with the truck. If he didn't, we're better off staying here."

Shawn went, full of anxiety. They looked very exposed in the clearing. Corey promised to post a sentry down the path. Shawn could hear Sarah Jean crying again as he started off.

There was no trail down to the road, but dawn was faintly breaking. All he had to do was to follow the slope of the land, staying as close to the bottom of the ravine as he could find good footing. The bottom was wet with runoff, but the season made it easy enough to push his way through the scrubby growth on the sides, where it would be impassable in a few months, when the leaves would be thick and the small twigs no longer brittle and easy to force through. Once they had the truck, they would have to decide how to get the people out of the other tunnels. Send someone to scout. Maybe use decoys to draw off the police.

He did not see the road until he stumbled out onto it. At first he could not find anyone, and he was wandering around hopelessly when a boy stepped out of the bushes holding a gun on him. He had a bad moment until New John spoke. "Shawn? Where's Corey and the rest?"

"You got through! Great. I came to scout. Where's the truck?"

New John showed him. A boy was lying on the metal floor wounded, and Carole was stretched out beside him. The others were crouched under a waterproof canopy except for Big Ned, who was tending the wounded. A bullet had passed through the boy's collarbone, but he would manage until they got him to a doctor. Carole had taken a burst from a shotgun. Her chest and belly and back were ripped open. She was dying. Slowly the blood ran from her across the metal floor and out the end.

Shawn squatted beside her. "Maybe the truck should take off and get you to a hospital. The rest of us can hide."

"I'll be dead in an hour. Listen to me. Everybody's got to clear out." She spoke softly. "Was in tunnel D. The gas killed both babies." He had to lean over her to hear. The smell of shit from her burst intestines. "They choked to death in our arms. Joanna went crazy. They clubbed her down." He took her hand. Cold, damp. "I felt ashamed, being taken in so easy. Me a warrior, and disarmed like

that! I made a break for it." Dark blood smeared her
mouth. He knelt and kissed her.

"Did they hurt Joanna?"

"Couldn't tell. She was out cold."

"Did you get hit escaping from the tunnel?" he asked
the boy.

"No. We had to shoot our way through the gate. I got
one of them."

Big Ned nudged him. "Listen, you want one of the men
to go up and fetch them? They got to move fast. We
aren't safe. They must have a report out on the truck."

"I'll go back. I know the way." He was afraid there
would be an argument with Corey about leaving, with
Joanna in the hands of their enemies. The day did not
lighten fast because the sky was covered with a low shield
of clouds. A small rain fell and stopped, fell and stopped.
But there was light enough now so that he could see his
way, and though the scramble was steep uphill, he made
good time. He was tired. He was tired beyond caring. His
muscles felt thick and sore. He kept pushing himself
uphill. He was scared all of the time in his belly like a
poison working. He was scared all of the time that he
would come and find them gone.

They were waiting in the clearing in a nervous cluster.
One more woman with a rifle had come up the path to
join them. She had already given them the news that she
had seen two more tunnels attacked with gas and the
people inside made prisoner. She had set fire to the lab
and then fallen back.

Shawn looked carefully at Corey. He was quiet but
together. Everybody started down the ravine. By the time
they reached the truck it was just after seven, not really
light, a dull morning and raining steadily. The boy was
still lying in the truck, but Carole was gone.

"We buried her the best we could," New John said. He
had been crying. They got into the truck. The floor was
still sticky.

Big Ned and Corey got up front, Ned to drive and
Corey with the maps to figure out their course. Everybody
else squatted in back around the wounded kid. They were
anxious and glum, all expecting a roadblock. It was tense
in the truck because they couldn't see anything, and every
time the truck slowed down or came to a stop, everybody

strained to hear, and those who were armed held their rifles at the ready.

"I hope Dolores wasn't in tunnel D," he said to Ginny. She was leaning wearily against John with the baby finally asleep from exhaustion in her lap.

"I hope she was. That's where Joanna took Leaf. If they're separated, she'll be terrified."

Shawn shook his head and told her briefly what Carole had told him. Depression thickened in the back of the truck. They were all close to exhaustion and despair. Nobody made conversation. Nobody had anything to say.

It was nine when the truck stopped for the last time and the motor was shut off. Corey came around to open the doors. "Out, quick. Ned has to ditch the truck. We're in Hoboken. We don't dare try to reach Manhattan in the truck. We can rest and eat here, and wait for Ned to get back."

The Hoboken commune was in an old frame house. Shawn fell onto a mattress, kicked off his boots and peeled his wet pants and fell to sleep. He did not wake till late in the afternoon. By then Ned had come back and Ginny was acting as barber. A sign on the wall in Corey's big block printing read: SOMETIMES THE RED MAN MUST PAINT HIMSELF WHITE. Corey's hair was cropped already. His ears stuck out. He looked younger and skinnier. Looking at him, Shawn did not believe he had slept at all. The bones seemed to be coming through his skin in desperation. His eyes glittered and saw no one.

At least Shawn was sure Corey did not see him. He wanted Corey's gaze. He kept telling himself his sense of guilt was irrational—that Corey would probably have been captured along with Joanna if he had not been up on the hill, but he still felt as if everything, everything were somehow his fault. He kept realizing that Carole was dead. No one spoke about it. They could not afford to think of her yet. But he felt immobilized by guilt.

After Ned had been shorn, Shawn sat down in the chair and Ginny spread the towel around him before beginning to slash and cut. The floor was deep in fallen locks, brown and black and now his yellow hair. The first report over the radio came on the three o'clock news. They figured the radio report to mean that what was going to be raided had been hit already. The radio described raids by the police of two states on the headquarters of an illegal armed gang of deserters. It promised more information on the evening news.

Scouts sent out from the Hoboken tribe were back by supper. One of the Manhattan communes had been hit during the night, caught by surprise, and everyone busted except for one boy who had jumped naked from the fire escape to the next building and been taken in by a girl. Several carloads of kids from the farm had arrived in New York. Nobody who had been known to be hiding in any of the tunnels had turned up.

Corey was functioning on his will. His face frightened Shawn, but he kept moving and giving directions and asking questions and calming people. "We have to move into New York. Have to disperse the communes. They're down on us, and it's time to set things in motion so they can't pick us all off and round us up. We have to send runners to every commune. Got to get the word out.

"In the meantime, we have to find out what's happening to our captured brothers and sisters. What's being done to them. We go to Manhattan in groups of two."

Ginny went to fetch the baby, but Corey stopped her. "This commune has voted to receive the baby Sarah Jean as their child."

"But she's the only child our tribe has left."

"We are all Indians. There's work to be done." Corey's hand tightened on her arm. She sat down. He went on, "Who knows when we'll meet together again. Maybe on the streets. We knew they would come down on us. Now we'll find out how well we used the time we had, how well we built ourselves a movement and a people."

They all kissed and embraced each other. He had the feeling Corey still did not see him. He was acting, he was strong, but he was locked in himself. Then they got ready to leave by twos. Ruthie was persuaded to stay in Hoboken, but Ben insisted on his right to go. Shawn was quietly certain that Ruthie did not want to argue any longer, but that she would follow her brother by herself.

New John and Ben left first. Shawn stood to go. He looked at Ginny, but she was still sitting where she had been, and Corey was also looking at her. Corey gave a little jerk of his chin. "Come on," and she followed him out without ever looking aside. Five minutes later, Shawn followed them with Big Ned. As they walked into the tubes, he felt as if he was really passing into the underground. The catastrophe numbed him. He was glad that there was much they had to do.

THEY held the council Thursday in a hall where rock concerts went on every weekend, disguising it as a concert. The rock group was sympathetic, and Billy's boys tied up the manager backstage. An hour before announced concert time, the Indians started arriving, filled the auditorium and the box office was closed. It had been engineered in such a fashion because there had to be a general meeting, but the chances of all their best people getting busted in one big raid were grave. Shawn had done a lot of the footwork—after all, it was his show-biz world they were borrowing—and the Indians arrived with previously distributed tickets and were checked by face at the door.

People buzzed to each other, obviously uncomfortable with the format of everybody sitting in seats instead of the familiar circle, speakers addressing the group instead of each person speaking what he had to say in his turn. Billy had foreseen that and approved. No time for rigmarole and mystic formulas when they faced destruction. They had to sit still and listen to be moved into action. Tonight was to be the step beyond games. He needed the mass effects, the ambience of audience caught in large currents to pull them across.

Having kept the arrangements in tight hands, he had placed his warriors around the edges and across the sides of the stage for visual and psychological effect. They looked tough and disciplined. They were his pride and delight. From adolescent misfits, sour and lazy and rank with self-pity and spongy daydreams, stupefied and vain and whining and on the make, he had created real urban guerrillas. He had forged a responsible, trained corps. They were the fruit of months of hard work, so let them stand where everyone could see and admire and want to emulate. If he considered them an elite, it was with a consciousness of what material he had squeezed that cadre from. If they were an elite, an elite could be made out of any material with sufficient work, intelligence, direction and pressure—pressure from the inside and the outside. It had been a matter of upping the ante for the prestige that all kids wanted from their peers. Now let his warriors, his best troops, be prominently displayed around the hall as one of his best arguments in the fight that was coming here tonight.

The walls and the stage were heavily hung with posters and pictures of Third World revolutionaries. Beside the portraits of Che and Mao were innumerable Bolivian and Guatemalan and Algerian and Vietnamese and Angolan martyrs and fighters. That too was part of upping the ante. It was not merely a matter of needing alternative heroes. The past struggles in the United States could have filled the walls with dead radicals. It was not merely a matter of feeling solidarity with others who were fighting the same enemy in various parts of the empire.

It had to do with wanting to be somebody else. It had to do with the middle-class guilt that all these kids had instilled in them, a sense of powerlessness in themselves, futility, the subtle socialization through guilt and shame and the daily quiet gnawing fear of the loss of love through which they had all been persuaded they wanted to shit in the potty and keep their hands off their peckers and eat their food and not kick or punch each other. And go to school and sit in school and not wet their panties and keep quiet and keep still and be good and perform well. It was not enough not to fight. If you went inert, you got sent down to the lower tracks to be packed into hell and welfare. No, you had to perform. Neither an overachiever nor an underachiever be.

So they all wanted to be somebody else, someplace else. They hated where they came from too much to want to think about what a revolution by and for such people might involve. He was giving them images of manhood to enter that vacuum.

The meeting began with terse reports of what had happened—the two raids and a general dragnet on the streets. The cops had hit another commune two days before, but the commune had already dispersed and nobody had been taken. Marilyn, chosen by lot to head security for March, gave her report. Evidence suggested the Indians had been informed on by someone who had lived in the Hudson Street commune and spent time on the farm.

Two people fit that description: Ellie was a high school dropout who had joined the Indians the year before. She had been arrested in demonstrations at the schools between semesters, with the bunch of high school kids she was working with. Tim was an experienced warrior and bread distributor who had been trapped by narks on February 14 and was being held without bail and was expected to be court-martialed for desertion from the street militia in Cleveland. As far as they could find out, Ellie was in an institute for juvenile offenders upstate. Tim seemed likelier, as he could face a death sentence for desertion, as well as life imprisonment under the federal legislation against psychedelic drugs. They had been unable to trace his whereabouts.

People were scared as they listened to the reports, he could feel that. Not scared for their necks, not scared for their politics, but little scared: scared for their comforts and their tribes and their friends and their daily pleasures and hassles. Scared of a change, that was what it came down to. He could thank the enemy for breaking up the communes, because from organizing tools they had become homes for wayward adolescents, and everybody would have been content to play ring around the posy for the next ten years. Now the people were shaken out of their comfy social burrows.

The meeting moved slowly, like a fat old dog looking for fleas. He forced his patience to stretch and stretch, letting the tensions speak themselves, waiting until the room was on the edge of impatiently demanding an answer, a plan. Then just as he was ready to move, just as he glanced over at Matty to give the sign, Corey rose out of the audience like a waif and jumped up on the stage. He took the microphone, going to sit on the apron with his legs dangling over.

"Sisters and brothers, this is the season of the steamroller, of the club and the net. But we are water, and we will flow away, and re-form ourselves together in our season.

"Brothers and sisters, we have taken ourselves, frantic freaked-out kids with the man's programing in our heads, fear and poison in our bodies, and we have made a new people. Now the man is breaking the center. We must flow out. Those who are deserters have to go underground, and we must have solid ID for everyone in danger. But those of us who face only small detainment have to be strong enough to pass through organizing. It is time to go home for a while. It is time to go back where we came from, bringing the message and spreading the tribes.

"Today is March 18. The year's big call up comes after July 4. We have almost four months to organize a massive refusal. We have four months to pull friends out of the system. In the summer we will come back together in a new wave, five times as strong. It is time to show the strength of water and flow away from the man's steamroller. To stand is to be crushed, but to flow out is to gather new strength. We have to be ready for the most massive organizing and recruiting campaign we've ever tackled.

"What we have to do is break into small groups here in the auditorium, and each person should hassle out with his tribe what he should do: the danger he faces, his resources, his tasks. We must develop clear organizing strategies. We can help each other to choose not just the survival route, but the growth route, in spite of the club, in spite of the raids, in spite of our sisters and brothers now in the man's jails."

As Billy strode forward to grab the mike, he was not really angry. He was exalted, he was more high and ready than angry, but anger was his manner. Corey could not avoid this confrontation. Let him try to turn this clash into cornmeal mush. The lines were drawn past his old ability to soften and confuse them. The lines were drawn before everyone.

"Warriors and tribesmen, we have just heard the council of defeat. The enemy is attacking us, so we should surrender our territory and scatter before the heat. Who here doesn't dig that our only strength comes from being united? As individuals, they can pick us off. As tribes, we can fight back. We should go underground, says a former leader. But our friends went underground, into the tunnels, went into hiding instead of fighting, and where are they? The only good defense is offense. The only people who got off the trap of the farm were those who fought their way off. They're here tonight. Where are the others?"

He had touched them on a nerve. He felt it. "The proposal of my opponent is basically that since the enemy is attacking our organization, we should disband it before he attacks more. Why should we quit? We lost members of two communes, sure, but two months ago we had that many less members. Why are we growing? Because we fight the man. Because we attack instead of letting ourselves be rounded up like sheep. Because we are militant and protect our people, and everyone knows it. It's no time to abandon what we've stood for that brought people to us—that brought in every warrior in this room. The enemy won't change his mind about squashing us if we're stupid enough to do his job for him and disarm ourselves and scatter back to the homes and stinking neighborhoods where we could not survive before. Go back, pretend it never happened, maybe the man will forget. Maybe we should all turn ourselves in and enlist.

"No, warriors and tribesmen. We aren't that weak. It's time to strike back. It's time to take the offensive. It's time to attack.

"We'll defend our territory. We'll call out the high schools. We'll have actions in the streets, and we'll tie up this fucking city. The man won't know which way to swing his club. The whole city will be cracking. We'll make the Lower East Side so hot, the man won't be able to patrol it. We'll force him out and patrol our own turf. That's how we'll save ourselves—as a tribe. Not as chickens running for shelter. As Indians fighting together for our communes and turf.

"Call out the high schools! Call out the tribes! Into the streets and onto the housetops. This is our city. The streets belong to the people. Let's take them!"

People were on their feet yelling. His warriors were beating on the floor in unison, with a weird hollow drumming effect that made the hair on his neck rise. Childish rituals. He could taste the excitement, he was himself high and riding on it, yet he knew the crowd's excitement and his own were alien as mouse and giraffe.

Never sentimentalize your material. The bricklayer who overly cherished bricks would never build a wall. And other homilies. Speechmaking rotted the brain. But over time he had dealt with his own repulsions, his clumsiness, his shyness before groups.

A couple of his warriors followed to support him. All that arranged beforehand, the general pitch. They were doing okay. He did not have to listen but could watch the crowd instead. Tilting his glasses, pressing them hard into his cheeks to make out the haze of heads farther back, he read face by face through the rows, counting votes by expressions. Yes, he would carry them.

Corey got the mike again. He should not have been able to. He just gently took it, and the warrior, Matty, who had been speaking let him. Billy thought quickly, procedural point. No, let him go first, then come on himself to clobber.

Corey stood with head jutting forward, his face gloomy and sullen and his eyes glaring out from under half-shut lids. He looked awful. Billy moved up to stand beside him, towering over. Lack of sleep, fear for Joanna, hair cropped almost to baldness: Corey's charisma was damp and low. For once, they were equal in this fight. Corey would pull no miracles of flesh and charm and brother-me sister-me words. He had no miracles to shake out of his skinny body like the bullfighter's red satin cape magically whipped out of his bony ribs. Nothing but empty hands that cut the air mechanically as he spoke. His voice had gone dry. He turned and saw Billy standing over him, and for an instant their eyes met with a full glare of hostility on both sides.

"We grow dizzy with our own rhetoric. We give ourselves visions that blind us to the real situation. There are not *yet* enough of us to fight the state. There are not *yet* enough of us to bring down this city. We don't want to take over the system, but to abolish it. There are many ways to fight, but with weapons is the worst right now, because we can't win. We should never fight when we can't win."

Some of the warriors booed and pounded on the floor in derision. The bad luck, the shame of the farm fell on Corey.

"We must not be blinded by our own metaphors. We call ourselves warriors, we call ourselves guerrillas—so we can understand we've left their machine and are out to destroy it. But we must not be trapped inside our words. There are times to be visible and times to be invisible. We are afraid to leave the comfort of our communes and our tribes, but we must go out and organize everywhere."

"It's you who's scared now!" a woman shouted. "We don't want to run away. We want to fight. Sit down!"

"We must not let our own words and our habits and our past trap us. We must not just react to the enemy but act freely out of our own need to grow, and the need of those still inside the beast for liberation. We must go back and come out again. This is the path of growth. That is the real path of the Indian now, more difficult than rushing into the streets, because it will take greater strength and more purpose than we've ever shown."

It was not working, it was not working. Corey hated being booed, and he showed it. His voice sounded petulant. He retreated into self-righteousness. Their mood was running against him, and he could not come to meet it. He was not moving to effect the compromise that would heal. The more the warriors booed him, the more he repeated himself, embracing his martyrdom.

"It's going to be hard to go back where we came from because we were all so proud we left. But we have to go back for the others and bring them out too. We don't have the strength of metal but the strength of water. We must trust our own strength and take the difficult path of dispersing in order to reunite."

Billy stepped nearer. Enough, enough. Corey was still holding the mike and tried to speak to him directly: "Billy, don't hold too hard to the line. We need to loosen, to change as the situation hardens—"

Billy pulled the mike from his hand. He turned to the audience, stepping to the edge of the stage. "Who dares to say we can't fight? Who dares to say, now that the chips are down, that being warriors was only a game, only words? Look around you. These are fighting men and they're ready to fight. It's always easy to find excuses for your lack of nerve. We all have reasons to be afraid. Let's stop pointing fingers. We all get tired and lose our nerve. We get confused and think up reasons not to act. It seems to us too much has been asked, that the price is too high. We want to rest for a while, to take it easy. That's how defeat comes: when we're defeatist beforehand. Of course there's danger. Only a fool would pretend there isn't, and only a fool would deny what you know: that it will be tough and dirty on the streets, and many of us will go down. But we'll push the pigs off our turf and liberate our streets if we hang together. If we're defeated, then is the time to counsel retreat. Then we can disperse and run away. But we're not defeated. We've been attacked, we've lost a few prisoners. But here we are, look around! Are you beaten? Tell me!" Shouts of "No!" "Vote, then. Let me hear you! How many are ready to fight?"

The shout was deafening.

People hated the smell of defeat, and Corey gave it off, standing backstage with one tall guy. Shawn! Billy felt in his euphoria like giggling. Shawn had cut his hair and dyed it brown. There was a warrant out on him. Put on a pair of specs and a secondhand suit. He was talking fast and earnestly at Corey, who did not appear to be listening. Corey would not accept defeat—not this personal setback. Billy had won the solid man's victory of strategy: could Corey see that?

Every man came at last to the end of his nerve. But Billy did not run on nerve. His was the leadership now, not grabbed, not connived for or leaped into, not fallen upon him by chance, but slowly built for. An organization that supported him and whose embodiment he was before the others lent him weight. The other leaders rapped and trafficked in charm and the lure of their ease. He stood for discipline and he moved for power, and he would lead the tribes through. The outsider became the insider not by selling his brain and not by currying favor, but by building a slow necessary core about himself until the outside was the inside and the head of the pyramid was where he stood.

Ginny popped out from between two warriors. She looked strange. He figured that out as she crossed the stage through clots of excited people: a skirt and sweater. He had not seen her in a skirt since high school. Her job was over. Gone with the farm. So she was free now. Ginny had never been initiated as a warrior, but what about a nursing corps? With her efficiency, she could put that together in a couple of days.

He strode over to intercept her. Said hello awkwardly, how are you, getting the perfunctories over. Sketched out his idea.

She did not smile. "Certainly you'd get that organized, but I don't think I can take it on now."

"You're not going to try to go back to the farm!"

"I think we'll be on the road. But I'll let you know if we stick around." She slipped past and went on to Corey, her smooth hair sleek under the lights. She walked quickly in her sure, slightly flat-footed way, and poked Corey in the shoulder. There was a flurry of consultation between Shawn and her. Then she took Corey's arm and tugged him off, Corey moving as if drugged, with Shawn just behind them.

A bolt of anger fixed Billy. The weak soft squishy core of her. Of course she took the losing side. If Corey had won with his giving-up-in-advance strategy, she would be hanging around Billy, acting all butter and broth and nursey. Maybe what she had liked in him had been his awkwardness and his freakiness, and now that he had mastered his life, learned to function on his strengths and neutralize his weaknesses, she looked at him blankly and moved away. Mother searching for baby boys to hang at her breast. Forget her, forget her. She belonged on a farm, all right. She would never escape the soft doom of her automatic taffy-sticky maternal machine. Now he must think clearly about the tactics of the next days. Time to break up the general meeting and call his warriors into special session. He was better off without sources of confusion licking at the edges of his mind. He had offered her a chance to be useful, and she had refused it. Someone else would fill the position before the evening was over. Call it the hospital squad. Maybe draft Marilyn.

The demonstrations focused on two major demands: Free the Indians (the occupants of the tunnels and the raided commune) and Stop Police Dragnets—Let the Community Patrol Itself. The high school strike was about 60 per cent effective except in places like Staten Island. It was being coordinated by a committee of kids active in the schools, usually around anti-pigeon agitation and disruption of the recruiting assemblies and placement exams. They were nice hip kids, but their vision was limited. They wanted to demonstrate effectively and show their support for the demands: they anticipated, perhaps, that that might have some effect. They actually hoped for the release of the prisoners, at least on bail. They did not understand there was no possibility of avoiding violence, because the demonstrations were going to be smashed. Therefore when the time came, he would have to bypass and discredit them. In the meantime he let them run their show and filled service functions.

That was the one thing he could count on: If a bunch of people took to the streets asking for something they could not get in any other way and would not get that way either—whether it was to vote, or to have a voice about what wars they would die in, or to protest arrests or beatings or curfews—the police would go crazy and try to blind and maim and cripple them. A field day for sadists who felt unappreciated. To have a streetful of young boys and girls to beat was a cop's wet dream.

For years the culture had been telling everybody through every boob tube that only youth was sexual and beautiful, and that all an over-twenty-five schmuck like you could do was buy Brand X to look a little more youthful. Schmuck, schmuck, the boob tube said all evening long, you're powerless, sexless, fumbling, clumsy, mindless, unable to decide. Average man = schmuck. Average woman = bag. Buy our product at once, and maybe nobody will notice what a drag you are.

Because products wear out, right? Who wants last year's car or last year's dress or last year's avocado refrigerator? You want to look like a fool? You are a fool, but do you want to look like one? Look young, baby, or nobody will want to buy you any more. As a commodity, you can go out of style.

Thus is a people conditioned to hate its young and focus its frustrations down upon them in a vast dream of those half-dependent, half-independent children demanding and rebelling and threatening. A slow damp daydream spread among the ranks of the *Daily News* readers and readers of *Life* and *Time* of the rape, the torture, the humiliation of uppity sixteen-year-olds. Dozens of women's magazine and Sunday supplement articles advised in jargon, how to handle "them." They were different, alien. You were warned that you could not hope to communicate with them or understand their ways without the guidance of certified experts who had degrees in studying them, like biologists, specializing in tree monkeys or fighting fish. Them. Versus Us: the first step in the psychological conditioning for war.

The weakness of the young was that they did not believe in death. Their basic experience of relationships was all in the rhetoric of protection and nurture and punishment for their own good: parents to child, teacher to pupil, counselor to counseled. They were used to the repressive atmosphere of the schools, but that was a persuasion of fear, shame, manipulated competitiveness, failure to please and fear of failure. They were angry enough, but they were not yet serious.

Inside their skulls they thought they could go back, and the weakness in Corey's strategy was that they could for the most part—back to New Rochelle and Shaker Heights and Winnetka with fond memories of playing red man in the streets for a season or two to keep with memories of other team sports that were supposed to build character in adolescents. Corey had no place to go back to, so he could not imagine the co-optative softness of the average suburb. He had to be pushed aside, because he could not see that his plans would gut the movement.

Instead the kids would be thrust over the line so that they could never go back. They had to be forged in seriousness by the simple understanding that they must win or die. They must experience the brutality inside the empire that it exercised over subject peoples outside: armed repression, mass murder. Then they would become real revolutionaries. They would fight.

In the meantime who was yelling for their blood, who was organizing counter-demonstrations and waving flags and out on the streets looking for kids to beat up and heads to break, but all the working class who thought they were bourgeoisie, who felt the squeeze of inflation and the grinding pinch of depression, who bore the weight of taxes to support the whole shebang, and who were conditioned, frustrated, mad, fagged out, not willing to let go of one piece of the mortgaged jerry-built house or the tin-can car with six taillights, who felt the thrust from below and wanted to stomp.

All their lives they labored at a job, at two jobs, to buy only the gimcrackery in five shaky rooms, and why should they give up one fubsy lamp? Concessions to blacks, to kids, to the people howling about pollution, to the overseas proletariat would come right out of their pockets and off their backs: they sensed that. No corporation was going to reduce its take by one half of one per cent to pay for the demands of anybody. The cost of the war, the cost of a settlement was ground out of them. The blacks and the kids were to use their bodies to stop up the gaps, to sit out of the labor pool and be properly conditioned or barely maintained. But if they tried to shake things up, the folks already caught in the bind would be ready to start stomping. For twenty-five years they had been sold a crusader's world of Armed Might Versus the Red Hordes and now at last the myth was flesh and blood in the streets. Perhaps the Russians hadn't finally landed, but you didn't have to go farther than a subway token would carry you to Kill a Commie for Christ.

There were bombings around the city. Banks, induction centers, defense research institutes and corporate offices went up with a mighty bang. The Indians were not much into that. But others were. The newspapers hinted of conspiracies, but each bombing and each arrest suggested new targets. Every day a new army of one would go forth to blow himself or some piece of the city sky-high.

After sporadic though lively actions in the neighborhoods the day that the schools went out on strike, the first big confrontation was a march (for which the high school committee was refused a permit by the city) up from Washington Square Park. The Tactical Police Force was massed waiting, and attacked as soon as the park was full. Bands of warriors outside started diversionary tactics immediately. They turned in fire alarms, broke the windows of banks, turned over cars and set them on fire. The streets were full of running kids, but the cops were clubbing, arresting, and then clubbing at leisure.

Still, no more than a hundred were arrested in the park, as far as his men could estimate. Thanks to the diversions, most of the troops got out quickly enough, to remass some on Second Avenue and some in Union Square, where the whole scene was repeated, although the attack was expected and the cops did not succeed in surrounding the mass again.

All told, it was the cops' day. For most of the demonstrators, it was broken-field running and quick moments of revenge on trashbaskets or cars or windows, then more footwork and maybe a lump and maybe effects from the gas and maybe a fractured skull or a broken arm. Many kids staggered away weeping. It was not just the gas or the pain. In every confrontation, some kids always ended up weeping from shock, surprise, disgust. A barometer of their innocence. Lambs revolting in the slaughterhouse who still did not expect to be eaten.

He saw it especially in the way a girl sometimes would stop and stare at the cops, shocked, in the midst of everything, that somebody really wanted to split her head wide open, to kick her in the belly and splash her blood over the street. They watched television nightly in the bosoms of their families and went to spy movies in which the sexual thrill was the electrocution or dismembering of actor after actress and still did not understand that violence was the pornography of their culture. They were learning.

Once it got dark, a chilly wind put an edge on the air and the troops got hungry and began to go home for supper. They did not abandon the field in rout. They went running in loud tree-swinging packs into the subways, vaulted the turnstiles and shoved into cars that they dominated with their noise and élan, till the regular homebound citizens stared at them and drew apart and saw them as dangerous. The tribesmen were still combing the streets for the injured. The floor boards in their storefront hospitals were slippery with blood, and still the kids were brought in, noses broken, scalps lacerated, ribs cracked, shoulders dislocated, one boy with a contact lens broken in his eye by a club, blinded and oozing blood.

They retaliated the next day with a quick-striking demonstration against the leading manufacturer of tear gas, whose corporate profits in the field of weaponry for police departments, sheriffs' offices, and state patrols had risen with the number of citizens actively protesting the conditions of their lives.

It was not a mass demonstration. Several parties of warriors moved in from different directions, acting as separate groups with objectives and the looseness to change them if blocked, and moved out as quickly as they had come. Billy found the demonstration beautiful: that was the word that kept coming to him. Most of the warriors were dressed as they would be normally. They looked incongruous enough against the sleek marble and brass and opulent glassiness of the building. A few individuals were costumed to blend, either dressed as building workmen or as clerical workers, with specific targets such as the air-conditioning system and butyric acid capsules to disperse through it. Butyric acid created an instant nauseous stench. It literally gassed the inhabitants out of the building with its stink, and it would take the chemical company a bit of time and effort to air out their offices.

As the employees poured out, another group napalmed a dummy in the marble courtyard, demonstrating the uses of yet another product of the wonders of modern chemistry. Then they split and moved out. Inevitably there were some arrests, but for the most part they got in, acted and cleared out without casualties.

The next afternoon there was a rally in Tompkins Square Park. More than the high schools turned out. Massive police presence would always start things humming down here. Like Harlem and Bed-Stuy, an occupying army was visible strutting about. The heat protected no one from the casual violence of the streets, the junky robberies, the purse snatching and attempts to hustle unwilling women. They came down on village business, they clamped down on normal street action. They arrested the small entrepreneur—the grass peddler. They went after the loudmouth who protested. If a commune had a woman raped or a man rolled, they busted the commune. So you might get robbed six times and never report it. Not even your landlord would be naïve enough to suggest you should.

Yes, he knew his turf. Unlike Corey, he did not intoxicate his head with visions, but he looked around him and made do with what he found. So he thought, warming his hands at an improvised fire on the little hill in the park where the kids usually played. He had bought chestnuts from a vender, and he squatted to eat them, listening to the reports of his lieutenants. The chestnuts were good only insofar as they were warm. They were dry and mealy. Finally he gave them away to a hungry street kid and got up, wiping his hands, and moved out with half a dozen of his men to a position on a roof.

He kept watching for Corey. Corey had to try to cut himself back in. He could not hang out of big action like today. But Billy received no sure reports on any of the three of them. He decided to send a runner to Hoboken to find out if Corey was sulking there or trying to set up a rival command headquarters. He could not afford to dismiss a possible source of confusion from his consciousness. Suppose Corey was already trying to start a splinter group.

There were maybe fifty, sixty thousand street people and high school kids and Indians and the flotsam of the neighborhood. The rally maundered on with a dozen speakers, one from each organization that had signed the call, two rock groups, a folk singer and a minister. The police moved into position, but aside from push and shove on the crowd's fringe, they let the rally proceed.

The sun shone from a pale blue sky flat and shallow as a saucer. It felt like spring. The air was resilient. Dogs were barking in packs after a solitary bitch or sniffing around each other in swirls of dirty fur. Every so often a kid set off a string of firecrackers.

At times the mood felt tense and militant, at times relaxed. Gusts of hard and soft wind came off the crowd to his rooftop. He could see a young mother nursing her baby against a tree. A group with bells and tambourines were chanting Hare Krishna, ignoring the speakers. Other neighborhood people were passing joints or eating lunch on the soggy ground. Couples were nuzzling on blankets. People were greeting each other and exchanging phone numbers. In continuous circulation people stared around carefully, eye catching on eye, looking for friends, looking to see who was there, looking each other over and picking each other up. At the same time kids were carefully tucking their hair into helmets and preparing damp hand-kerchiefs against tear gas and passing around jars of vaseline against mace. Affinity groups of street fighters were sketching out their plans of mobile tactics in the mud, or with marking pens on the walks. Speakers and singers and rock groups did their thing and handed on the inadequate PA system to the next mumbler. All at once it was over, and time to make up minds.

People could go home (the rally was over: we have made our points); people could attempt to march uptown; people could break into mobile bands.

In ten minutes, before he had done more than send a few runners to check on deployment, all the choices made downstairs were academic. The people who thought they were going home and the people who thought they were marching uptown, and most of the people who thought they were breaking into small groups, were all caught in a close, desperate thrust and counterthrust, waves of pressure going through the crowd. The police had decided to prevent the march from setting forth, and instead attacked the crowd and drove people back on each other. People were trampled and began to scream. The front lines of would-be watchers pressed on the police, who were standing with clubs held before them in close formation.

When the crowd failed to dematerialize but pushed on the lines of police, their lines parted to let out a flying wedge, and clubs breaking bodies and mace cans firing, the TPF drove into the mass. It was as effective as a brass-knuckled fist into a soft belly. People were maced and blinded and panicked and went down to be worked over at leisure inside the wedge. People began throwing bottles and bricks into the lines of cops, and then a wedge of demonstrators armed with sticks and poles and bench slats drove across the middle of the wedge, isolating the vanguard of TPF in the crowd. All he could see was a moil of bodies.

The tear-gas trucks drawn up began to fire a dense cloud into the west side of the park. The police charged the crowd from the north again. There was a shot, then two more. So many people were screaming, he could not tell what was happening. The cops were attacking with clubs and mace, the gas was drifting in huge clouds low over the bodies. Then from a roof or a window, someone hurled a molotov cocktail into the massed cops. Then they were screaming too and began to shoot at the houses on the north side of the park, smashing the windows and raking the façades with bullets. The police helicopter that had been whirring back and forth descended close to the roofs.

Time to get into action. He ran with his men down the stairway and out through the back. The main thing was to start an orderly retreat. He no longer had a sense of being on top of events. Mounted cops were charging the crowd, riding over kids, and some kids were scattering marbles. A horse reared and panicked, and another went down with a broken hind leg. Gas was blowing in dense burning clouds. Everywhere unconscious or groaning demonstrators were being carried off. A woman came screaming out of a house that had been fired on, carrying a bleeding child, and was shot down on the stoop.

It was an hour before everyone was out of the park. They left behind fifteen dead demonstrators, two dead children and three dead cops. Most of the bodies had been shot and then trampled, but one girl had bled to death from a severed artery in her neck, and two of the cops had been beaten to pulp with bricks and fists.

Blue twilight. Something like three thousand held in pens on twenty thousand dollar bail. The police were on a rampage. Half the cop cars in the city were cruising the Lower East Side, arresting any kid who had on a bandage, arresting any kid who looked to them like a demonstrator—or a kid. Any long-hair. Pulling them off the streets and working them over in the cars and beating them in relays in the station houses.

The mayor put a curfew on the whole area south of Fourteenth Street. The bars and liquor stores and places of public entertainment were closed. People were stuck in the pads where they had taken refuge, gathered in stores behind shutters, hiding in cellars. When a cop car came down a street, life froze. When it turned the corner out of a street, that street came back to life. People shot out the street lamps so they could dodge from block to block. A moderate amount of looting went on.

Cruising cops were attacked with bottles and homemade bombs, and an occasional molotov cocktail. They replied by shooting up whole rows of houses. Sporadic gunfire sounded all night. The cops raided and shot up the storefront that had housed the high school committee and got nobody, shot up a storefront hospital and got a full house. A reign of random terror in all the cluttered filthy streets. People hid behind lowered blinds and ate cold cereal and peeped warily out the windows. The National Guard was mobilizing in the armory on Fourteenth Street.

The black high schools had gone out on their own demands two days before, and they had been beaten and gassed and mass arrests made. But at Food and Maritime— an ancient dead-end vocational high school where Lincoln had once spoken and blacks and Puerto Ricans took courses for obsolescent jobs and prepared for unemployment—when the boys refused to disperse, the police fired on them.

The next day the police used shotguns in El Barrio and Harlem and Bedford-Stuyvesant, firing on demonstrators, and there were more dead and many more wounded, although only by word of mouth could people find out. In the white neighborhoods the police continued to use gas and clubs. Friday night, Harlem went up from west to east, and Brooklyn exploded.

The mayor did not hesitate to call in the Armed Forces, as the last mayor had been voted out for waiting too long to bomb last time. This candidate had run on a law and order ticket, and besides, it had become clear that a great deal of money was to be made by those who counted through rebuilding afterward. All day Saturday the city shook with the bombardment and planes came in screaming on their metal bellies, dropping load after load.

The Indians opened free stores and medical centers and armed whoever would take arms, marking out an area of the Lower East Side where they would no longer permit the enemy to patrol. They had plenty of rifles and shotguns and homemade gasoline-based explosives, some machine guns, and a few mortars. They had bought some half-tracks and armored trucks from surplus stores. Billy argued that they could inflict the most damage by attacking to the south—into the complex of government buildings and beyond into the financial district.

Detachments began moving south at three in the morning. It was a cold damp night with the lights of the remote skyscrapers reflecting off the leaden clouds. The wind swept up Allen Street as Billy led a company of his best warriors past the rows of shuttered stores selling men's neckwear. His random army was moving south by every street and avenue, as he led his men west along Grand. They had a brief but staccato battle with a group of TPF just east of the Bowery, in the blocks where tawdry shops sold wedding gowns and mannequins stood in the stiff white garments swathed in yards and yards of tulle and satin. Burning dummies lay in the street among the bodies of the dead as they advanced.

Men were moving in firing from the side of the Centre Street police headquarters already—the narrow north side with the carriage entrance. Headquarters was a misshapen fussy building with a dome and a clock on top amid allegorical statuary, made out of yellow gray sandstone that suggested a sidewalk on which many dogs had pissed. It brooded like a shabby hen over a neighborhood of Italian stores and used machinery exchanges. He stayed long enough to see the mortar emplacement and the beginnings of the assault. He did not care whether they really took the headquarters or not, although they might. This action must divert from their real objectives downtown, where the major fighting was already getting started at the Criminal Courts Building and the circle of government buildings around Foley Square and Federal Plaza. He climbed into an armored truck and directed the driver south on Centre.

Going south they were attacked by a helicopter, zooming down on them with a high nervous whinnying. It killed one of their men and wounded two others before they could bring it down exploding in the street. The battle was underway now. Fighting appeared to have broken out in several places.

He hopped off the truck. One hundred Centre Street—a building every Indian hated. That was where you ended up. That was where you were taken and where you might get out on bail and you might not, where you had your trial and where, after they found you guilty, if you were male they took you across to the prison on the north. Dark gray building with shiny marble at the base—chunky, linear, aspiring: a kind of heavy modernistic stone temple to oppression.

The troops assaulted from three sides. On the south from Leonard Street the kids had already taken the district attorney's offices through the windows, low enough to boost each other in. On the east across Baxter Street hunched a row of seedy luncheonettes and law offices and bail bondsmen, where warriors were holed up firing, and where that petered out, Columbus Park, mainly a cement lot that the kids from Chinatown beyond played in during the daytime. For the moment, it made a good staging area. In that Baxter Street wall an entrance for deliveries stood open, but it was still being held by guards from the prison. As he hurled himself across the street under sporadic return fire from the broken windows of Criminal Courts, a plaque crossed his field of vision: a black group founded in 1810 had placed it there to commemorate a former stop on the underground railroad. Freedom Now.

He had a certain amount of radio contact with the leaders of some bands of warriors, but he was in no position to have a strategy beyond turning his troops loose—his only in the sense that he had made minimal plans and secured the weapons—in an area where they might wreak damage before the end. He allowed himself no illusions about being a general. There was no discipline in this army beyond a handful whom he considered adequately trained. Whatever they had agreed to do in council, whatever directions had been handed out, on the streets the kids were doing whatever occurred to them, and if something looked exciting or groovy they would imitate it. Even with real weapons in their hands at last, even with explosions shaking the ground and bodies going down to the right and to the left, they were still playing guerrilla theater. He watched one boy pause to adjust his headband and preen his mustache before charging to his death in the driveway entrance, machine-gunned down and cut in two.

He moved around to the Centre Street side. Waves of troops came across the barren little plot of grass and the parking lot between Lafayette and the Criminal Courts. They are, he thought: the criminal courts. They have dispensed the moneyed white justice for too long. Selling people back their liberty. Kneeling and firing, he could remember crossing that parking lot to the cafe beyond to bring back paper cups of coffee and ham sandwiches to Indians who were on trial up in one of the courtrooms. He had never seen them again.

Free-standing pillars big enough to shelter several men firing and hurling grenades stood in each of the two entrances, but beyond them was an exposed run to the doors under fire. But their side had people. They had bodies. He was growing used to seeing people die. People were so liquid, so easily squashed. A cockroach was much hardier. Essentially they were into the building, and he called off some of the troops and sent them to aid the forces assaulting the new police communications building by the Brooklyn Bridge.

The National Guard began to arrive with tanks. There was fierce fighting across the square, in the pinkish granite amphitheater before the squat black glass Customs Court and the big black and white radiator cover of the Federal Building. The troops were coming at them along Worth. He hurled himself down in the dry fountain, round and rimmed like an ash tray. It made a good trench. The boy firing beside him was wearing an athletic sweater from a Catholic high school. The woman on his other side was a fat forty-year-old Puerto Rican who looked like a weathered Dolores. She was chewing sugarless gum, which she offered him, and firing continuously and wildly. The boy had the top of his head shot off a moment later. The blood splattered Billy's glasses. He had to stop shooting to wipe them.

Artillery had been brought up, and the Indians' positions in the open area under the Customs Court were being attacked. A couple of direct hits on the thick supports they were using as bunkers, and with a great crumbling roar, the whole building settled and collapsed like an elephant going down on its knees.

This was it: reality at last after so much fantasy. He was really fighting. Billy with a gun. Fact at last. Why did it feel so . . . thin? He could not connect. He was functioning well. He kept in touch with his captains as best he could. He supervised the use of the mortars. He rallied and advised retreat. He did what he was supposed to. He was not afraid, except sometimes in his belly and then with a moment's almost overwhelming nausea. His head was not afraid. But he could not quite grasp the events. They broke into bizarre images and faded from him.

Most of their army fell among the office buildings. They never managed to get farther than Duane, where they blew up a couple of banks. When they retreated to their turf, the guard came after them and formed a cordon around the Lower East Side. The remaining Indians delimited an area they would try to hold. Posters all over the neighborhood went up at the same time as the barricades on their sixteen-block chunk. They tried to take the Con Edison plant, but the National Guard was already entrenched there, and they sustained bad losses in the assault. The guard came in with tanks and armored cars.

After burning barricades came burning houses. The tenements went up like paper. Among the roar of shells and the rattle of machine guns and the crack of rifles and the explosions of grenades and homemade bombs, his troops moved back from house to house. After the first day none of them succeeded in slipping out of the encirclement, but they fought well. Black kids, Puerto Rican kids, hippies, high school kids and Indians fought in small bands in the rubble from house to house and went down.

He lay shooting from the ground-floor windows of a one-room apartment with the Virgin Mary over the bed and a pot of red rice and beans moldering on the table. Ben lay on the bed in a dark puddle. He was probably not conscious any more. He no longer responded to Ruthie when she crept back to speak to him. Then they could no longer leave their post, Matty and Ruthie and he with Korean War surplus rifles, one German machine gun and a decent supply of ammo.

He felt calm and tired, but with a hollow high in his chest. He had sustained the test of combat. All he had ever claimed for himself was that he might be a useful weapon. He had proven himself. He had set an example and fought well. Again and again he had held a forward position, letting others fall back. They were losing, but they had proved themselves to the others around the world fighting and dying.

He might have been a monster. He had been in line to serve the empire. He might have become a contented scientist writing the formulas for nerve gases by day and going home to water the lawn or grow rare fungi or play poker or string quartets at night. He might have studied the trajectories of missiles or the stimulating problem of how to differentiate the various objects upon re-entry to the earth's atmosphere, warhead from dummy. He might have been studying how to package the black plague conveniently for dispersal. He might have been working on a chemical that could perform the equivalent of a prefrontal lobotomy on a whole population in ten seconds. He could have been busy and secure and happy in his work, solving technically interesting problems that damned the vast numbers of mankind to death or continued slavery and starvation.

He looked over at Matty, who was sweating hard and whose hands looked almost green against his rifle. He looked at Ruthie, whose face was smeared with tears that had dried and whose blouse was soaked with her brother's blood. She was biting her lip with concentration, staring through the sight. The last thing he heard was the whine of a shell from a tank that was moving across the ruins of Avenue C toward them, where they lay shooting from the ground-floor windows with the Sacred Heart of Jesus in four colors on the wall over them. The next shell made a direct hit.

Marcus as an Underdeveloped Country

THAT winter had gone okay. None of his people died of starvation and only one of exposure—from getting caught in a blizzard. First off, Marcus felt they'd finally learned their hunting ground. They had learned how to make it outside and live off the picked-over land. Besides, they had food and medicine and weapon drops from the Indians. They had added to their band. They had raided a school excursion and got girls. Marcus was relieved. He had the explicit fear of homosexuality of the street child: the fear of being used by a bully male and losing his manhood, the fear of being turned to a simpering, pimped object for money. Even in the hardest pinch of the winter, things were not so tough. He vaguely remembered Robin Hood tales. They even had fun.

It was good-looking country, and they knew it better than anybody since maybe the redskins who'd lived there. Marcus wondered sometimes about them, imagining their bones under the loam of rotting leaves. They named every trail they found or made, every stream where they drank, every overhang or cave where they slept, every mountain with a good lookout point.

Every night they built their small fires. The kids would be sprawling around making music, dancing, boasting, competing in memories of the city, talking about their families who might be living and might be dead, but that they never would see any more. Sometimes he worried that the recollecting might be bad for morale, but morale in general was high. No one had killed himself since that first bad winter when they had been four days hungry. Hell, now they were all used to doing without food for a day or two. The boys didn't panic at that any more.

Naturally it was hard in the winter—a mean cold that froze him clear through to his bones: he was never not cold, never, for month after month. He remembered when he was a little bitty child, when the landlord would cut off the heat in the winter or the furnace would blow, and his

192

ma would take him in bed and warm his back and rub his
arms and legs between her hands. For months now the
cold never eased up and he never got used to it. If he was
lying by the fire and his face was scorched, his backside
was still freezing. His woman, Terry, had lost toes from
frostbite, though he had sat up half the night with her
trying to rub the feeling back in. They couldn't cover
ground fast in the deep snow, and always they were
nervous about their tracks and dependent still on the food
drops.

So he felt the first signs of spring as he never had, the
rocks and then the earth sticking out through the mushy
snow, the patches of mud, the green shoots they fell on
like rabbits, some sour, some sweet, some bitter, some
that made them sick. Green is for eating—fresh green.
Little animals skinny and ragged from hibernation, little
animals hungry like them, began to come out. They started telling stories in the evening of what they were going to
do as the weather got warmer: how they would go swimming down by Piss Lake and by Mau Mau Lake where
the bottom was sandy, and how they would go fishing and
catching frogs and there would be more berries than they
could eat. In all the camping sites there would be fat
tourists with picnic baskets and refrigerators full of gro-
ceries and suitcases full of clothes, and it would be easy
living and plenty of times for just acting like kids for a
change. George swore he was going to grab onto one of
those put-put outboard motorboats and give them all a ride
on Mau Mau Lake as fast as the engine could go.

It was still lean pickings, but it was clearly spring, and
clearly it would be summer. Then just when they were
beginning to feel alive and kicking with the changes, it
came down on them. They began to be hunted.

With spring the tourist cars, the local cars on the park
roads did not come back. Only cop cars and cars belonging to the park administration. Small planes and helicopters kept crossing overhead. When they went down for
their next rendezvous and food drop, no one was there.
Nothing. It gave Marcus a chill. Naturally he cursed
around and said Whitey had let them down and they
should have been expecting some such stab in the back,
but they had all grown used to having a connection with
someone out there. They looked forward to the drop, to
the ritual negotiation, to the social contact no matter how

guarded and full of careful poses of putdown and hostility and menace, to the things they needed and had been waiting for and the things that surprised them. It was their regular holiday.

All the time now a helicopter was hovering in their sky looking for them, veering slowly back and forth like a hornet cruising or a nasty horsefly. There were too many of them to take cover easily. He considered and considered what they must do. Finally they talked it out and decided they had to split into three groups. Marcus worried about that a lot. He was two years older than any of the rest, and he was responsible. He was the man. He was the leader. He could not split himself into three and go with each of the groups. He tried to guess what would be best, though it weighed on him, and he appointed Shirley leader of one of the groups, because even if she was a chick she was older and smarter than the others, and the third group he gave to Willy, and then they chose up their teams.

He took his girl, Terry, and Joe and his woman and George and Tiger and Skinny and Ho (from Horace) and little Gladys, who was only ten and the sister of Joe's woman. It gave him a sick lonely feeling to go off from the others, and then an hour after there were only the nine of them, and the others were swallowed up in the woods. Who could guess what was happening to them? He could not know any more and he worried, but he kept it to himself. He kept the gang moving fast so they would forget. Still, it was easier to find food in the smaller group. They heard gunfire and dogs from time to time, and patrols passed on the major trails.

If only the leaves would come out on the trees! There were just buds. Every morning, he looked at the branches over them. The sun was hot on their heads, though the air was cool. Water was a problem sometimes when they were hiding up on the peaks. Often when they set a trap, they could not get back before the animal had rotted, because they had to run before a patrol.

One morning high on Muhammed Ali, they saw one of the planes dropping a load of explosives down the valley by Piss Lake, where they had used to camp in the summer, watching for tourists to raid and fishing and swimming and having a high old time. They could see flames for a while and then not any more. They all squatted on the ledge arguing whether they should find out what happened, if it was just walking into a trap to go down. Finally Marcus decided they had to take a chance, because suppose it was some of their people in trouble and needing help. He took George with him and they went to scout, while everybody else promised to wait around on Muhammed Ali till they came back.

They were quick runners, so they made it down to the spot in under two hours. They didn't have any trouble finding it. They just followed their noses. Things were still smoldering. George got sick and puked on his shoes when they started looking at the bodies, but Marcus was so petrified by fear and rage he was all right. Five of the bodies were crisp and burnt. That left two, including Shirley, and he called their names loud as he could for a while, though his voice scared him. He didn't want to die that way. He was of two minds. He half hoped they'd escaped, and half he was afraid that Shirley had run off and deserted the others, and that he had chosen wrong. Then Joe, who was down at the lake washing the puke off, saw two more bodies in the water. Probably they had run in, trying to put the flames out, and drowned or burned—who could say? They were sure dead. One was Shirley and the other must be Fats, though it was hard to tell any more.

George said that they ought to bury them real quick, or they'd get caught down here and fried too. Marcus said no. They had to get out at once. Surely some patrol would come to do a body count—they liked that kind of thing. Then they multiplied times five and put a story in the newspapers. Besides, the enemy could not know how many of them were in hiding. Maybe they'd think they'd incinerated them all, and leave them alone in the mountains. Then they'd be all right; they'd make out somehow.

He debated on the way back what to tell the others. It would not be good for them to know. But what could he make up? George could not be trusted to keep his mouth shut, even if Marcus gave him a good scare. The picture would haunt him. He would have to tell it to somebody, and then no one would believe Marcus any more. He could not save them then.

The gang had been so different: all that jockeying for position. Nobody wanted to push him out of being leader here, but how heavy the leadership weighed. At first he had acted like the big man, taking the biggest slice. Now if there was not enough, he went hungry. It was a burden: all of them on his back. He felt more than two years older; he felt a century older. His woman was too young to shake his troubles. He made George push himself, trotting faster and faster, because he was scared now, scared scanning the face of Muhammed Ali, that his people would be gone. He was scared to find them fried bacon smoking in the sun. Yet when he arrived, he yelled at them. He yelled out the news all at once and fell back.

After that sometimes they ran from patrols, but sometimes they fell in behind them. They waited for a chance to pick off a straggler. Now the men hunting them were soldiers. They wore uniforms and carried all kinds of equipment, rifles and grenades and walkie-talkies and radio apparatus and even cameras.

One time Joe was lying up among some rocks with his woman watching a patrol. Marcus was on the other side of the ravine with Tiger and Skinny, while everybody else was off food gathering. He watched the patrol stop and take up a covered position, and then they fired some kind of rocket at the ledge. They got both Joe and his woman. He did not understand. The soldiers could not have seen them. Joe had not fired or shown himself. It was not possible for them to know. But he did not stop to think about it, just high-tailed out of there with his boys.

They were more careful after that. Staying way back, they waited for times when the soldiers were not alert. A lot of the time the soldiers shot up patches of woods where there was nobody at all but chipmunks and deer and jack rabbits. Finally Marcus and Skinny and Tiger captured a soldier. They had been following a patrol from the top of the ridge for three days. The soldier had stopped to take a crap and he was long about it. They hit him on the head and carried him off, but it was hard for them. He weighed ten tons.

The soldier was scared and not scared. His name was Ed. Ed kept saying it was a big laugh. He kept telling them they were nothing but punk kids. He was twenty and from Akron, Ohio. He said the soldiers were Special Forces—special counter-insurgency troops—and this was part of their training. Tiger said it was fighting, not training, and didn't they understand this was guerrilla warfare? Ed said that was pretty funny, guerrilla warfare with a bunch of colored juvenile delinquents, and that more of his buddies would get killed driving around on Memorial Day weekend than in their whole time hiking around the park. Matter of fact, they liked this assignment. They got a lot of time in New York City, and now that the weather was getting better, it wasn't so bad tramping in the mountains.

Ed kept saying they should realize they had not captured him, but he had captured them, and they should all go in with him and quit playing hide and seek in the mountains. If they didn't quit while they were still in one piece, they'd all get blown to bits by next Friday. He kept talking like it was a big joke, and Marcus kept thinking about the bodies of the other kids by the lake, about what was left of Joe and his woman splattered on the rocks. "We fight till the last of us get killed."

George just got up and spat in the soldier's face.

"Jesus Christ," Ed said with disgust. "What shitty luck being captured by a bunch of crazy ten-year-old spades."

Only Gladys was ten. Her sister had been Joe's woman. She sat like a skinny brown chicken with her knees drawn up to her chin and her hand with the knife going stick, stick in the earth.

Marcus questioned Ed about how come the soldiers had been able to send that rocket at Joe when he was hidden behind the rocks. Ed explained that they were trying out all sorts of brand-new body detectors. They had one that worked by detecting body heat, and another magnetically sensitive device that located pieces of metal from a good distance. That one had not worked so well, because enough tourists had come through the hills to leave scraps of metal and old beer cans pretty nearly everywhere, and for a week they had been shooting up bushes before they sent that one back upstairs. The heat detector, however, was pretty effective, and it sure could pick up one of them hiding in the hills from a couple city blocks away. Professors had been developing these gadgets for locating natives in jungles for years, and now they were getting a good testing. "You kids are just amateurs. You got the whole might of the U S and A on your tail, picking you off like flies. You better wake up."

"The whole USA ain't worth my mother's ass," Marcus said. A pang went through him. Alive, dead, busted, free. He felt that if he could only see that fat old woman for

five minutes, even his mean sister with her stinking hair
straightener and her strutting around, he would be so
happy he would go straight through the ceiling. He felt a
sharp disgust at living. Weary, weary. But his people were
looking at him. They had to move out.

They tied up Ed's mouth with his undershirt and took
whatever they could use off him. Then they beat him to
death. Except for Gladys with the knife, they did it
methodically and without much excitement. They were all
too depressed by the business about the body detectors.

Tiger started in, "Maybe it high time to clear out of
here. Quit hanging around these old mountains and find
some other place to hide out."

"Yeah?" Marcus gave a short disgusted laugh. "We so
invisible. All we got to do is just walk out down the
highway. They used to seeing just millions of raggedy
black kids running around in packs in these parts. We can
just mix with the crowd naturallike, so nobody will give us
two looks."

After that everybody shut up, but they went back to
their old way of just trying to keep out of the path of
patrols. When they came to blasted patches, they did not
walk out into them but skirted them superstitiously and
turned another way. They never ran into any other of
their people, and they did not come on any bodies. He
thought of the third band as dead, but part of him kept
hoping, part of him would not give up that they were
hanging on, too. Then Gladys and Skinny got picked off
when they were tracking a deer, and just three days after
that, Terry got caught in a clearing where she was picking
some greens, and the plane dropped some kind of bomb
that exploded all these hundreds and hundreds of little
pellets. The pellets just tore right into her.

Marcus and Tiger carried her between them all day.
She was in awful pain. He sat up with her away from the
others, because she was moaning and wailing and the
bleeding just went on and on. He tried everything he could
think of to ease her and to stop that blood running out.
Terry was a thin buck-toothed girl with a light yellowish
cast to her skin, and she hadn't even started to have hair
yet. She was kind of silly, and she would still cry for her
mother sometimes, and she was always bitching because
the Indians didn't bring them nice clothes to wear. But she
was okay. When they were hungry and couldn't find a

thing to eat, she would just keep on looking for nuts and leaves and bark they could chew on, long after the others had given up.

Now she kept gripping his hand and asking, "Marcus-honey, am I hurt real bad? Please, I feel so cold."

He kept telling her she was going to be all right, but he knew she didn't believe him, and he knew better too. She just kept on bleeding. Just before the sky began to turn gray, she conked out.

Ho just disappeared. They found a big hole in the ground but they couldn't tell if he had been blown up in it or not. It was a pretty big hole.

Finally there were three of them left. Marcus and George and Tiger, only them out of everybody. They ate roots and leaves, and they were hungry all the time. They didn't dare hunt, and they seldom could stop long enough to set traps and take animals. They did not ever leave each other's sight.

Tiger said one morning, "Tomorrow time for the drop. We going to the rendezvous this time?"

"What for? Exercise?" Marcus asked. But they were hungry all the time. What the hell! If they walked into a trap, it would be done with. He could close his eyes and die. He was so weary. Besides, he knew that what they really hoped for more than the food or the medicines or the ammunition, was that they would show up and find the members of the missing third band, and then there would be more of them again. Dying he wasn't scared of. What kind of life was it running like a mouse around these damned stinking hills, while the white bastards practiced their machines on them?

Still they moved in cautiously. He was sure all the time it was a mistake, because they were depressed and short-tempered with each other. It was like licking a wound. Nobody was there. They hung around back in the woods watching nothing for a while. Then Marcus wigged out. He got so mad he couldn't stand it. He ran out into the clearing and started yelling, "Crazy motherfucking white bastards, why don't you kill me! You shitty white murdering bastards!"

"Hello?" A white girl with a small rucksack strapped to her back crawled out. Sort of dumpy-built white girl with brown hair. She explained she didn't have much for them. What she had was on her back, a few days' dried rations, because she had hiked in to find them. "Where are the rest?"

"Dead. What do you think? Dead. We all that's left."

She had a map. It was all worm tracks to him, but they managed to figure out where she was talking about. In two days they were supposed to be waiting where they could see the road, and Corey was going to try to have a truck there for them. She told them things were not going to be a great improvement out there. The Indians were being hunted too.

The three of them squatted down and had a vote. George was for taking her with them and going back to their turf. This could only be a trap. Why should they trust her? They'd made it so far, they could go on making it.

Tiger wanted to move out. If other people were fighting, then he would go and fight with them, pink or purple or even white. He reminded them they had seen black soldiers with the others. Here he was going to go out of his skull with them being picked off one at a time. If Tiger was ever left alone, he'd just jump off a cliff or run into a patrol firing. Look what old Marcus had just gone and done. Suppose the enemy had been in ambush? They were all going stir crazy, and it was no good.

Marcus squatted on the ground considering. He looked the girl over. She was wearing pants and a man's padded jacket, and she carried her rifle as if she was used to it. Her hands were rough and callused. Listening to them she leaned against a tree, and she was calm. She was alert and together and calm. She was not scared of them. She was standing in her own cone of silence waiting. Alone she had come in looking for them, and that was a crazy stupid thing to do, and she had done it well. If they went back with her, what she had done wasn't crazy. That was her bet. Corey had come through on his promises to them. And he just plain wanted to get out. There were too many bodies here already.

"They said some of their women were warriors. Are you a warrior?"

"I guess I am now."

He voted to go out with her. George just stood there shaking his head and grinding his teeth together. "We all gonna die. Don't you know that yet? Can't that sink through your thick black head? Gonna follow a white cunt out to where they can pick you off, squash you like a roach scuttling up the kitchen wall. This here is our turf. They let us down once, those Indians, they gonna let us down again. I remember every body the enemy got. Here's where I fight."

He wanted to force George to stick with them, but he knew he did not have the right. They weren't going to safety: he didn't believe that. So he had to stand and watch George go off by himself among the trees, while his eyes ached like raw meat. Then they started walking with Marcus leading, the girl behind and Tiger bringing up the rear. They went cautiously, but they kept going all night. They did not dare stop while it was dark, because, in full daylight planes and helicopters would be cruising overhead all the time.

During the day they rested in a heap of big round boulders. They dozed but could not really sleep. They were too wary. Marcus kept hoping George might come after them, and he did not want to miss him. They spoke in whispers.

"What's your name?"

"Ginny."

Tiger asked her if she wanted to fuck. She said she was too scared. Besides, she thought it would bring them bad luck.

"Do you belong to anybody?" Marcus asked her.

She stuck her chin down into her jacket. He thought she was smelling somebody else in it, maybe the man it belonged to. "Sometimes I think so now."

The drone of a plane coming low. They pressed among the rocks and lay still. Marcus always found himself holding his breath. That made him angry. To be so stupid and so scared. Freezing like a rabbit. The ground vibrated under him. Like a hawk the plane circled and circled, and he felt its eyes. But it passed away in droning circles. Unless it was radioing for bombs?

Ginny went on trying to explain her mind after the plane had gone, as if she had thought of nothing else in the meantime. "I think I finally have learned how to love the people I love. It isn't belonging, but it's serious. I'm trying to make a baby with someone. It has to be his. So I can't sleep with anyone else."

"It's not such a hot time for making babies," Marcus said.

"I think it's now or never, with this one. And I'm getting sick of never."

She was a plain girl mostly, but as sturdy as a good rocking chair—sturdy as a big old table for eating on and putting your feet up. She was not flashy-attractive like a white girl should be, she was only funny and sturdy. He grinned at her. "Maybe after you have that baby, I'll come by and give you another, in a contrasting color."

She laughed. "I'm not even sure I got this one yet. But I used to be good at growing vegetables."

When dusk came on, they started again. Tiger asked, "How come you guys knew to come in and get us?"

"We saw you on television. One place where we stayed, they had a television, and we saw your program."

"What you mean, our program? What you talking about, girl?" Tiger stopped and stared at her. His eyes were big and the eyeballs white in the dark. Marcus knew what he was thinking, and he was suddenly scared too. Suppose the chick was crazy?

"They have a new adventure show, it's one of the most popular shows on TV. It's on every Monday at eight, and a lot of kids stay up to see it. Everybody watches. See, it's the adventures of K Company, but K Company really exists. They're one of the Special Forces companies assigned to mopping up in the Catskills."

"You mean they're filming us getting bombed and burned and shot up?"

"They do a lot of filming right on the trails and from the helicopters, but they fake a lot of it, too. The critics say it's a new art form—a mixture of news, documentary and drama serial. There are lots of shoot-'em-up scenes. Part of what excites people is that they never know if what they're watching is real action, real black kids getting blown up, or if it's staged. You can think whatever turns you on the most. Corey says it's the last stage of the spectacle—a sort of living-room bread-and-circuses with the cop-out of letting you pretend it's not real."

"Those bastards. Too bad we didn't get to kill more." Marcus fingered his belt. "They got a sponsor for us?"

"A men's deodorant, a soft drink and plastic wrap. So we decided you'd sold enough soda and it was time to get you out."

All night they kept on and into the next morning. They had to keep going in the daylight to reach the road. Then they crawled into the bushes and waited. It wasn't good cover, but it was all there was. They could not afford to miss the rendezvous. All day they lay hungry and exhausted—too exposed to risk sleep. Finally the truck pulled over and they ran for it, to be taken up into the back.

WEARY and battered and haunted by their dead, they were trying to move through into unoccupied land somewhere to the west where they could stop and heal themselves. Maybe they were even willing to settle for a reservation. To scuttle into some empty place and collapse there, together. That was the nub: together.

Shawn and Ginny had worked hard on getting the tribes dispersed, and they had in large part succeeded. Many of the Indians had gone underground or had rendered themselves invisible. They were ready to be tapped when the time ripened. But they had run into a widespread stubborn refusal.

The ideological split between the Fire People and the Water People, the kids who thought the only hope lay in immediate guerrilla warfare and those who favored a massive diffuse organizing strategy, was re-enacted in tribe after tribe. The more threatening the situation grew and the graver the danger of imprisonment and death, the more the kids seemed to want to stay huddled in familiar rooms arguing theory with each other, each reaffirming his own militancy and dogmatism in the face of his "enemies," the other faction across the room.

Perhaps, Corey thought, he had emphasized too much building a people instead of training organizers, and now he had kids who feared the loss of their sense of clan more than they feared dying. They were like animals that below a certain minimum population will not mate any more and become extinct. He had set out to disperse the tribes and ended up heading a migration. So they fled under the strafing of the planes and the ambushes of the different corps of police and militia and National Guard and Army units, leaving their broken dead scattered across the land. When he closed his eyes, the bodies sprawled before him—obscene, gaping, maimed, even pretty, often pathetic in their tousled haphazard tumble. Lovers lying in the green wheat fields riddled with bullets.

Yet as they fled across the vast bowl of the plains, where going twice as fast seemed to keep them in the same place, the young came out to join them, out of the Nebraska towns the highways had been built to curve around, towns with cottonwoods and spires and grain elevators sticking high out of the wheat. Towns spread on the bends of sand-colored rivers riffled with bars. Towns coming down from bluffs into sudden river valleys, throwing out a bridge to a collection of random frame buildings on the other shore.

"We're the Pied Piper." Shawn squatted on the other side of the breakfast fire, stirring coffee boiled in a can. His hair had grown out a mixture of dyed brown and yellow like leaves turning in the fall, and he was tanned the color of cowhide. "They swarm out like lemmings. It's driving me crazy. What are they looking for?"

"There's nothing to hold them where they are. They aren't attached." The kids in the towns that had been emptied of their content and left to decay only needed a body in movement to draw them out of those houses where they were precariously lodged, loosely attached, ill at ease. A faith flared up in the columns that if there were enough of them they would survive. Even Corey felt that way sometimes. "They won't kill all the kids. They can't. What animal kills off its own young?"

Ginny was sitting cross-legged with her hands resting lightly on her belly. Her skin was dappled with freckles, so that her eyes stood out of her face a clear honey brown. "The corporate animal. People are functions. Institutions spin off corporations. You can always replace a body or a brain that stops functioning efficiently with another just like it. Can't you? That's what they think the world is."

Then they came to a valley near Salt Lake City and found an Army encamped blocking their way.

Corey was made of wire. His skin was paper. Always he was weary. He walked four times as far as the column, because he went back and forth, back and forth, shepherding. He had been superficially grazed and wounded a dozen times but never hurt badly enough to keep him down the next day. He ignored that kind of danger. He did not believe they could kill him that way. But constantly he nagged at Shawn and at Ginny to stay out of danger as well as they could, especially Ginny.

At night as he lay in her arms, her body felt soft and

vulnerable to him, a thing metal would want to tear. They were short on food, they were hungry all of the time, and now he could feel her bones against him, till she almost felt like someone else. He tried to restrain his anxiety, to keep himself from calling her name again and again in rising hysteria when she passed out of his sight. That reminded him too much of Joanna. All things reminded him of Joanna. So he stifled his voice and instead his eyes swung in his head, while he looked and looked for her in silent panic. Watching him always, Shawn would understand. Shawn would come to his elbow and say quietly, she's over by the stream, she's resting in the bushes.

For a long time he had not wanted to give her his child. Though they made love, he did not want to make a baby with Ginny. But as they slept together night after night on the ground in the old blanket, he began to tell her secret things, sacred things, things of his childhood, things his mother had told him about the stars and the earth and the moon and Coyote—old silly dark things that ran in his head. He told her his first vision, and the coming of the buffalo. Then he gave her the child that was the small swelling in her belly, between the hipbones that should not be visible, that he should not be able to feel. The things he was telling her were for the child. He was telling stories to the minnow child hidden in her flesh and the woman who held it and held him.

They camped waiting for the scouts to come back. Marcus led the scouts. Marcus and Tiger were their eyes and ears and long tentative fingers. They could slip through an encirclement and back without raising a random shot. Time after time Marcus had brought them through. Now again he came back with a report. He had found a way up and out of the valley on a narrow exposed trail. They would have to wait until dark. They would have to fool the soldiers into thinking they were still camped in the valley, blocked there. They held council and debated. A group of seventy women chose to stay. They would dance and keep the fires burning. They would try to fraternize with the soldiers and persuade them not to attack.

One of the couple of survivors told Corey about it two days later in the mountains. After all, the soldiers were young like them, just like them. It was easy to talk in the dark across no man's land. They had long conversations.

Some of the soldiers came over. The girls taught them to dance as the Indians did, and the soldiers took off their uniforms and danced naked in the firelight. They turned on with bread and with the grass the soldiers had. Some couples went beyond the light of the fires and lay together. Before dawn the soldiers went back, in time for the attack. As soon as it was light, the planes came over.

When helicopters found the main column again, they dropped leaflets urging the Indians to surrender. They would be allowed for a brief period to turn themselves in safely, the leaflets promised. They offered a parley. Some of the leaflets mentioned Corey by name and said he must come to parley for the surrender, that the terms would be explained by a former Indian who had been captured at the raid on the New Jersey farm.

If the leaflets had said *Joanna*, he would not have believed them. He would have seen a trap. But because the leaflets did not mention her by name, he knew it was really Joanna. She had managed it somehow. Yes, they had put his name in because she had said he was a leader, in order to find him. Probably she had pretended to know him casually. He said nothing, nothing, except that he would go to the place specified in the leaflets and hear the terms the government was offering.

Ginny knew at once. "How can you be so sure it's her?"

"Who?"

She laughed at him harshly. "You pretend so badly. But be careful. Be careful! I think it's her too. But we think so with different parts of ourselves—you with the strength of your hoping and me with the strength of my fearing. Reality is someplace else. If you are disappointed, what will you do? Don't throw us away."

In an abstract way he wanted to comfort her. After all, he was still with her lying in the blanket. He reached out his hand and touched her cheek, and a slow tear came out of her eye and ran over his fingertips. He stared into her face, her clear honey-colored eyes melting into his gaze. She wanted to believe, he could feel her wanting to hope and believe. Odd how she had changed and not changed. The same round face with the pointy chin, same clear eyes and little nose, same freckles and smooth hair a shade or two darker than her eyes and soft as down. Her expression was changed. But her desire to feel him loving her was just the same. She had been good to him. She was strong now. He even believed that she loved him and that her love meant him well. She was like a round hut in which he was safe, in which there was little that could hurt him, less that wanted to. She had come to him when the world had broken on his head. It had been her decision to be there. After all, she had chosen him in his weakness and despair and defeat. She must have known Joanna would come back.

Now Joanna came like the sun and stood between them. Wanting awakened in him again. He became a man instead of the ghost of a shaman, and he kept his secrets in himself.

There was still that swelling—the baby. Now he did not want to think about it. Time enough when it appeared yelling. Sometimes he thought of it strongly as his. Imagined she would give it to him. Sometimes he thought of it as hers: she had wanted it, and now she had it. He let himself remember at times that Shawn wanted her, that Shawn had let him take her because Shawn felt guilty and could not assert his desire. It would be all right. He would arrange it all. Perhaps there would be Ginny and Shawn. Perhaps he would get around all of them, fix things with Joanna so he could keep them both. Maybe Joanna would still feel guilty about Shawn, so she would have to accept Ginny. But at any cost, he would have Joanna back. So he withdrew into himself and waited, while on the last night Ginny lay beside him sobbing in the dark and he pretended sleep, made himself into rock to wait.

He could see Joanna's red hair in the pass before he could see her clearly. He could see her red hair as he came down the pass toward the rendezvous. She sat on a rock in the morning sun. They were between the two armies, the army of metal and the army of flesh. As he came close and she was still there, he wondered how he had seen her hair, because she wore a straw hat that covered it and threw patchy shadow on her face. She looked different. She slumped there waiting. She glanced occasionally at the pass, oftener at a book she was reading. He tried to make himself strong to endure what she had gone through in prison and among the enemies. Maybe his had been the easier road in spite of all, and he had to think of that now in order to reach her.

She was wearing bright cotton pants and a striped shirt

that looked clean and new. They must have issued her clothes for the meeting. She looked bigger and older. She had put on weight. Prison and lack of exercise.

"Hello, Corey." She nodded, squinting against the sun, and gave him her hand to shake formally. It was hot and dry.

He could not touch her yet. He could not put his hands on her, although they itched and the fingers curled on nothing. Were they watching from nearby? "Is this an ambush? Do you know?"

"Don't be silly. They could have shot you any time coming down. They want to give you a chance." She sounded impatient and a little bored.

As soft as he could, he asked, "Are they listening?"

"You've become very paranoid."

"A lot of killing does that." He was angry for a moment. He saw the thing he hated most to see: the body of the last of their babies, Sarah Jean, with the blood pouring out from her torn chest, and the heart exposed and still spurting blood, throbbing like a small animal, like a red frog. Her mouth open. Her eyes open. He sat down beside Joanna.

She moved away a little. He was almost too shy to look at her. Then he made himself. Joanna, Joanna, Joanna. Her hair was cut shorter and processed in some way that took the kinks out. It was neatly and fussily curled around the bottom of the hat. It did not look quite real. It needed to be loose in the wind.

"Take off your hat."

"The sun bothers me." She stirred under his eyes. "I've gotten fat, haven't I?"

"The more, the better. You look good to me."

"I put on a lot of weight in the hospital. Insulin therapy does that."

"The hospital? Were you sick?"

"I was in bad shape when they took me in. I started a fire, you know. So I had to go into the hospital for treatment. First they tried electroshock and then insulin." She grimaced. "I really hated electroshock. It was all pretty grisly the first couple of months."

He could not speak. His throat turned into a bone. He took her hand and held it against his mouth.

She detached it. "I was in very bad shape. Doctor Hayes, the psychiatrist I had after the first month or so, was very good. He brought me through the tunnel. It's like being born all over again, it really is. I suppose that sounds like nonsense to you, until you go through it yourself. I feel as if he's my real father. I put up such a fight at first, not to let him get through to me, not to let him reach me. But he's such a wonderful, devoted doctor, he wouldn't let me discourage him. It was like learning to read, except this time I was learning to read myself."

Her voice went on. He could not speak. He sat in a stiff huddle beside her. She was somehow bigger than him and puffy. Maybe she was puffy with the words they had injected into her. He had to listen and wait—wait for Joanna to come out.

She giggled suddenly. "I'm supposed to be talking to you about terms and all that. You have to come in, to bring in whoever is still running around up there with you, before it's too late. But I really wanted to tell you about all I learned about myself. I think you could be helped, Corey, I really do." Voluntarily she reached out this time and patted his arm.

He seized her hand inside his. It sat there, hot and dry and impassive, in his grip.

"I want to try to help you, Corey, honestly. Because I came to understand why I did what I did with Shawn. Well, I was trying to castrate you."

"Never mind about that shit. I understand it my own way now. I haven't been faithful either. I don't want us to get stuck talking about that stuff now. What matters is getting you back."

"But I did castrate you. I mean, you were impotent then."

"Only that time, Joanna. It wouldn't have lasted."

"But you were. All week. You don't have to deny it."

"Oh, Jesus, don't think that. Come here." He tried to draw her closer.

"It was the whole matter of my penis envy. I had no good female models. I wanted to be a boy and I tried to turn myself into one. For instance, sleeping around and running away from home and trying to reject myself—pretending my name was Joanna, pretending I could become someone else. My name is Jill, and I wish you'd use it. Wanting to be a warrior—what was that but wanting to be what my father was? It was that whole fixation on the Army. But there was a positive side in me, even then. For instance, Dr. Hayes pointed out that I was captured because I was in Tunnel D with the babies. That was my effort in a crisis situation to act out my femininity."

"That's bullshit. Sylvie deserted her post. You got stuck. It was an accident."

"You speak of accidents because you repress these things. I don't need to, any longer. I'm ready to face myself and accept who I am and live in the world."

"Joanna, Joanna, what do they have to give you that you want? A pair of new pants and a clean shirt? Words that make your tongue go flap, flap? That awful stuff they put on your hair to make it lie flat? Your hair is naturally wild and beautiful."

"I have problem hair, but I accept that now. I don't exaggerate it. I was like a child who's naughty to attract attention. I wanted to be loved because I was bad, instead of acting in such a way that I would attain real relationships with people."

"Shut up!" He made his voice softer. "Don't parrot their garbage. You've been processed, and you've taken it in, so that you could survive. But listen, Joanna, you're a few feet away from freedom."

"You listen to me, Corey. I'm where I want to be now, and I don't mean sitting on this crappy rock. I've got a scholarship to a decent school. I'm going to be a teacher. I'm going to be something on my own."

"Joanna, your people are up there in the mountains waiting, Shawn and Ginny and Marcus—remember Marcus and Tiger from the Catskills? Your people are waiting to take you back. The enemy has hurt you, but the pain will go away and leave you tougher and stronger. Freedom and your own people."

"How can you talk about freedom, when you've come to negotiate surrender? Now look at this damn paper. You have to sign it. Or take it back and have a council and bring it down tomorrow." She thrust something at him, fine print, lists of conditions.

"Don't think that. I came down to get you! Joanna, look at me! Look at me!"

She turned her head, and her brown eyes met his, squinted against the sun's glare. Eyes like hubcaps. They gave him nothing human. Only himself reflected twice looking back. A robot that looked a little like Joanna. A plastic doll with rubbery skin and a smell of plastics about it. He was suddenly running before he knew he had stood up. He turned, tearing up the stiff pages of the treaty. She frowned after him.

"Corey, come back here. Sit down. We have to settle things. Corey!"

He hurled the fragments of paper at her. He wanted to throw them in her face, but they drifted lazily in the sunny air and idled away. A funnel was closing on his head. Claws in his chest. The air was glass. It was crushing him as he ran blindly, and a choked scream escaped him like an injured bird drag-flapping off, like a wounded crow. He screamed again, again muffled, and fell to his knees. The rocks were spines under him. His hands scraped at his pounding chest. The pressure had warped his head.

Then he was lifted up. Shawn pulled him to his feet and hoisted him and carried him over his shoulder. His head hung down and he could hear Shawn panting as he trotted. Corey's head banged against Shawn's back. Then his sight riddled with red and black holes and receded, as he willingly let go of consciousness and slipped down into the swift dark river and was carried away.

"It's better to die than to become plastic. It's better to be shot than to be reconditioned. It's better to live your own death than somebody else's life." That was Corey's message to the people. He could not tell them the terms because he had not received them. He said unconditional surrender. Some went down. Most stayed.

Ginny had taken her knapsack and cooking pot and gone to Marcus. She was mad at Shawn too. She stood up and said that she was leaving, and she wasn't going to surrender either. She was going to try to get through the encirclement. Why wait for death? As long as there was a chance, take it. But she did not go. She spent her time persuading other people to leave, and some of them did slip out by ones and twos to try to escape. She wanted Marcus to leave with her, but he wasn't ready yet.

Corey paid no attention. He had only to look at her belly, and he did not believe she was about to go off from him. He found himself blocked. He could not make himself move. He was frozen with despair and the lush desire to die. He knew he must steal time, the terrible luxury of time, to fast and wait. He must cleanse himself of his despair and wait for the knowledge of what must be done. His desire to be alone was like an intense thirst. He did not care for anyone. He did not care for himself. Abstractly he worried for his people, but he could not connect enough to bring that to action.

Early in the morning he climbed to what felt like the peak of a nearby mountain. Clouds filled in the valley and the ravines as he climbed, and though he scrambled above them into the sun, he could see nothing but the immediate brownish rocks and the shaggy white ceiling of cloud below. He fasted and sang chants and waited. He slept and was wakeful. But he did not even dream. He passed through hunger into weakness and then into a dry lightness, like a desiccated leaf. He rose into the clear purified state in which vision came. Yet nothing happened. He remained still and empty and waiting.

The gods lose interest in a loser, he told himself. No vision came because he had squandered the one he had been given. Nothing moved through him. No power used him as its nexus for coming into the world. He remained only Corey—thin as wire and dry as paper, sitting cross-legged in the sun on a pile of rocks with a cold wind going through his ribs like a buzz saw. Below somewhere was the bloated shell of his other self, his love, his desire, his fearful dependency. Below somewhere too were his wife and his unborn child and his friend.

Vision would not come. After a while he could not keep his mind quiet. His mind came out of him in the form of a gnomic old man who skipped round and round him with the sun firing off Ben Franklin specs and explained and explained in a voice as monotonous and inevitable as the multiplication tables.

He had only thought of getting the kids out of the system. The system was such a nightmare to him that he had not tried to decipher its machinations, but only to make people feel the weight that pressed on them. Everything they might have offered as program seemed reformist and compromising in the face of apocalyptic revolution. Yet you could not win a violent revolution in the center of the empire with rifles against tanks and planes, if the Army would fight against you. You could not win with an isolated minority.

The secrecy, the paramilitary measures they took against police infiltration finally made them vulnerable to raids. The model of warfare, without the firepower to wage it, had seduced their imaginations. The kids who came in search of them were moved by their own alienation and the lure of their style, but for the passive others, the angry others, there were only the horror-story caricatures of the mass media to shape their responses. They had done no propaganda. They had been too turned off by the great square glimmering vacuums to do other than turn away, so they had no allies. If they would not consume, the society would turn and consume them. It would all work out in terms of profit and loss. Stability would return. The labor market would be less glutted. Whose children were these? Children of the gray box, children of the print-out, children of the death ray, of the comic book and the Pentagon. Their deaths would move only each other. Their putative parents grazed on meadows of corporate newsprint and grew fat and took pills to soothe their stomachs.

No vision came to him. No god, no totem, no devil on the mountain. No vision of the kingdoms of the earth or his psyche. On the fourth morning he made a small fire to cook the dried soup he had brought with him. Then as his strength came back, he went down the mountain.

Where his people had been encamped, he found a vast parched place, as if a desert had fallen over the land he remembered. There were no trees, no bushes, no birds, not a green or living thing. There were signs of great heat. The earth itself seemed shriveled. A fine ash blew in the breezes here and there. Baked clay and rock.

Now he must be seeing visions. Now finally he must be mad. He stopped to eat some chocolate and raisins, squatting, and then retraced his path up the mountain and jogged down again.

The same. He walked onto the new desert. Then at last in the distance, he caught sight of people and ran toward them. His heart was pounding with exhaustion. He would locate his people and collapse. There were workmen, he saw, here and there on the plain sucking up the fine ash in large trucks and hauling it away. Men were unloading black earth from trucks and planting bushes and orderly rows of saplings. A steam shovel was digging the bed for a small lake.

THIS PARK IS NOT PAID FOR BY YOUR TAXES

A big red, white and blue sign explained that the new park was to be financed out of bonds that would be paid off from visitors' fees.

He must find out what they had done with his people. He had to find Ginny and his son and Shawn. He ran through the dust and the fine ash blew into his nose, making him choke and sneeze. Finally he staggered onto new earth. A man was operating a bull-dozer there, spreading out the new ground evenly so that the workers coming behind him could put down the rolls of turf like carpeting. Corey dragged himself panting toward the machine.

The driver, a small man with red sunburnt skin, slowed down to gaze at him. Pushed up the goggles that hid the eyes: blue-gray eyes quick as minnows against the ruddy skin. "Well, if it isn't Ned's pal, Corey. How do? What brings you to these parts?"

"Big Ned's father! Help me. Have you seen Big Ned?" He knew better as he asked. Big Ned had been exploded in Nebraska crossing the Platte. A shell had blown his head right off, and his body had fallen in the water and slowly sunk away.

"Now what would he be doing around here?" The old man tilted back his hat to scratch his head, puzzled.

"Help me, Mr. Howard. I can't find my wife and baby."

"Son, you're sure in trouble around here, I can tell you." Mr. Howard did not halt the bulldozer, but drove it forward.

He backed away. "Watch out, okay? What are you doing here, Mr. Howard? How come you're not in Fink's Bend? Could you shut that thing off?"

"I'm sorry for what I have to do, Corey. You young folks brought on the recession and they closed up the blue-jeans factory where Mrs. Howard was employed. We went on relief and times were hard. Then the government came recruiting for these clean-up jobs."

"But my people? Where are my people?"

"They got removed to make way for a new camping park. Now, look, for the first time in over twelve years I'm holding down a regular job and the old woman's

coming out as soon as we can swing it. I have a job to do
here, Corey, and it's too bad, but a job is a job." He drove
the bulldozer right at Corey.

He did not run. "That's okay, Mr. Howard. Don't feel
bad." Ned's pa was getting taken to the cleaners. He'd
bring his family out and the prices would go sky-high and
eat up his wages. Then they'd finish up the job and lay
him off and there wouldn't be work to be had. Now there
was only time quickly to ask for his death song, that it
come to him, and that he die well.

He stood straight, held out his hands and sang between
polluted earth and unpolluted sun:

> I rode the buffalo
> but now I have fallen off.
> I lie on the ground.
>
> Grandfather buffalo,
> others will ride further.
> Grandfather buffalo,
> others will ride further.
> Some finally
> will break through
> to the other side.

"Orders are orders. Look out, now!" Big Ned's father
stepped on the gas and the blade grew huge before him.
Corey sang out loud:

> "Some finally
> will break through!"

The blade hit him with its dull weight, making him fall.
As it rolled over him smashing his bones, his heart burst
free like a rising crow, and he fainted.

WHEN it had been dark all the time, Shawn had wanted to die. She had found him and led him out. She had found first him in the dark and then Marcus, but she could see. Marcus wanted to die too, he was so badly burned. Only Ginny did not want to die, and she did not want them to abandon their bodies. She held him gently, formally. Her belly kept him off. So long as he was blind, he felt neutered in his helplessness.

She was gentle with them both and angry at them. She would not love them, because they had not been willing to leave in time, because they had not been willing to escape. She told them they were in love with apocalypse, like all men, more in love with myths than with any woman. But he felt suffocated. He thought of colors. If he could see only one color, any color, it would not matter which. Or if he could see in tones of gray, like an old movie. Or just light. He found it hard to sleep, now that it was always dark. She lay beside him, cradling him but unable to be touched, and she did not sleep either. Marcus moaned with pain.

They were a sorry family. Scar tissue made raised patterns on Marcus' right arm and chest. He walked with a dragging limp. In his sleep he still moaned and shuddered. Ginny was big as a house and short of temper. She balanced her swollen belly on swollen legs, hobbling among the rocks. If Shawn came near her, she arched and hissed like a mistreated cat. He was not so bad as he had been. His eyes were still weak and sore. He wore shades all the time in the day. But even if his vision was blurred and perhaps always would be, he could see: colors, shapes, her face, rocks, an eagle circling, the intricately cracked mud of an arroyo, clouds, dust wraiths, the tea color of Ginny's hair, the red-rimmed sadness of Marcus' eyes, crickets hopping, a jack rabbit, the map of pain in

livid pink and plum on Marcus' bark-colored skin. The
jack rabbit had a hard-on. It was early in the morning.
Jack rabbit eyed man, while man squinted weakly at jack
rabbit.

At dawn Saturday he walked down into the little town
and caught his ride in a truck to the gas station on the
highway. He worked there weekends. He could see well
enough to fill tanks and wipe windshields and test for oil.
Wednesdays he helped them unload stock in the little
town. The town was named Pancake. It was on the map.
They had to fill up the road maps with something, so
wherever there was a house, they put a town on the map.
The map showed a dirt road going off the highway and
ending there. It did not show the trail climbing to the
abandoned cabin they had taken over. After he helped
unload, he would pick out some supplies. Then he would
hike carrying them the two miles mainly uphill to the
cabin. They lived on what he made. Ginny took care of a
patch of vegetables, the only living things in the world she
was not angry at. Time went by slowly, whining like a
circling mosquito.

Often she talked, but not to them. She was talking at
Corey. Her bitterness crackled like burnt skin. "I thought
I was strong enough. I thought I was whole enough. But
his will to die was stronger than all my caring. He wanted
her more than he wanted anything he pretended, more
than any of the dreams or than any of his speeches or our
ideas. More than the whole tribe put together. When he
knew he couldn't have her any more, he left us to die. It
all comes down to the same old private-property thing.
His own thing meant more to him than all the rest. Tons
of bodies fertilizing nonsense."

It was hot that day though it was fall, if they had fall
here, and sweat stained her cotton dress. She had not been
able to get herself into pants for a long time, so he had
bought her two tent dresses. Now they were faded and
stained with sweat. Actually the rest of her seemed smaller than ever, shrunken, with the huge belly crushing her
under it. She would sit and hold her belly. "Maybe it's a
monster. That would be just like him to give me a monster. God knows what all that firepower did to it." She
was joking bitterly, but he knew she was really afraid. She
felt alien to the embryo. She claimed it kicked her vicious-
ly. She was afraid of the coming birth, but she refused to

leave the cabin. She made him order her books on child-birth and read them all. Six books on having babies were cast around the cabin.

She was alone and animal in her pregnancy. She shut him out. She was kinder to Marcus, because Marcus had gone so far into his pain he did not threaten her as a man. As long as Shawn had been blind, she had suffered him to touch her, to hold her, though she would not make love. But when his vision began to seep back, she turned him into the other, the enemy, and shunted him away.

Sometimes he told himself he could just leave. Get on a bus on the highway with his weekly paycheck and take off for the horizon. Starting all over and over and over again. When the land was worked out, leave it. Move on to spoil new land.

He stayed put because they were the remains of the only thing besides his music he had ever committed him-self to. Because if he could not be close to them, he would not manage with anybody else. Because he was worried about her and Marcus and the baby.

He bought a harmonica from a guy in the gas station. He made simple music now. Marcus and he sang together, and sometimes they made up songs. Marcus beat time on the boards of the porch. After a while he made a drum from a paint can. As Ginny grew closer and closer to term, Marcus took over what was left of the vegetable garden. The men worked on the house, trying to mend it, and began to talk politics. They discussed every decision minutely and took each of them again. They welded their separate histories into one and poked and prodded and turned it over. It became engaging. It was something they hurried back to together, like an interminable chess game. Not against each other; against history. Feeling very an-cient and very young, they began to joke around. Ginny got even more irritated and tried to shut them up. "Stupid pricks! Men are always floating castles on a cloud of hot air! How dare you call that politics?" She sulked in her hugeness.

"If you're a mouse fighting a tiger, maybe that's the wrong question, what did I do wrong?" Marcus said. "We thought guns made us real, but it was people, and we didn't have them. Move the people, and the system really is a paper tiger."

Shawn said, "It's still we win, or everybody loses. Time

is almost gone. It's the last great free-for-all robbery of everybody's earth. They're into polluting the ocean. The great famine is here."

Marcus said, "People would always naturally be more comfy going to meetings with their brothers and sisters and arguing their itsy-bitsy doctrinaire song-and-dance routines, than going out in the streets to talk to the people. We couldn't get a message out. We had to rely on you guys."

"People get arrogant so fast. They confuse pain with virtue. Or if they're like me, they let other people make the decisions. Two sides of weakness."

Shawn thought he had come to understand a lot of things he had done wrong, and he tried to talk to her. "I left you alone with him too much. I could never figure out what I wanted enough to say it to you. I felt guilty about Joanna. Drifting with things is a habit it takes almost dying to break, Ginny."

She was sitting on the porch sewing a torn blanket into a baby blanket. Her eyes when she raised them from the stitches went straight to the bleak wall of mountains.

He went on, "I let Corey tell me how to be used, because that was less work than taking hold of myself. I let him take you over because to fight it I would have had to stand up and say I wanted you and act, for a change."

"As soon as he thought he could have her back, he shut himself off. He forgot he had loved me. He forgot he had come to me, broken and wanting me. He forgot his promises. I never asked him not to love her. I only asked him to go on being with me. What I hate is that I believed in him. I was taken and used. That's what I hate—that I trusted."

He came back to Marcus with his self-analysis, but Marcus wasn't having it either.

"Quit nit-picking your soul, you big old baby." Marcus whacked him none too kindly across the ass with his good hand. "Wait for the birth. With the milk she's going to loosen. Her love will come down again. But if all you're learning is how you should have done this and should have done that, and how to start carrying on like Corey did with Joanna, I think Ginny and me will just bury you out in the yard with the other unsuccessful pumpkins. Hang loose, Shawn. Horniness is stupefying your mind."

The pains began in the early evening. At midnight she

made them both get out of the cabin. Marcus and Shawn took their sleepingbags and lay down outside. Shawn could not sleep. He got angrier and angrier staring up at the sky, the smear of nebulae. Finally he rolled up his bag and came back in.

She glared at him from the bed. "What are you doing in here? Leave me alone. Get out!"

"No." He squatted against the wall. "I'm staying with you."

"I don't want you here."

"I want to be here. I'm in better shape to insist."

"Get out! I have a right to be alone."

He shook his head. "No. We're in this together."

She laughed sharply, her laugh prolonged into high hysterical giggles. "It sure doesn't feel that way!"

He remained squatting against the wall. She lay on the iron bed with its cracked ivory paint, waiting for each contraction, trying to go with it. She was soaked in sweat. Every time a contraction hit her, she writhed on the bed and the metal net of the bedspring jangled. He thought he could feel the waves of her pain crisping the air.

"Why don't you get out of here? Just leave me alone."

"If I wanted to leave you alone, I could have hitched out of here a month ago."

She was silent for a while. "Why didn't you?"

"Because I feel married to you."

"Oh, possession again."

"Come off it, Ginny. The three of us are all that's left. The three of us are married. Have I ever hung on, except when I was blind and you had to lead me?"

"You didn't have sense enough to hang on even then. I had to hold on to you. . . But it's his baby."

"No! It's not his. It's not even yours. It's ours. Let Corey be the goddamn father. A ghost is a perfect father. Something that comes and goes without touching you. I want to be its second mother. And Marcus its third."

"If there's numbering, Marcus is number one. Number one motherfucker, number one mother. For instance, Marcus is remembering right now about how Ginny suppose to be breathing, and Ginny, she is just moaning and forgetting." Marcus leaned in the doorway.

She groaned and heaved to and fro on the bed. Shawn could not tell if she had listened. Briefly she wept, and he came and wiped her face and neck with a washrag dipped in water from the metal basin.

"Listen! Listen to me. I keep thinking I'm going to give birth to a weapon—a little tank. Or a monkey. I'm going to have a furry hedgehog that will lick itself and run off into the brush." She paused for a contraction. "People can't live any more. There's room for machines and a little room left for animals. I don't have too much hope for animals. But a sort of hedgehog or a shrew or a weasel that eats insects to start it all again! To go a long ways back, past apes, past monkeys, past mammals altogether with their strutting snarling males and their nurturing suffering females. Back to a furry hedgehog that eats insects and lays eggs, and try it again!"

"People can be good. Think about the farm." He wiped her forehead again. "Sure, kids brought hang-ups, but they weren't at each other's throats. It wasn't what we did right that destroyed us."

But she only sobbed with pain and writhed on the bed.

"Ginny, hear now. You got to do that breath-thing right, you know, the way it tell in the book." Marcus came to the foot of the bed, smiling with pity. "Don't you remember, in the mountains you go on how much you want to make a baby? You knew he was only half with you, but you got him to give you one, you know? Now you're like a child that started down the big slide, and halfway down, that child is scared and wants to get off and starts clutching at the sides. Now it hurt you to be trying to hold back."

"I don't want to live in this world! Maybe you should cut me open. Take the baby and let me die! I thought I was stronger than I am."

"Human beings aren't naturally strong enough or nasty enough to live in this world," Marcus said. "You got to remember how to breathe."

Shawn wiped the lank wet hair off her forehead. "We have to get down out of here and find out who's left. We have to start again open and slow. We have to keep at it for twenty years."

"But we failed. Corey said we were the last generation. We tried and we lost." She tossed from side to side, hands scrabbling on the swell of her belly.

"While there are people, we haven't lost. We were right and wrong, but the system is all wrong."

"Come on, now, Ginny, you got to push. You come nine months of the way home, and now the baby wants out and you got to swing with it." Marcus limped toward the edge of the bed and sat down on its edge. "It too late to stop. We all walked through the big fire, and we are changed inside and outside. Sometimes we have to swing with the big changes." He held up his good left hand. "Remember the exercises. Come on, stop playing stupid, girl. Come on, you got to help. We been waiting on you for months. Time to get moving. Time to push that baby out and teach him to walk and clear out of here. We can't reach nobody but the mosquitoes and the rabbits up on this hill."

So they sat on either side of the bed with her and did the counting and the breathing with her, and the sweat ran down them all. All night she labored, and sometimes she broke and wept and screamed, and they had to calm her back to the rhythms, back to going with her contractions instead of fighting them. But the baby did not come. Shawn was afraid and Marcus was afraid and they sweated their fear till the cabin smelled of a harsh animal reek. When their stares crossed, when Marcus' dark eyes met Shawn's, they pushed away from each other.

Shawn was afraid that she would die. Never would the thing be done. Nothing could be worth the suffering. She would die and leave them. She would become a pile of meat. Marcus and he would be left alone together, and they would commence fighting and biting on each other until they were dead of each other's poisons like two rattlesnakes. To all their dead would be added more. He could not bear it.

He could not give her up. He gripped her hands and let her dig her nails into him until his palms bled and he found his own muscles straining to move the baby.

Finally two hours after dawn, the final contractions thrust out the slimy wet head and Marcus drew out the baby, red and iridescent and screaming with life, slapped it for good measure and cut and tied the cord. Ginny lay in her blood, spent and torn. Shawn laid his cheek against her limp fallen hand and wept. Faintly her hand stirred to touch him. When he looked at her again, she was smiling. The baby wriggled damply against her belly, and she was staring and smiling.

Marcus quickly sped through the six baby books to

make sure he had forgotten nothing he must do. Shawn felt useless and yet full of energy and light, a turned-on bulb, a ridiculous helium-taut balloon. The baby lived and she lived and it was day for Marcus and for him, it was day for all of them.